Praise for *Framed: A Thriller*

"Original, clever, deftly written, and a simply riveting read...
Framed showcases the author's genuine flair for narrative-
driven storytelling that fully engages the reader with every
twist and turn. A consummate legal thriller...the stuff of which
high-tension movies are made."

—*MIDWEST BOOK REVIEW*

"Grayhall's prose is clean, precise, and emotionally intelligent.
She writes with the clarity of a scientist and the empathy of
a novelist...Readers who admired *Erin Brockovich* or John
Grisham's *The Pelican Brief* will find *Framed* equally gripping
but more intimate."

—*SAN FRANCISCO BOOK REVIEW* (5 STARS)

"Patricia Grayhall's thriller, *Framed*, delivers a pulse-pounding
story that skillfully intertwines environmental corruption with
a high-stakes bank robbery trial. With masterful pacing and
a twist that will leave you breathless, Grayhall keeps readers
guessing at every turn. The perfectly calibrated romantic
tension adds another layer of complexity to this intricate plot,
making it impossible to put down. A must-read for thriller
fans!"

—MICHELLE COX, AUTHOR OF *THE HENRIETTA*
AND INSPECTOR HOWARD SERIES

"Gripping, timeless, and timely, *Framed* pulls readers into a world of deception, betrayal, and mortal danger...and doesn't let them go until the very last twist."

—Anastasia Zadeick, author of *Blurred Fates*

"Grayhall injects several surprising revelations—and a shocking twist at the end—that most won't see coming...The story is brisk and lean...as these fully dimensional characters seek the truth."

—*BookLife Reviews*

"Grayhall's smooth, easy prose and the manner in which the two women navigate...secrets will keep readers rapt...A taut rendering of one woman's fight against Big Oil."

—*Kirkus Reviews*

"A brilliant blend of medical and legal thriller...Grayhall does a masterful job at weaving the suspenseful plot...She delivers a page turner that keeps the reader guessing until the very last page, with a genius ending that does not disappoint."

—Julie Hatch, author of *The Very Best of Care*

"*Framed* is a clever romp...packed with suspense, romance, and social relevance...and then just when you think you've reached the finale, the unexpected ending bowls you over."

—JUDE BERMAN, AUTHOR OF *THE DIE*

"This engaging and well-written novel, highlights what the law can do to right wrongs, and how it can be used as a weapon in the wrong hands."

—LORI B. DUFF, ESQ., AUTHOR OF THE *FISCHER AT LAW SERIES*

"Patricia Grayhall's new thriller is a textbook example of a page-turner...The end has a surprising twist, even for me, an avid thriller reader."

—SOPHY SMYTHE, AUTHOR OF *THE MEDICAL CODE*

"A thriller that a modern Agatha Christie might have written."

—MARILYN ZIMMERMAN, ESQ., AUTHOR OF
IN DEFENSE OF GOOD WOMEN

FRAMED

FRAMED

A THRILLER

PATRICIA GRAYHALL

RAIN CITY PRESS

Published 2026

Print ISBN: 979-8-9937017-0-7

E-ISBN: 979-8-218-73553-1

Rain City Press

6830 NE Bothell Way, C155

Kenmore, WA 98028

Interior design by: Damonza Studio

Cover by: Damonza Studio

*"We do not inherit the earth from our ancestors
but borrow it from our children."*

—WENDELL BERRY

CHAPTER 1

ON MONDAY, JUNE 17, 1985, Dr. Victoria Nelson's descent from respected physician to accused felon began as an ordinary working day.

She approached her patient's exam room and checked his intake sheet outside the door. Mark Evans. Twenty-five years old. Apprentice process engineer. Three children under five. Dizziness, sore throat, headaches. She sighed and closed her eyes, imagining lunchboxes packed at dawn and bedtime stories interrupted by headaches. He was the fourth patient from World Petrol she'd seen in a week. What was going on at that refinery?

Smiling, she entered the room, where a tall, slender young man stood to greet her. His youthful face was smooth, but his complexion was unnaturally pale, with dark circles under his eyes.

"Hello, Mr. Evans. I'm Dr. Nelson."

She shook his clammy hand, roughened by work. "Please make yourself comfortable. I'd like to hear more about these headaches and dizziness you mentioned on your form."

He sat down, and she took the chair opposite him, waiting.

Mark cleared his throat. "Well, ma'am, I'm learnin' how to run and fix them distillation columns, compressors, and reactors. The operator usually calls me in to open the equipment when something springs a leak. The fumes that come off it? Lord, they tear up my nose and make my throat burn somethin' fierce. Sometimes, I get so dizzy I can't hardly stand straight. Feels like I'm gonna throw up. And yeah, I get headaches dang near every day."

She nodded and leaned forward. "That sounds very difficult to tolerate. Do you use any respiratory protection or masks that help you breathe safely?"

"Yes, ma'am. We grab masks when we can, but they're old as dirt and don't seal right half the time. I can still smell them fumes comin' off the columns. Honestly, I don't think the operator likes me much. He always gives me the worst jobs."

She shook her head. "I'm sorry." She'd heard this before and chafed at the company's practice of giving the dirtiest jobs to the newest, lower-ranking hires. Like many others she'd treated, Mark was exposed to dangerous volatile organic compounds—benzene, toluene, xylene—and hydrogen sulfide and sulfur dioxide from crude oil. These chemicals weren't only unpleasant but also posed serious health risks.

Her frustration rose. It was like hitting a locked door again and again. She'd seen quite a few patients like Mark in the past few months. She had plans for a laboratory that would enable her to measure their exposure directly in blood and urine samples, but the lab was nowhere near ready. When she spoke, though, her voice held no hint of frustration, professional to the core.

"We'll discuss your work environment further, but first, let's review your medical history to make sure we're not missing any other factors that could contribute to your symptoms."

After a detailed history and thorough examination, she

said, "Mr. Evans, your symptoms are likely related to chemical exposure. The first approach would be to reduce your exposure to these toxins by using proper protective equipment, including a well-fitting respirator, appropriate gloves, and improved ventilation."

Mark's face dropped. "But . . . they . . ."

Her face softened. "I understand it may be difficult for you to ask. I'll get things moving by contacting the plant's industrial hygienist and helping you to open a workers' compensation claim."

Mark rubbed his face, and his forehead creased. "Now hold on, ma'am. That could stir up some trouble for me. I don't wanna go makin' waves with the company and causin' a fuss. I ain't got no fancy engineerin' degree. They're trainin' me for this job, and it pays way better than anything else 'round here. I have three little ones at home, and I can't afford to lose this job."

She held his gaze. "This isn't about causing trouble, Mark. It's about ensuring you're there for your kids in twenty years." She watched his face register the implications.

"So, it's serious?"

"It could if it continues. But you're here. We've got you." She smiled reassuringly. "What would help you feel safe in taking the next steps? You can hold off on filing a workers' comp claim for now."

Mark let out a sigh. "I'm not sure. What do you think I should do?"

"Okay, you can ask your health and safety staff for two things: a respirator fit-tested for your face shape and size that only you use, and PVA gloves. They provide better protection against chemical absorption than nitrile gloves."

Mark hunched his shoulders. "Alright then, ma'am. Could you write that down for me? I'll give it to my boss."

Tori nodded. "Absolutely. I'd also like to see you again in about a month to check your progress. Remember, your health matters—not just for you, but for those three little ones who depend on you."

Mark bit his lip and met her gaze. "Yeah, I know. Thanks."

∾

Dr. Nelson was standing in the hallway scanning her next patient's thick chart when she startled at the sudden weight of Dr. Jensen's hand on her shoulder. He was a small man, but the medical director's touch felt heavy.

"Do you have a moment?"

His jaw was set, and his tone made it clear this wasn't a request. Her stomach knotted.

"Sure," she managed, the word barely escaping her throat. Encounters with Jensen were rarely positive.

He ushered her into an empty exam room. As the door closed behind them, its click echoed like a prison cell locking.

"I've had another complaint," he announced, his slate-gray eyes drilling into hers with a cold intensity. "This time from Dodge Chemical. They claim that their workers' compensation claims have doubled since you arrived, with most of them being medically supported by you."

Her heart raced, and she felt a moment of panic. Then, her patients' faces flashed through her mind, giving her courage. She straightened.

"They're all legitimate claims," she countered in a steady voice. "Dodge is notorious for neglecting worker health and safety."

He waved his hand, contemptuous and dismissive, as if swatting away an annoying insect. "That's their business. We hired you to serve the area's major employers by conducting executive exams, administering drug tests, and providing medical surveillance. We did not hire you to antagonize those companies by increasing their workers' compensation costs."

That's not what I thought when you hired me.

This wasn't the mission she'd signed up for. The gulf between her and Jensen yawned. She considered medicine a service, but he thought it was an industry. She felt a burning sense of betrayal in her chest and struggled to keep her voice firm. "What about serving the patients?"

He ignored her, moved to the door, and yanked it open. "Dial it back," he commanded over his shoulder. His lack of response to her questions screamed louder than any rebuke could have. She was left alone with her principles and the crushing weight of an impossible choice.

CHAPTER 2

TORI'S HEART HAMMERED against her ribs, and she struggled to breathe normally. Another panic attack. Each breath was more elusive than the last. With trembling fingers, she fumbled for the small bottle in her pocket. She tipped out an orange pill and tossed it back without water. It scraped down her dry throat. Only two left, but she wouldn't refill it. Her anxiety had been a constant companion lately, a shadow that grew longer and darker with each passing day. Her hefty responsibilities—running a clinical practice, trying to establish a toxicology lab, and racing to complete a cancer study in communities poisoned by petrochemical giants—pressed on her shoulders like concrete slabs. She was already sinking under the weight, even without the medical director threatening her and telling her to stop advocating for her patients and doing the very essence of her job.

She closed her eyes and drew in several measured breaths, centering herself before pushing open the patients' exam room door to see her last patient of the day. Her heart sank at the sight of the man who greeted her.

This retired petrochemical worker had been fighting

asbestos-related lung disease under her care for over a year. He was barely more than a skeleton draped in loose skin. His complexion had the ashen pallor of approaching death, and his once-full cheeks were now concave hollows beneath sharp cheekbones. Despite his deteriorating state, Mr. Taylor's eyes brightened at her entrance, his cracked lips forming a smile.

"Good afternoon, Mr. Taylor." Tori's voice was gentle as she settled beside him. Her hand rested briefly on his shoulder, mere bone beneath her fingers. "How are you feeling?"

"Not great," he rasped, each word seeming to cost him precious energy. Once robust from years of shouting over machinery, his voice had faded to a whisper. "I can't make it up the stairs to my bedroom. We moved the bed to the living room."

He rasped a wet cough. Tori let the truth remain unspoken. His decades of smoking had only accelerated what the asbestos had wrought.

"I'm sorry," she said, maintaining eye contact that conveyed more compassion than words. "It sounds like it's time to set you up with home oxygen."

Tori removed the stethoscope from around her neck and motioned for him to lean forward in his chair. She lifted his shirt and could count each vertebra and rib. As he breathed, the crackling sounds that filled her ears were like cellophane being crushed. "Sounds about the same," she noted, keeping her voice neutral.

When she snapped his recent X-ray onto the viewing box, the irregular white mass that invaded the dark space of his lung leaped out at her like a predator, crouching and waiting. She inhaled deeply, steadying herself before turning to deliver the unwelcome news.

Across from him, she leaned close, her hand resting on his bony knee. "Your chest X-ray shows a growth on the lining of your lungs. Given your many years of asbestos exposure and smoking, it may well be cancer. I'll refer you to a pulmonologist for a needle biopsy to determine the exact cause."

Mr. Taylor's eyes flickered. He shook his head slowly. "I don't want a needle biopsy." He straightened as if to face an unseen enemy. "I'm a goner anyway."

A knot formed in Tori's chest. This was a man who, despite his suffering, never failed to bring her homemade cookies and share a corny joke during his visits.

"Are you sure, Mr. Taylor? Do you want to think it over?"

"No, ma'am," he said with unexpected firmness. "But will you talk to my wife and me together? Tell us what to expect. I'm not spending my last days in a hospital."

The medical director and his warnings be damned. Her resolve hardened.

"Of course," she promised. "I'll do everything in my power to ensure that workers' compensation covers your care, regardless of your decision." She appraised the trembling but defiant man before her and judged he needed to hear this. "And that your wife receives death benefits."

∽

Later, as twilight painted the sky a deep blue outside her window, Tori sat in the cramped office, finishing her dictation. The shrill ring of the telephone sliced through her thoughts.

"Dr. Nelson? This is Amy at the reception desk."

Tori suppressed a flicker of irritation. Who could need her now? Her patients were gone, and all she wanted was to leave the clinic and dive into her cancer research. She sighed and pressed the phone closer to her ear. "Yes?"

Amy's voice dropped to an urgent whisper. She sounded frightened. "There are two men in suits here. They say they need to see you immediately."

Tori's pulse spiked, and her legs turned to jelly as she forced herself to take a deep breath, as dread filled her. Was the medical director firing her? Had he called security to march her out in disgrace?

The elevator descent took forever. When the doors finally slid open, two men stood waiting, still as statues. One taller than the other, older, and exuding an air of authority, stepped forward and flashed a badge.

"I'm Special Agent Renfrew with the FBI." He motioned to the man standing next to him, young, with short copper-colored hair. "This is Special Agent Brennan. Dr. Victoria Nelson, you are under arrest for armed bank robbery."

Tori froze, her heart hammering. "What?" she stammered, her voice barely above a whisper. "There must be some mistake!"

The red-haired agent wasted no time. His grim expression didn't waver as he grabbed her arm and spun her around with practiced precision. The cold steel of handcuffs bit into her wrists as he recited the Miranda rights in a monotone: "You have the right to remain silent. Anything you say can and will be used against you in court."

She didn't hear the rest of the recital because her mind was reeling as if she were watching someone else's nightmare unfold. She felt she was looking in from the outside, a distance away. The room blurred at the edges, and her knees threatened to buckle as they pulled her by the elbow toward the front door.

"Wait!" she cried. "Where are you taking me?"

The taller agent's response was steely and cold.

"To the FBI field office for processing. And if the Federal Detention Center is full, we'll take you to the Harris County Jail."

CHAPTER 3

THE MORNING AFTER FBI agents led Dr. Nelson out of her clinic, Jo Turner, an associate attorney at the environmental law firm of Fredrick and Engle, left Houston Intercontinental Airport. She drove southeast toward the Houston Ship Channel, reflecting on the conversation with her senior law partner the previous week.

As she'd gazed out the conference room window of their downtown Washington, DC office, she crossed her long legs and dangled one high-heeled shoe from her toes, daydreaming about the upcoming weekend.

She'd snapped back to attention when David, the senior partner, spoke of a call he'd received from Mary Williams, a resident of Oilton, Texas. Speaking for herself and a group of her neighbors, she had told him of a cancer cluster along the Houston Ship Channel where dozens of petrochemical companies belched toxins into the surrounding neighborhoods. David tilted his head toward her.

"Jo, don't we have a potential expert witness in that area? Dr. Nelson, wasn't it—studying cancer incidence nearby?"

She uncrossed her legs and swiveled to face him. "She is.

We talked only a couple of weeks ago. She's worried. The local cancer rates in her initial analysis look alarming."

David nodded. "There may be some business for us. Why don't you go down there and talk to Dr. Nelson? Meet with the residents who called me, and anyone else who is interested."

Jo felt a surge of excitement. This was why she did this work. To have a chance to put things right. "I'd be glad to. I'm up to date on my current cases. I can spare a few days."

"Great," David had said. "I'll have my paralegal call the residents and tell them you're coming. Sounds like we might have a toxic tort case brewing."

Jo steered her Ford Escort rental into Oilton, the refinery looming ever closer with each block. Just beyond the neighborhood's modest homes, flare stacks pierced the gray sky, their labyrinth of pipes twisting like veins. A faint gray haze hung in the air, and a low, unrelenting hum came from the catalytic cracking units. The compressors' vibrations could be felt even in her car. She pulled up in front of Mary Williams's house, a small, weathered home with peeling white paint. Despite its wear, the front yard was tidy, and the grass freshly cut. Bright red geraniums in clay pots lined the wide porch where an older woman rocked gently in a chair.

Jo pushed open the car door, and a sharp stench of rotten eggs hit her like a slap. Sulfuric and acrid, it stung her eyes and nose. She blinked against the irritation and, grabbing her briefcase from the back seat, she made her way toward the house.

The woman on the porch rose from her chair, gripping the railing for balance. She wore a faded floral-print dress and flip-flops that slapped against her heels as she shuffled to meet Jo. Her movements were deliberate, her frame bent. Up close, Jo noticed worry lines creased deeply between her brows. But they softened as Mary's faded blue eyes met hers with a warm, gap-toothed smile. She extended a frail, arthritic hand. Jo clasped it gently between both of her hands and smiled back.

"Hello, I'm Jo Turner," she said. "I'm an attorney with Fredrick and Engle. We spoke on the phone. It's great to meet you in person."

"Glad ya made it," Mary replied. Jo was struck by the rasp in her voice. "C'mon in and get comfy. We saved ya a chair, and I whipped up some cold, fresh-squeezed lemonade."

Jo followed her into the house. In a tidy living room, half a dozen men and women sat on well-worn furniture. Their faces turned toward her, curious eyes sizing her up. Mary gestured to an empty metal chair with a cracked vinyl seat and shuffled off to the kitchen.

Jo sat down carefully under their watchful gazes and smiled in greeting as she set her briefcase beside her. A few returned her smile. Mary returned with lemonade, the condensation already frosting on the glass. She handed it to Jo before easing herself onto the couch between two other women. Jo noticed one of them had a persistent facial tic that tugged at her mouth every few seconds.

"Well, now," Mary said, with an encouraging clap of her hands, "why don't y'all introduce yourselves to my lawyer here, Miss Jo Turner?"

The neighbors complied, each taking their turn around the room. Two older men, dressed in worn overalls, introduced themselves as former refinery workers, while the four women shared that they had lived near the petrochemical plants for decades. Their lined, pinched faces revealed the strain of lives spent in the shadow of the sprawling oil refinery.

Jo was impressed. Mary had gathered this group of potential

plaintiffs on short notice, even in a town where challenging Oilton's dominant employer, World Petrol, risked reprisal. She scanned the room, meeting each person's gaze with steady resolve.

"Thank you," she said, acknowledging their introductions. "I'm here to listen and learn." Her voice was calm and purposeful. "Our firm in Washington, DC, specializes in lawsuits against companies suspected of violating laws and harming the environment. I understand you're deeply concerned about the cancers and respiratory illnesses affecting your community."

Mary leaned forward. "That's exactly why we're here." She hesitated for a moment before continuing. "I'll start." There was a catch in her voice, and she cleared her throat. "My husband, Barry, never smoked a single cigarette. For thirty years, he worked twelve-hour shifts at that plant and hardly missed a day, until he got lung cancer." Her voice cracked on the last word, but she pressed on. "He used to tell me about those fumes, so strong they'd make him nearly pass out."

Ralph, a retired maintenance worker with weathered hands and a furrowed brow, nodded grimly. "That's no exaggeration," he said with conviction. "Those fumes could topple a horse."

Mary paused to collect herself, her eyes shimmering with unshed tears. She swiped at them before continuing. "Barry was only fifty-five when he passed." Her voice was heavy with grief. "It was awful to watch him go like that. Toward the end, gasping like a fish out of water. He never got to meet his grandkids or take those trips we'd dreamed about for his retirement." Her expression turned grim. "His doctor tried to file a workers' comp claim for his cancer, but the company's insurance folks shut it down. Said it was unrelated."

Maureen, a woman so emaciated she nearly disappeared inside her baggy man's work shirt, reached over with skeletal fingers and touched Mary's arm in silent solidarity.

Jo swallowed hard, her own painful memories surfacing unexpectedly. Her father had died of brain cancer when she was only eight years old. She'd come to believe his exposure to toxic chemicals had stolen him away from her family. It was why she fought so fiercely for people like these. "I'm so sorry," she said gently, her voice thick with emotion.

Another retired worker raised his hand abruptly, unable to hold back any longer. His voice carried both anger and urgency. "I know for a fact there've been leaks of cancer-causing chemicals like 1,3-butadiene, especially when the polymer explodes inside over-pressurized pipes. It's not just us workers breathing in styrene and benzene. These toxins are also released into the community, often at night when no one can see the smoke."

Janine, the woman with the facial tic, spoke up next. The tic worsened as she talked. "That's right," she said bitterly. "They think they can hide it—but you can smell it plain as day! That rotten-egg stench with its sickly-sweet undertone? It seeps into your clothes and right through your windows."

Jo noticed Maureen had slumped on the couch, her emaciated frame taking up even less room in the oversized shirt. Her eyes were closed. "Maureen?" Jo said. "Are you okay?"

Maureen opened her eyes and sat up with visible effort. Her voice was faint but steady as she answered. "Just feelin' a little lightheaded," she said. "I've got leukemia, and I never worked in those plants." She paused to gather strength. "But I've lived here my whole life. And my cousin—she was married to a supervisor but never worked there either—she died from leukemia." Her thin finger pointed toward the window, as if to accuse the air, and her voice grew sharp with pain and anger. "That stink out there? That's death you're smellin'."

A chilly silence fell over the room, broken only by the distant hum of the refinery. Mary wrapped a protective arm around

Maureen's shoulders, which looked as fragile as bird wings. "Would you like to lie down for a spell, honey?"

Maureen nodded weakly, and Jo rose to help. Together, they guided her down the hall toward a quiet bedroom. Behind them, the others sat in heavy silence.

CHAPTER 4

WHEN JO AND Mary returned to the living room, the conversation crackled to life like a long-dormant fire. Georgia leaned forward.

"My babies . . ." Her voice faltered. "Three little ones, they all gasp for breath every time that poisonous smoke rolls in. Last week, Caleb turned blue. I held him 'til dawn, praying his lungs wouldn't quit." A single tear traced the crease of her cheek.

The woman in sweatpants, Linda, ground her cigarette into an ashtray. "Asthma is bad, but try feeling like someone's drilling through your skull for days. I snap at my kids, my man. Hell, I even yelled at Ralph's mangy hound yesterday."

"Ain't you always sweet as burnt toast?" Ralph jabbed, but Jo saw his smile fade when Linda turned away, swiping at her eyes.

Georgia continued, desperation etched on her face. "My man works down at the chemical plant. He makes good money and doesn't wanna leave. But these asthma meds are bleedin' us dry. So dang expensive, we're choosing between medicine and meals by the end of the month. I'm 'bout ready to pack up, take the kids, and go before they stop breathing altogether."

A movement at the door drew their attention.

"I couldn't settle, hearin' y'all jawin'." Maureen's entrance silenced the room. She moved like a ghost, her thin frame sinking into the couch. "We're dyin' here," she rasped, eyes burning into Jo's. "What's your fancy legal firm going to do about it?"

"I'm deeply sorry for your struggles." Her voice was unsteady, and the words sounded inadequate to her own ears, even though profoundly true.

Jo swallowed hard and tried again, sounding more natural. "It's terrible what you've been through. What you're going through. My law firm will fight to hold these petrochemical giants accountable for the devastation they've unleashed on the environment and families like yours."

She glanced around the room to make sure she held their attention. "Large damage awards can force them to view you as people deserving of justice rather than blindly focusing on their profit margins. We'll start with one of the largest and worst offenders, World Petrol. If we win, the case will send shockwaves through the entire industry."

"How long is that going to take?" Maureen asked, hope battling with doubt in her face.

Jo sighed. It was possible, she thought, that Maureen might not live to see the outcome. "It takes months, if not years. To start, our expert, Dr. Victoria Nelson, is working on a study that I believe will confirm what you already know in your bones. Cancer stalks the neighborhoods around these petrochemical plants."

Maureen waved her hand in the air. "That's what we've been screaming into the void for years."

"Yes, you have, and you deserve to be heard," Jo acknowledged. "But to build a case, we need medical and scientific evidence that connects your suffering to the specific poisons they're pumping into your community."

Ralph interrupted, bitterness infecting his words. "Good luck with that." His laugh grated like rusty metal. "You know what outsiders call the stench around here? The smell of prosperity. Prosperity. That's what drives these companies. They bury the truth deeper than toxic sludge."

"Yes, they do," Jo said. "A small law firm like ours typically partners with other environmental advocates, including other law firms, the government, and organizations such as the Sierra Club. We can demand the company's air monitoring records during pre-trial discovery. Even with Reagan trying to muzzle OSHA and gut the EPA, we'll work every angle to uncover the truth."

"Have y'all had any luck bringing corporate giants to justice?" Ralph asked with a flicker of hope in his weathered face.

"Yes. We've forced coal companies to answer for ravaging the land, poisoning their workers, and contaminating the water of entire communities." Jo looked around at their faces, hungry for justice. "But I won't lie. It's a long, hard road. And often workers fear for their livelihoods."

Several shook their heads, muttering darkly.

"However, change begins with brave souls like you filing lawsuits and demanding that your government prioritize the protection of people rather than corporate profits."

Maureen's shoulders sagged. "Yeah, if we live long enough."

"The jobs at these plants pay well," Ralph said. "Folks around here aren't going to like us bringing in doctors and lawyers to rock the boat. Some neighbors, even those coughing up blood, wouldn't dare speak against the company."

"I understand the fear," Jo said. "Your courage humbles me. But these billion-dollar corporations can afford to provide both good jobs and clean air. I need your stories. Your medical records. Your anger. Let me carry them into the courtroom."

"How much is this all gonna cost us?" Janine asked, her facial tic taking off again.

"Our law firm works on contingency. If we win, we will get a percentage of the monetary award. If we lose, we take nothing."

This produced some raised eyebrows and nods of approval.

The discussion burned through the afternoon. Jo collected their contact information and signed all six as plaintiffs, adding consent forms to release their medical records.

After sharing a Lone Star beer with Mary, Jo trudged back to her car, her mood dampened by the stories of families trapped between poverty and poison. She tried to lift her spirits by focusing on her meeting that evening with her old friend, Tori. They'd spoken over the weekend, and Tori had invited her to stay at her home in Houston after the interviews. Jo was looking forward to it. The comfort it promised was welcome at the end of a day filled with so much misery.

As Jo drove west on I-10 toward Houston, the oppressive gray haze and the acrid stench of burned matches and sulfur began to lift. The road was clear, and she drifted into memories of her long friendship with Tori—a bond forged years ago at Boston University, where they'd shared a dorm room and so much more. Jo had been captivated from the start by Tori's brilliance, athletic grace, and effortless beauty. With her golden hair and striking features, Tori could easily have been mistaken for a young Candice Bergen. But Jo's first crush had gone unrequited, as Tori had a boyfriend, Rick, and married him after her first year at Harvard Medical School.

In college, their days were filled with study sessions with friends in cramped dorm rooms or on sun-dappled benches along Commonwealth Avenue. The early 1970s was an electrifying time to be young and idealistic. Second-wave feminism was surging, women's marches filled the streets, and anti-war protests echoed across campuses. Those heady years shaped their progressive ideals, even as life pulled them in different directions: Tori into medicine, Jo into law. Now, under Reagan's presidency, she watched with regret as so much hard-won progress slipped away.

Jo reached Houston forty minutes later, stopping at a gas station before heading to a payphone to call Tori. No answer. Jo was puzzled. Tori had sounded eager for this visit when they spoke last week. They'd planned to catch up on their lives and discuss the findings of her cancer study. She battled a growing sense of unease as she grabbed a quick burger and salad at a nearby diner before trying again. Still no answer. She could hardly turn up on her friend's doorstep, bag in hand. With a sigh, she resigned herself to finding a hotel for the night.

Once settled in her room, Jo called her girlfriend back in DC, as she always did when traveling.

"Sam doesn't love you anymore," Kate teased. "He's sitting in my lap right now and has decided I'm his new favorite person."

Jo smiled, imagining her Doberman sprawled across Kate's lap like an overgrown puppy. "Uh-oh," she said with a chuckle. "Sam and I will have words when I get home."

They chatted about Jo's day and her worry about being unable to reach Tori.

"Maybe she forgot?" Kate suggested.

"That's not like her," Jo replied, biting her lip. "She's always so reliable."

"She might have had a medical emergency. She is a doctor."

"Maybe," Jo conceded. "But I checked with my office, and she hasn't left any messages about canceling."

"Can you come home early then?" Kate's voice carried a note of hopeful longing that tugged at Jo's heart.

"Maybe," Jo said after a pause. "If I can't reach her tomorrow."

After their usual murmured endearments, they hung up.

Jo couldn't settle. She sat on the edge of the bed, rubbing her hands up and down her pant legs, unable to shake the feeling that something wasn't right with her friend.

The next morning, Jo called Tori as soon as she'd finished in the bathroom, hoping to catch her at home before work. Still no answer. She had breakfast in the hotel dining room and wondered if she'd need to check out today. Back in her room, she reviewed her interview notes until she was sure Tori would be at her clinic, only to be told Dr. Nelson was not in that day.

Her frustration mounted. Keeping an eye on the clock, she wrote a summary of her trip and, just before checkout time, rang the front desk to request a late departure. Then she tried calling Tori at home one last time before leaving.

Finally, Tori picked up.

"Tori, I've been so worried! Where have you been?" Jo said, relief flooding her voice.

"Oh, Jo," Tori's voice was breathless. It sounded as though she'd been crying. "I'm so glad you're here. You won't believe what's happened."

Jo's shoulders instantly tensed in response to the distress in her friend's voice. "What is it? What's happened?"

"I've spent the last thirty-six hours in jail," Tori said. "The FBI arrested me for bank robbery."

Jo's world tilted on its axis.

CHAPTER 5

JO SAT PARALYZED, trying to understand what she had just heard. That the FBI suspected a physician with a thriving career, married to an entrepreneur, had robbed a bank boggled her mind.

There is no way the Tori I know would ever risk all she's worked for to rob a bank—absolutely no way.

She paced her hotel room as far as the phone line reached.

"Tori, this must be an egregious error."

"That's what I kept telling the agents as they hauled me off to jail in handcuffs." Tori's voice was weary.

"What led them to arrest you?" She ran her hand through her hair and flopped onto the bed. Someone started vacuuming in the hotel hallway, and she strained to hear Tori. She picked up the phone and sat on the uncomfortable chair by the tiny hotel desk, further from the door.

"At the initial hearing with the magistrate, I learned they had a surveillance video and two still photographs. They likely got my photo from my driver's license. Eyewitnesses apparently identified me from a photo lineup." There was a sob in Tori's voice as she choked out, "I'm so scared, Jo."

"Of course you are! Still, I can't believe you are even a suspect. You have no criminal record and probably not even a parking ticket. You have no motive. It makes no sense." She rubbed the back of her neck with her free hand and took a deep breath. She needed to think like an attorney. She was an attorney, dammit. "Did the FBI claim to have found any physical evidence to link you to the robbery?"

"I'm sure they searched my house. But they wouldn't have found anything."

There was a knock at the door and a call of "Housekeeping." Before Jo could answer, a woman unlocked the door, but she withdrew when Jo waved her away.

"Did your husband get you a lawyer?" Jo asked. She recalled Rick's chiseled jawline and fraternity swagger—the cocky charm that had swept Tori off her feet and down the aisle.

"No," Tori sighed. "I asked him to, but Mr. Big-Shot-MBA couldn't navigate his way out of a paper bag in a crisis."

Jo rolled her eyes. Typical Rick. All flash and no substance when it mattered.

"So what sprung you out of jail?"

"The judge allowed sureties for bail—$100,000 worth. But I'm in real trouble here, Jo. I need a good criminal attorney. It's not like I have any contacts in criminal law. Can you help me?"

Jo scratched her head. Environmental law was her battle-field—wetland preservation and corporate pollution, not criminal defense. "Jesus, Tori, I'm still reeling from shock, but I want to help. Let me reach out to my professional network to find you a skilled criminal defense attorney."

A weighted pause hung between them before Tori whispered, "You don't think I did it, do you?"

"Of course not," Jo answered without hesitation. "It must be a case of mistaken identity." She gnawed at her bottom lip as she thought. "Let me find you a shark of a defense lawyer. I'll make some calls right now before I come over."

Tori's relief came through the line in a breathy exhale. "Thank you."

Jo sat frozen, the receiver still warm in her hand. It took several minutes and a few deep breaths before she could regain her composure. She picked up a pen and rolled it absently between her thumb and forefinger, her mind racing to process what she'd just heard. This wasn't just shocking news: it was incomprehensible. What had happened for the FBI to arrest Tori, of all people—her brilliant, blameless, idealistic friend?

Jo's thoughts spiraled back to the Tori she knew: the woman who had bulldozed her way through Harvard Medical School when few women dared, who had conquered an internal medicine residency at Massachusetts General, and who had earned a master's in epidemiology from the Harvard School of Public Health while exploring the mysteries of environmental toxicology. Tori had built a career that most women could only dream of, shattering glass ceilings with every step. And now? Now she was accused of robbing a bank. It was absurd. Unthinkable.

Over the years, their friendship had thinned to sporadic phone calls each year, but Jo had never doubted Tori's brilliance—or her integrity. Recently, they'd reconnected through work when Jo contacted her to serve as an expert witness for her law firm. Jo had been thrilled to collaborate with her again, especially with Tori on the cusp of publishing groundbreaking cancer research that would bolster their case. But this? This would seriously affect Tori's credibility as an expert witness.

There wasn't time to wallow in disbelief. Jo snapped into action. She dialed her office in DC, instructing her paralegal to dig through her Rolodex for contacts—former colleagues, law school professors, anyone who might help make sense of this mess. She began making calls. One name surfaced repeatedly. Brian Kirkland. Jo dragged the weighty Houston phone book from her bedside table, flipped through its pages until she found his office, and scheduled an appointment for herself and Tori to meet him the following morning.

Whatever was happening, she wasn't about to let Tori face it alone.

Jo's blouse stuck to her with sweat before she cranked the air conditioner to full blast in the sweltering Ford Escort rental and sped toward Tori's house. Before she'd checked out of the hotel, she had rung her old criminal law professor. His words echoed in her mind, sharp and impossible to ignore. "It's rare for a woman to rob a bank, but when she does, it's usually for practical reasons—paying bills, for instance." He'd paused. "Maybe Dr. Nelson has some secret, like an expensive drug habit?"

Jo had scoffed at the idea. Tori? A drug abuser? It was absurd. But then his maddeningly detached tone continued, "Sometimes women resort to bank robbery during periods of personal turmoil. They're motivated by control, reclaiming power when life feels out of their hands."

The thought gnawed at her as she gripped the steering wheel. She'd lived with Tori for two years in college and had rarely seen her unravel under stress. But people change. Life changes them.

Still, none of this made sense. How had Tori—a successful physician with no criminal record—ended up in a photo lineup shown to eyewitnesses at the bank? This had to be some colossal mistake. But if it wasn't, what on earth could have driven Tori to such a desperate act?

CHAPTER 6

TORI HUNG UP from her phone call with Jo and pressed the heels of her palms against her eyes to stem the tide of emotions threatening to overflow. The bank robbery arrest had catapulted her life into chaos, a tornado that had uprooted everything familiar and secure. Even her home had been violated. The FBI had searched it, leaving drawers open and items haphazardly strewn around. Jo remained her lone anchor in this storm.

She drifted into the kitchen, the hardwood cool beneath her bare feet as she mechanically prepared coffee and sat at the kitchen counter, staring out the window at nothing. Her stomach protested its emptiness, but food held no appeal. Instead, her mind replayed the nightmare of the last day or so, starting with the FBI dragging her away in handcuffs as the clinic receptionist stared in stunned disbelief.

At the Harris County Jail, a stone-faced female officer with dead eyes had conducted the strip search with clinical detachment as if Tori were merely an object to be processed. "Take the tampon out," the guard had commanded, her voice flat.

"It's just a tampon," Tori had protested, her cheeks burning.

"How do I know that? Take it out," came the emotionless reply, the guard's stare unwavering.

Under that unflinching gaze, Tori complied as her dignity crumbled. The guard's only response was to thrust a wad of rough paper towels at her—no replacement, no compassion. Her medical credentials, years of education, and spotless record meant nothing. She was just another number in the system now.

The holding cell in Harris County Jail was a tableau of misery. One woman hunched over the exposed toilet, her face buried in her hands. Another lay corpse-like on a cot, eyes fixed on the ceiling, staring blankly as if willing herself to disappear. Tori claimed a bench, its surface cold and unyielding. The pale woman on the toilet moaned intermittently, her body wracked with what Tori diagnosed as withdrawal symptoms. That night, Tori summoned the same grit that had carried her through sleepless hospital rotations as she tossed and turned on the lumpy jail mattress.

Morning brought no relief. When Tori tried to flag down guards to get medical attention for the suffering woman (and necessities for herself), they swept past without acknowledgment.

"They won't come. Don't bother," murmured a cellmate, resignation heavy in her voice.

As she sipped her coffee at the kitchen counter, another memory intruded. Rick's voice was sharp and accusatory. "What the fuck have you gotten yourself into, Tori? It's outrageous."

"Do you really think I would rob a bank?" she had asked him, hoping to penetrate his callousness.

"I don't know what you'd do anymore," Rick had shot back. "You've been so weird lately."

She had hoped he'd fight for her, to move heaven and earth to raise bail and get her an attorney. But when she stood before the magistrate that morning, she had no attorney. Rick had done just enough to arrange a surety for bail from their joint account, as if it were an unpleasant chore.

His indifference had stung. How had it come to this between them?

Even more importantly, what would happen to her now?

Persistent stomach growls reminded her again how long it'd been since she'd had a proper meal—two days, perhaps more. She put her empty coffee cup in the sink, opened the fridge, and pulled out a frozen dinner. After microwaving the meal, she sat at the counter with a glass of milk, staring at the steaming plate. Her fork hovered over the turkey as her mind wandered to the week ahead. Patients. Appointments. Her cancer study. And then, the image of the FBI hauling her away in handcuffs flashed in her mind like a cruel joke. Everyone must know by now. She dreaded the stares, the whispers, the questions. That is, if she dared to show up at work.

Her stomach tightened at the prospect. "I can't deal with it," she muttered. She dropped her fork and rose to grab the wall phone, dialing her medical assistant.

"Dr. Nelson! Geez, we heard the news! Are you okay?" The voice on the other end was breathless, concerned.

"Yes, I'm out of jail," Tori said. The words sounded peculiar as they came out of her mouth. "It's a case of mistaken identity, but I need to resolve this mix-up before returning to work. Please cancel all my patients' appointments for the next two weeks."

A pause crackled through the line before her assistant replied hesitantly, "Of course. We've already canceled this week's appointments, but—"

Click. Click.

Tori stiffened, alert. *Is someone tapping my phone?* She couldn't handle another problem right now.

"Thank you," she cut in abruptly and hung up.

Her hands trembled as she rummaged through her handbag

for her pillbox. She shook a small orange pill into her palm and stared at it, hesitating. This was the last one. With a sigh, she swallowed it and forced herself to take a few more bites of food. But eating the rest was impossible while her thoughts so loudly competed for her attention.

Thank God for Jo, her rock. Jo stood by her side even after admitting to Tori her unrequited college crush, proving their friendship was stronger than awkward confessions and disappointment. But Tori hadn't told Jo all her secrets—hadn't told her about Jude, the woman who had so rocked her world over the past several months. Their complicated situation must stay private—at least for now.

Thinking of Jude, she hadn't shown up for their lunch date on Friday, the same day as the robbery, and hadn't answered any of her calls since then. Tori had chalked it up to one of Jude's work emergencies; her job often kept her out of reach for days.

But now? A growing suspicion that Jude had learned of her arrest and was keeping her distance began to form. She worried away at the thought until she could no longer sit still. Leaving most of her food untouched, Tori threw on clothes and headed out to find a payphone. Just in case those clicks on her home phone meant what she thought.

Jude picked up after four rings.

"Jude, I'm so glad you picked up." Tori began urgently.

"Hi, Tori. I'm so sorry I missed our lunch date on Friday." Her voice sounded genuinely apologetic. "There was an emergency at work. I've been putting in sixteen-hour days and barely slept for two nights. I knocked off early today to get some sleep."

Tori exhaled, her tension easing. "God, I'm so sorry. Did I wake you? Was anyone hurt?"

"No," Jude replied. "But you know how it is when things break down."

Usually, Tori asked for details, but not today.

"Jude," she began, gripping the receiver tightly, "I need to tell you something that might upset you."

"What is it? What happened?" Concern sharpened Jude's voice.

She hasn't heard.

Tori took a deep breath. "The FBI arrested me Monday night. For robbing a bank."

Jude gasped so loudly it hurt Tori's ear. She flinched.

"Oh, my God!" said Jude. "Why? Are you okay? Where are you?"

"I'm home now," Tori said, tears threatening to spill over as she spoke. "Out on bail. But jail was hell." She felt ready for another bout of crying and fought to control it. "A friend's helping me find a criminal defense attorney."

"This is insane," Jude said, panic creeping into her voice. "Why would they arrest you? Is someone trying to frame you? Does this have anything to do with us? With what we're doing?"

"I don't know," Tori admitted grimly. "But listen—don't call me at home anymore. I've heard clicks on my line. Someone is monitoring my calls."

"This is so outrageous!" Jude was silent for a moment. "When can I see you?"

"Not for a while," Tori said, reluctantly. "We need to lie low until I figure out what to do."

A weighty silence lay between them before Jude whispered, "Be careful."

"I will," Tori promised. "You be careful too."

CHAPTER 7

AS JO APPROACHED Tori's house in Houston Heights late Wednesday afternoon, she drove through dappled shadows cast by the mature trees lining both sides of the street. She parked on a gravel strip to the side of a two-story Victorian, painted a vibrant blue with cream trim, and entered a well-manicured lawn. She admired the baskets of flowering plants that hung on the front porch and wondered how Tori and Rick had time to maintain all this beauty.

The wooden floorboards of the expansive wrap-around porch creaked as she approached the door, and Tori opened it before Jo knocked. Jo was dazzled by her smile that revealed perfect teeth and enchanting dimples, but when it faded, worry lines creased her brow. Tori's face looked drawn and her eyes, a deep sapphire blue, had lost their familiar sparkle. She pulled Tori in for a tight hug.

"Hello, my friend." When Jo stepped back, she noticed Tori's eyes glistened as she wiped away a tear.

"I'm so relieved you're here."

Jo hugged her again. "It's going to be okay. We'll sort this out."

She followed Tori into the spacious, light-filled interior of the home, where she found a pleasing mix of antique and modern furniture. It didn't appear to be the home of a couple struggling financially. *Thinking of couples, where is Rick?* Shouldn't he be around when Tori had only just returned from her ordeal?

Tori led Jo into a guest room with a ceiling fan, cool blue drapes and bed covers, a comfy chair by the window, and even a telephone by the bedside. *She thinks of everything.*

After Jo set her bags down, they returned to the living room, where she and Tori settled on the overstuffed couch. They munched on pretzels and sipped from chilled glasses of sweet tea, the soft whir of the ceiling fan providing a gentle backdrop.

"We have an appointment tomorrow morning at nine with Brian Kirkland, a criminal defense attorney."

Relief flooded Tori's face. "Thank you, Jo. I knew I could count on you. Is he good?"

"I don't know him personally, but I've heard nothing but good things about him from my colleagues. Hopefully, he'll have more information about what led to your arrest."

"Where is he based?"

"Downtown Houston. I could drive you?"

"No. Let's go in the Volvo. It's probably got better air conditioning than your rental."

Jo was glad to see a slight smile on Tori's face.

"Tell me about everything from the beginning."

In a calm, level voice, Tori told her about the FBI showing up at her clinic in the late afternoon on Monday, handcuffing her in the clinic lobby, and hauling her away in their van. But behind Tori's tired eyes lurked fear as she described her day and a half in the Harris County Jail holding cell.

"I feel so awful for those poor women in that place," Tori said.

"It sounds hellish," Jo said. "I wish you'd called me."

"Everything was so confusing, I wasn't thinking straight. Besides, Rick had access to our account to post the sureties the judge required."

Jo sipped her iced tea and set it on a coaster before venturing into sensitive territory.

"I'm surprised Rick isn't here with you. Is he at work?"

"Um, no. I've been meaning to tell you . . ." Tori looked away and ran her thumb up and down the condensation on her glass. After a moment, she met Jo's eyes.

"Rick and I have been having difficulties for quite a while. We've hardly spoken in the last six months, and the tension only escalates when we do. We were seeing a marriage counselor, but it was a charade." She sighed. "I wonder what I ever saw in him."

Tori took a sip of her tea. "We've separated, and I've filed for divorce—my choice. Rick reacted with anger and bitterness. He's still angry. Three months ago, he got his own apartment. He occasionally shows up at the house since he has nowhere else to store his stuff."

This news paled in comparison to Tori's arrest for bank robbery, but it still packed a punch. When Tori married Rick ten years ago, Jo had privately thought he was not right for her. This felt like vindication, but the marriage's failure still left her saddened. She touched Tori's arm lightly. "I'm sorry. And now? How do you feel about it?"

Tori flashed a brief smile. "Relief, actually." She sighed. "The tension was so bad, it poisoned the air even when we weren't speaking or in the same room. Now, when he's away, I breathe freely. The work on my cancer research flows, the hours fly by, and I get so absorbed, I forget to eat." Tori rose. "Speaking of forgetting to eat, let's make supper."

Jo was starving after her journey and willingly took the hint that Tori didn't want to discuss Rick or the separation further. "Let me help," she said, springing to her feet and gathering their glasses. "Then walk me through your cancer study. I'm aware of only the broad outline of it from our call months ago."

Tori gave her the second full smile she had seen that day. "I'd be happy to."

In the kitchen, Jo stood at the large central pine table, tearing lettuce and cutting tomatoes and carrots for a salad. Tori put lamb patties on the indoor grill for burgers and whipped up a dressing for the salad. They mainly worked in silence, lost in their thoughts, until they both jumped as the wall phone rang.

"It may be the clinic," Tori said, before answering the call.

Jo went to the large porcelain sink to wash her hands, but snippets of the one-sided conversation reached her over the sound of running water.

"Yes, it's true. I have no idea. No, I need some time. Yes, of course."

When Tori hung up, the worry lines had deepened. "What do I tell people? I've had to cancel my patients' appointments. I'm presenting my study findings to cancer specialists at MD Anderson's medical grand rounds next month—the first time I'll publicly share my results. The word is getting around about my arrest. It's just . . ."

The phone rang again.

"Don't answer it," Jo said, touching Tori's arm.

"It could be the university." Tori picked up the call with a curt, "Yes?" She rolled her eyes. "No comment."

She slammed the receiver back.

"Now the reporters have my unlisted home number."

Jo threw her arm around Tori's shoulders and squeezed. "Don't answer the phone anymore tonight. Let's eat, then walk me through the research that has you so excited."

CHAPTER 8

FORTIFIED WITH DINNER, Jo prowled through Tori's home office, taking in the rich, dark wood molding that framed the tall, narrow windows. One entire wall was devoted to a built-in bookcase of matching wood, its shelves sagging under the weight of the heavy medical tomes. The room's scholarly atmosphere was jarringly interrupted by a utilitarian tan metal filing cabinet, the hulking presence of a beige IBM computer monitor squatting on a large beige box from which ugly cables sprouted, and the chaotic jumble of papers strewn across Tori's massive oak desk.

Tori gestured for Jo to sit in a straight-backed chair she'd positioned alongside her desk, then sank into her well-worn leather chair. The computer hummed as it slowly booted up.

"At least one of your interviewees is almost certainly part of what we call a cancer cluster." Tori's voice took on a professor's cadence. "Along the Houston Ship Channel, dozens of petrochemical giants and oil refineries transform crude oil and natural gas into chemical building blocks, the invisible architecture behind everything from plastics and polyester, fuel in your car, to fertilizer for our crops. Modern society both benefits and suffers from it."

Jo nodded. She knew this already, but was happy to see Tori's face transform as she spoke. It pleased her to see the worry lines etched by Tori's legal troubles vanish, replaced by the animated expression of someone in their intellectual element.

A whirring and clanking from the big beige box under the monitor interrupted Tori's flow, and she glanced at the screen presumably to check everything was in order.

"I assume the petrochemical workers also find their way to your clinic?" Jo prompted.

"They're practically half my practice," Tori replied. "These men and women come to me convinced that what they've breathed, touched, and absorbed has poisoned them. I can medically validate their suspicions in about one-third of cases— enough to support their workers' compensation claims. Her shoulders dropped slightly. "This advocacy hasn't made me popular with the petrochemical behemoths or my medical director."

"I can imagine," Jo said dryly.

"I've been mining the Texas Cancer Registry data like a detective at a crime scene," Tori's eyes brightened. "The scientific literature has long confirmed that vinyl chloride and benzene exposure correlate with liver, brain, and blood cancers in workers."

Jo nodded. "Yes."

"But what's been keeping me up at night is what happens beyond the factory gates." Tori was dead serious. "That acrid stench permeating Oilton? Outsiders call it the smell of money, but for nearby residents, it translates to cancer rates well above state and national norms. My study will be the first to link these invisible killers to the communities they affect."

"Our firm is counting on that," Jo said.

The computer finally came to life, bathing Tori's determined face in an ethereal blue glow. Her fingers danced across the keyboard with practiced precision.

"Look at this," she said, gesturing toward the screen. "Cancer incidence along fifty miles of the Houston Ship Channel dramatically outpaces Texas and national averages. But," her fingers tapped the keyboard again, "to establish correlation, I had to dig much deeper."

"What variables complicated your analysis?" Jo asked, leaning in and resting her chin on her hand. She admired how Tori refused to rush to judgment about causation without solid evidence. It is what would make her testimony so devastatingly effective as an expert witness in court.

"These companies deliberately cluster in neighborhoods where poverty reigns and people of color predominate," Tori explained, her voice hardening. "Communities that already struggle with limited access to healthcare and nutritious food."

"So, their cancer rates might be elevated, regardless?"

"Precisely. Additionally, cancer isn't a single entity, but a Hydra with many heads. It's multiple diseases likely triggered by a complex interplay of factors."

Jo sighed. "Yet the International Agency for Research on Cancer estimates environmental factors are behind 90 percent of all cancers."

Tori's laugh was sharp and humorless. "Meanwhile, World Petrol's industry scientists insist environmental factors cause a mere 5 percent. They've assembled an army of researchers willing to obscure any connection between cancer and fossil fuel production."

Her fingers struck the keyboard again, conjuring new data. "When I isolate which cancers show elevated rates, a pattern emerges: mesothelioma, lung, brain, leukemia, multiple myeloma, melanoma, bladder, and prostate cancer."

She pivoted the monitor toward Jo, who absorbed the tables of damning statistics and drew a deep breath.

"The million-dollar question is how do you prove these rates aren't simply consequences of poverty, lifestyle choices, race, or inadequate healthcare?"

"By obsessively cross-referencing multiple data sets," Tori replied, her eyes gleaming. "I controlled for smoking, occupational exposures, stage of diagnosis—everything I could get data for. These factors explain some excess, but the strongest correlation remains proximity to the petrochemical complexes."

Jo leaned back, the chair creaking beneath her. "That's exactly why I've been talking to residents in Oilton. Once we secure enough plaintiffs, we'll sort out those with similar claims and perhaps have them certified as a class or simply file a mass tort suit. Your research will serve as the scientific cornerstone of our case."

"Right," Tori said, her excitement fading. "You mentioned that during our call. A lifetime ago now." A shadow crossed her face, her legal troubles intruding once more.

Uh-oh. Keep Tori talking. "This study must have been a monumental effort to tackle alone. When do you even have time to see patients?"

Tori's somber expression lifted. "I only see patients three days a week. But honestly, they're the reason I started this study in the first place." Her passion was unmistakable as she continued. "So many came to me convinced that pollutants from the petrochemical plants were making them sick—or worse, killing their neighbors. It was heartbreaking. That's why I urged Mary Williams to contact your firm. Isn't she just a gem?"

Tori's smile lit up the room, radiant and warm like sunlight breaking through stained glass. It sparked a bit of the same frisson in Jo as it did in college when Tori smiled that way.

"She is," Jo agreed with a grin. "And she's an excellent organizer.

"I thought she might be," Tori said, but her smile dimmed as her tone grew serious. "For so long, I couldn't say with certainty that the pollution was causing their illnesses. There wasn't enough evidence in the medical literature, just scattered case reports. It was maddening."

Tori's face brightened. "But now? Now I can back their claims with real data." She huffed. "Of course, World Petrol's army of well-paid experts will argue that I can't prove causation for any individual patient."

A strand of Tori's blond hair slipped into her eyes. She brushed it back with practiced ease, her blue-eyed gaze sharpening with determination. The laugh lines at the corners of her eyes softened their intensity, but Jo recognized the fire behind them.

Jo stretched and leaned back in her chair, lacing her fingers behind her head. "We'll deal with World Petrol's rebuttal when the time comes," she said firmly. Still, something nagged at her, an unanswered question in Tori's otherwise impressive findings. "Do you have specific data on what exactly people are exposed to near the plants?"

"It's a toxic cocktail," Tori said, frowning. "Benzene, formaldehyde, acetaldehyde, polycyclic aromatic hydrocarbons, chloroprene, vinyl chloride, trichloroethylene—you name it. And don't forget the micro-particulates that carry carcinogens deep into the lungs." She gave a little huff as she turned toward Jo. "However, Texas state agencies don't routinely test the air in these neighborhoods. That's why I'm setting up my lab to analyze body fluids and tissues for selected toxins."

Jo blinked in surprise. "That's incredible."

Tori opened her mouth as if to say more, but stopped herself with a slight shake of her head. She turned back to her computer screen.

Jo said, "I'm surprised there haven't been more studies on the health effects of air pollution in these areas."

Tori bit her lip before answering. "The only one I'm aware of is a small leukemia study involving female high school students in Port Neches, downwind from the refineries spewing benzene and other carcinogens." She shut down her computer and leaned back in her chair. "But there haven't been any with environmental monitoring. Even so, I've struggled to get funding for this research."

Jo could hear the frustration in her voice, and a flash of unease ran through her. *So, Tori was struggling for money*, though it had nothing to do with drug dependency. She suppressed the thought as Tori continued. "Most of it is coming out of my own pocket since the university isn't offering much support, and obviously, no help from Big Oil or chemical companies."

Jo nodded grimly. "That's tough. It wasn't always like this. In the mid-seventies, environmental research funding flowed freely until Reagan came along and gutted it."

Tori turned off the desk lamp and shot Jo an anxious look as shadows deepened around them. Her voice dropped. "I can't believe what's happening. I can't go to jail for bank robbery. Not before I publish my research."

Jo froze momentarily, hit with the same dread, before snapping back into focus. "No, Tori, you're not going to jail!" She reached out and gripped Tori's arm. "We'll make sure of it."

She withdrew her hand and studied her friend's face in the dim light of the floor lamp—a mixture of beauty, brilliance, and resolve. Tori was one of the most relentlessly determined people Jo had ever known; once she had a goal, nothing could stop her.

Not even powerful petrochemical companies, which might try to bury her work.

But she was sure of one thing: no matter what hornet's nest Tori had stirred up with this study and her plans for a laboratory that threatened Big Oil, there was no way she was letting her friend go to prison for a crime she didn't commit.

CHAPTER 9

ON THURSDAY MORNING, Tori followed Jo through the glass doors of Holmes, Kirkland, and Anderson, her palm damp against the strap of her handbag. The reception area's chrome-and-leather modernity felt sterile. Copies of *The Wall Street Journal*, *The New York Times*, and *The Houston Chronicle* were fanned across the glass coffee table but held no interest for her. As they waited, Jo nudged a cartoon of Reagan toward her, but Tori's lips barely twitched, her nerves too jangled for humor.

When Brian Kirkland strode in, his tailored suit and striped tie conveyed an air of expensive competence. The sharpness of his glance was softened by the crow's feet that framed his eyes, and the warmth of his smile and handshake reassured Tori.

He led them into the law library, which enveloped them in the scent of old books and was dominated by a massive wooden table. A tastefully branded notepad, a sharp new pencil, and a tall glass had been placed with geometric precision in front of three leather chairs at the nearest end. Brian invited them to sit and indicated they should help themselves from the water carafes. Jo poured Tori's before her own, the clinking of ice breaking the silence, and Tori nodded mute thanks.

The lawyer slid into a chair across from them. "First things first. Please call me Brian," he said. "Dr. Nelson, how shall I address you?"

She shrugged. "Tori's fine."

She liked him already. It irritated her when people assumed they could address professional women by their first names without permission. Still, her shoulders remained tense, hands clasped tightly in her lap despite Brian's attempt to put her at ease with small talk.

Brian segued into the task at hand, snapping open his note-pad. "Let's review what little we know, shall we? The court gave some information this morning." He pulled his reading glasses down from atop his head.

"You're accused of robbing Fallon National Bank of $6,555 on Friday, June 14th at 11:15 a.m. The robber, described as a medium-height woman with shoulder-length blonde hair, entered the bank with her hands in her pockets. She wore khaki pants, a loose-fitting blue work shirt, a ball cap, and large sunglasses. The bank was empty of customers, but three employees were present. She approached the teller, told her she had a gun in the waistband of her pants, and demanded that the teller hand over all her cash."

The room constricted around Tori as he read. "Oh, my God," she exclaimed, throwing up her hands. "I've never even owned a gun."

She and Jo exchanged alarmed glances. The charges were more serious with a gun involved.

Tori sighed, "Sorry, go on."

"We won't find out much more until after the grand jury decides whether to indict you."

"When will that be?" Tori asked.

"Within a couple of weeks," Brian said, taking off his glasses.

"And we can't get any more information about why I'm an accused felon until then? What other information could the FBI have?" Tore noted her voice had risen, and she took a few deep breaths to calm herself.

"I can tell you what the FBI usually looks for. Often, the teller slips a dye pack into the bundles of bills and activates it as the robber leaves the bank. When the FBI agents searched your house and office, they'd be looking for dye-stained clothes, gloves, or money."

"They would have found nothing to incriminate me," Tori said with conviction.

Jo leaned forward. "So why did they include Tori's photo in the lineup in the first place?"

"Ah, yes," Brian said. "The bank had grainy surveillance footage of the robbery from which they printed two still shots. All three bank employees confirmed it showed the robber. The still shots were then circulated around the business district, which, as you know, includes Tori's clinical office. Someone anonymously reported that the robber looked like Dr. Nelson."

"Anonymously?" Tori said. Who hated her enough? She ran over the possibilities, silently. The clinic's medical director. Her husband. Someone from the petrochemical industry with offices nearby.

Brian nodded. "Yes. Unfortunately, yes. I'm unable to access their identity."

"But isn't reasonable cause required to follow an anonymous tip?" Jo asked. "Arresting someone with no apparent motive, no prior criminal history, and I would assume no physical evidence linking them to the crime is unusual, don't you think?"

"It's weak," Brian agreed. "If confirmed, we'll use that to our advantage if the case goes to trial."

The thought of a trial sent a chill down Tori's spine.

"Something you should be aware of," Jo said, "is that Tori is studying cancer occurrence along the Houston Ship Canal, where several large petrochemical complexes are located. Cancer rates are elevated, likely due to their toxic emissions. Fixing that could cost them dearly. Her results are like a grenade lobbed at the corporate giants. Could her arrest have something to do with her research?"

Brian laid his pen down and fixed his gaze first on Jo, then on Tori. "How so?"

"Someone might want to put me in jail to prevent me from publishing my findings," Tori said.

"Hmm." Brian looked thoughtful, gazing into the middle distance. He shrugged. "I'll keep it in mind. Let's see what evidence the federal prosecutors have before exploring the possibility of corruption and conspiracy."

He flicked through his notes, then caught Tori's eye. "Let's review the morning of June 14th. Walk me through the entire day."

Tori gathered her thoughts. "As I told the FBI, I woke up about 6:30 a.m., made coffee, and turned on NPR to listen to the news. It was too hot and muggy for a run, so I made some eggs and toast. After breakfast, I took my coffee with me to work upstairs."

"Do you have an office in your home?" Brian asked.

"Yes, I work on my research project on Fridays," she said.

Brian scribbled notes on his pad. "Can you describe what you did on the project that morning?"

"I worked on a cancer study I'm presenting to medical grand rounds at MD Anderson Medical Center next month."

"Did you receive or make any phone calls that morning?"

"No. I turned off the phone's ringer to work without interruption."

Brian looked up from his notepad. "What time did you do that?"

"About 8:30 a.m."

"When did you turn your phone back on?" Brian asked, writing.

"Around 12:15, when I checked my answering service for messages."

Brian raised his head. "Can anyone confirm you worked in your home office during those hours?"

"Only my cat."

For an instant, the corners of Brian's mouth drew down, and he and Jo exchanged a glance. He cleared his throat. "What did you do after checking your messages?"

Tori hesitated before answering. "I turned off my computer, dressed, and left the house to meet an acquaintance for lunch."

"What time did you leave?"

"Around 12:30."

"Did anyone see you leave? A neighbor, perhaps?"

"I don't think so. I didn't see anyone."

"Where did you meet for lunch?"

"The name of the restaurant was Lori's Texas BBQ."

"Will the person you met confirm you were there?"

Tori took a quick breath in, suddenly regretting mentioning the lunch.

Brian jiggled his pen, waiting.

Tori kept her expression neutral. "She didn't show up."

Brian and Jo exchanged glances. It didn't look good that she had no alibi for the time of the robbery or shortly after.

CHAPTER 10

THEIR MEETING WITH Brian concluded just before noon. Tori signed the retainer agreement, and they exchanged farewells. Jo, whose metabolism required her to eat every three hours, was ravenous when they finally left his office. They stopped off at a famous lunch spot featuring Texas BBQ. She wolfed down her brisket, beans, and cornbread while Tori picked at hers.

"Do you like Brian?" Jo asked.

"He seems very thorough."

A neutral endorsement. Jo expected Tori to feel reassured, but instead, she acted distracted and anxious. Earlier, she'd said she thought her phone was being tapped. But after being thrown in jail for a crime she didn't commit, Jo guessed she had a right to be on edge.

"Perhaps the grand jury will decide there is insufficient evidence to indict you," Jo said, anxious to reassure. However, she knew grand juries most often decided in favor of the government.

Tori didn't appear to be listening. Jo followed Tori's gaze to a beefy, bald man by the window who was staring at them. Meeting Jo's eyes, he quickly looked away and shoved a forkful of food into his mouth.

Tori leaned forward and whispered. "Are people staring at me because they think I'm the bank robber?"

Jo smiled and whispered back. "No. Guys stare because you're beautiful."

Tori gave a slight shake of her head. "I don't like it. Let's leave. We pay up front."

᷎

They had settled on the couch, chatting and drinking tea, when the doorbell rang. Tori hurried to the door, and Jo followed, ready to protect her from unwanted intrusion.

Rick slouched against the wall, briefcase in hand. Stubble caught the light on his angular, unyielding jawline. Nature had blessed him with perfect symmetry, but since Jo last saw him, his features had hardened. Worry lines were carved across his brow, and his pale blue eyes had turned to ice.

"Hi, Tori. I tried calling, but the line was busy." The space between them hummed with unspoken tension: no kiss, no touch, not even the slightest lean toward his wife. He uncurled from the wall and made as if to enter.

"How was your meeting with the attorney?"

"Fine." Tori, unsmiling, opened the door wider.

No thanks to you, Rick, thought Jo.

A flash of orange caught her attention as a tabby cat she'd only caught glimpses of before, slunk into the hallway and sat by Jo's feet. It did not appear to welcome the new arrival. Its flattened ears and whisking tail mirrored Jo's own unease.

Rick shouldered through the door, and his gaze landed on her. "Hi, Jo. Tori told me you had lined her up with an excellent criminal defense attorney." His delivery sounded hollow, mechanical.

"Hi, Rick," Jo said, determined to put a neutral face on. "It's upsetting and unexpected, isn't it?"

"Totally," Rick said. He looked from one to the other. "Am I interrupting?"

"Tori and I were discussing her study."

Rick rolled his eyes skyward. "She's obsessed. I've told her she's asking for trouble."

Jo was quick to defend her friend. "What does that mean?"

Rick looked uncomfortable. Silence stretched between the three of them, broken only by the angry swish of the cat's tail, until Rick cleared his throat.

"Tori, may I have a word with you in private?"

Tori shrugged. "Okay."

As Rick moved, the orange tabby crouched, body low, tail lashing like a whip. Rick eyed it warily, giving it a wide berth as he sauntered into the living room.

"I'll go upstairs," Jo said, leaving them together.

She thought of calling her senior partners. They needed to know about Tori's arrest and the potential loss of their key medical expert. On the landing, fragments of Rick's voice drifted upward. She stopped.

". . . bail money . . . stretched too thin . . . how do you think I feel?"

The words floated up like toxic bubbles. Now, Jo heard Tori's indistinct murmuring, quickly interrupted by Rick's voice, sharp and angry. "Three hundred an hour?"

This did not sound like a man sympathetic to his wife's plight. He sounded worried only about how much her defense would cost and how it would affect him. Thank goodness she'd come. Tori needed her.

Jo closed the door and flopped on the bed, staring at the ceiling. She postponed calling her office. Instead, she conjured up memories of Tori in their university days. She had brought a homeless teenager into their dorm room for a week, helping her reconcile with her parents. She'd coached a fellow student failing organic chemistry through the semester to a passing C grade. She volunteered at the local animal shelter. Tori was the kindest, most selfless woman she had ever known.

One night in their third year of college, she and Tori sat cross-legged on the roof of their dormitory, sharing a bottle of cheap wine. Tori's shoulder had pressed warm against hers, denim jacket rasping against Jo's thin sweater. Her hand rested on Jo's thigh, casual as a dropped scarf, incendiary as a lit match. Jo's pulse hammered: D - A - N - G - E - R D - E - S - I - R - E.

"Do you ever feel you were put on this earth for a purpose?" Tori said, taking a swig of Mateus from the bottle with her other hand.

"Not really. Do you?" Jo said, already giddy, the wine going to her head.

"I do," Tori said. "When I was twelve, my grandmother told me I was special. She predicted I would do something substantial and important, move mountains if necessary, to improve people's lives." Tori chuckled and took another swig. "I believed her."

"You've moved me." The confession slipped out, wine loosened. Unconsciously, she took a breath and held it. Her unrequited crush on Tori had made her realize she was a lesbian, even if Tori was off-limits.

Tori took her hand off Jo's thigh. The cool night air rushed into the space where her warmth had been. Jo let her breath out.

"I enjoy helping people," Tori said. "But I'd like to do more."

"Is that why you're choosing a career in medicine?" Jo said when her pulse stopped thudding in her neck. "That's helping people one at a time, unless you discover a major medical breakthrough. You could pursue a career in law or politics if you want to make a significant impact as a change maker."

"Nah," Tori said. "Medicine's my path."

They talked late into the night, both waking up with hangovers and vowing never to drink Mateus again.

Jo returned to the present and sighed. The Tori she knew aspired to do good in the world. She was not a woman who'd rob a bank.

"Jo? Are you on the phone?" Tori's voice called through the closed door. She sounded hoarse, as if she'd been crying.

Jo's heart skipped a beat at the distress in her friend's voice. She leaped from the bed, crossing the room in three quick strides, and yanked open the door. Tori stood there, eyes red-rimmed, shoulders slumped.

"What's wrong?" Jo beckoned her inside.

Tori's voice quavered. "Rick is angry, blaming me for the arrest."

Heat rose in Jo's chest. *The bastard.* After everything Tori had been through, her own husband had turned against her.

"Has he left?" she asked, barely containing her contempt.

"Yes." Tori sighed.

Jo softened her voice, gesturing toward the bed. "Come sit down." Tori followed her and they sat side by side, their shoulders touching. Tori's proximity and touch no longer sent Jo's pulse racing like it used to. Those feelings had long since mellowed into something more manageable.

Tori clasped her hands in her lap. "Things were tense before the arrest, but now they're unbearable."

"He should be supporting, not blaming you," Jo said, indignation coloring her words. She wanted to say more, much more, about what kind of man abandons his wife in her darkest hour.

"He's concerned about the cost of the sureties and my

defense. And how my arrest will affect his job contracts." Tori's tone suggested that even she didn't believe these were valid excuses.

Jo bit back the scathing remarks threatening to spill. "I'm sorry, Tori." The words seemed inadequate, but what else could she say? Rick was still Tori's husband, damn it. Jo expected him to be concerned about how the arrest affected his wife's mental state and career, not just his own circumstances.

A flash of defiance sparked in Tori's eyes. "I don't need his bullshit right now."

"I understand," Jo said quietly, then shifted the conversation. "What's Rick doing for work these days?"

"He was working with another engineer to design a new portable computer. But other companies, such as Compaq, have beaten him to it. His start-up folded, but he recently secured a temporary contract to do IT work."

Jo's lawyer instincts stirred. "Are you having financial difficulties?" The words were out of her mouth before she heard the implication, and she flushed with embarrassment.

Tori's lips curved in a wry smile. "No, Jo, I didn't rob the bank because we needed money. To the best of my knowledge, neither of us is in dire financial straits. We keep our finances separate, though," Tori said. "I'm earning about $60,000 a year, and Rick hopes his temporary contract will lead to a job with a salary."

Jo reached out and touched Tori's arm. The cotton of Tori's sleeve felt soft beneath her fingertips. "I don't believe for a second you would rob a bank, even if your finances were dire."

Tori's smile warmed, lighting up even her eyes. "Thank you." The smile faded as quickly as it had appeared. "The thing is, I think Rick believes I did rob the bank."

Jo narrowed her eyes, outrage bubbling up. "Oh, for fuck's

sake, you've been married for ten years. Doesn't he know you at all? How could he even begin to imagine you robbing a bank?"

Tori put her hand over Jo's, the warmth of her touch distracting Jo from her outrage.

"Thank you. I'm so grateful you're here. It means so much to me."

Jo looked down at their hands, touched by the depth and strength of Tori's trust.

After lingering over takeout Indian food, Jo leaned back against the couch cushions, swallowing the last of her beer. *I ought to ring Kate before I go to bed.* The house carried the earthy smell of turmeric. Across the room, a rust-colored blur emerged from the shadows—the cat flowed across the hardwood floor, tail quivering as he vaulted onto Tori's lap.

"Little con artist," Tori murmured, her fingers working the velvety notch between his ears. "He appeared on my front porch one day. He had no collar or tags. I didn't feed him, but he showed up every night for a week, meowing to be let in. Wouldn't take 'no' for an answer." She glanced at Jo and smiled. "Meet Orange Cat."

Jo snorted. "Orange Cat?"

"Yes, really."

The cat cast a slow glance from one to the other while kneading Tori's thighs. His drifting, amber-eyed gaze unsettled Jo, as though he were deep in thought behind those languorous blinks.

Tori stroked him lovingly. "He's very perceptive. Wakes me from nightmares. Makes me laugh with his antics." She smiled. "Reminds me not to disappear into my head. And he's loyal." Tori met Jo's eyes. "Like you."

✑

Jo climbed the stairs to her room, Orange Cat padding silently behind her, apparently accepting her presence. The cat had a knack for appearing at just the right moments, his amber eyes gleaming with curiosity. She shut the door behind her, but he slipped through before it clicked, leaping onto the bed as if he owned the place. Jo barely noticed. Her thoughts were on Kate.

She picked up the phone from the bedside and settled into the chair by the window. The line rang only once before Kate's voice came through, warm and familiar. "Hiya, stranger."

Jo grinned. "Have you been sitting by the phone waiting for my call?"

Kate laughed, a sound that always gave Jo a warm glow. "Yes, I hoped you'd call. I miss you."

Jo smiled, letting the words sink in. *It's nice to be missed.* "Sorry, I didn't call last night," she said. "It was late when I came up to bed, and I didn't want to wake you."

"So you got in touch with your friend?" Kate asked.

"I did," she said. "The afternoon after we talked."

"That's a relief. Did you have a good visit?"

Jo hesitated, her fingers tracing idle patterns on the bedspread. "Um, there's been a development."

"Tori has switched teams and realized you've been the one for her all along?" Kate said, her tone only half-teasing.

Jo laughed. Even if Tori had undergone some miraculous epiphany, Jo wasn't that naive young woman anymore—the one who'd fallen for straight women and women who couldn't decide what they wanted.

"No," she said, shaking her head. "Far from it. Tori's in big trouble. She was in jail when I couldn't reach her the other night. The FBI arrested her for bank robbery."

"What?" Kate gasped. "Are you serious?"

"Yup," Jo said, still grappling with it herself. "Shocking."

There was a pause before Kate spoke, her voice cautious. "How well do you know this woman? You said it's been five years since you last saw her."

"That's true," Jo admitted. "But I know her well enough to say she'd never rob a bank."

"Then why did they arrest her?"

"An anonymous tipster said she looked like the robber."

"That's all?" Kate sounded incredulous.

Jo remembered Tori's paranoia about her line being tapped. "Listen," she said, "I can't explain everything right now. I promise to tell you the whole story when I get home."

"Are you still coming home tomorrow?" Kate asked, a hopeful note creeping into her voice. "Shall I pick you up?"

Jo sighed, longing for their easy banter and Kate's arms around her. But life had other plans.

"No," she said reluctantly. "I'll stay until the grand jury decides whether Tori goes to trial. Her husband's a jerk, and she needs my support. I hope to God her case gets dropped for lack of evidence. A lot is riding on it—including my lawsuit."

Kate huffed, but there was no real upset—just disappointment. "Okay," she said, "But Sam already thinks you've abandoned him."

Jo smiled, imagining her Doberman sulking by the door as if his favorite human had betrayed him. "Oh, he'll get over it," she said lightly before softening her tone. "I just hope you don't feel abandoned."

"No," Kate said after a beat, her voice light and mischievous. "I'm good. But you'll have to make it up to me extra nicely."

"Hmm," Jo murmured, smiling at the image of how she might do that. "Looking forward to it."

They exchanged goodbyes—sweet and tinged with long-ing—and Jo set down the phone on the bedside table with a sigh.

She returned to the comfortable chair, and Orange Cat jumped into her lap, uninvited. He rubbed against her chest before settling in with a contented purr.

"Well, Orange Cat," Jo said in the singsong voice she reserved for animals. She stroked his soft fur, "Are you going to vouch for your mama? That she was in her home office working on her cancer study the morning of the robbery?"

The cat lifted his chin at the sound of her voice and looked up at her. He blinked with wide, inscrutable amber eyes.

"No comment, huh?"

CHAPTER 11

FRIDAY MORNING, BRIAN'S voice crackled through the phone when Tori answered it. Jo came close, straining to hear. *"Defense attorneys are not usually informed when a grand jury will hear a client's case, but a colleague let slip yours may be heard as soon as the end of next week."*

HER EYES DARTED to Tori, who took a deep breath and looked away, but not before Jo caught the fear in her eyes.

"I'd like you to come into the office Monday morning to get more background information, in case the grand jury decides to indict you," Brian continued, his lawyer voice all business.

"That's fine. I've taken two weeks of leave from the clinic to deal with this, so whatever time works for you."

"How about 9 a.m. then? Bring your current bank statements. Will your husband come this time?"

Uh-oh. Jo had witnessed enough of their marital discord to know where this was heading.

"Yes to the bank statements. But my husband won't be coming. We're not on good terms."

Brian was quiet for a moment. "That may be a problem if

you are indicted. I should meet with him to determine his suitability as a witness."

Tori glanced at her friend's wry expression and sighed. "Okay. I'll see if he'll attend the meeting on Monday."

∽

Later that morning, Jo's fingers hovered over the phone before she reluctantly dialed her office. She asked the receptionist to connect her with David. As she waited, her mind raced. *Should I tell him now if he hasn't already heard the news of Tori's arrest? Or wait until after the grand jury hears her case?*

She sighed, her indecision weighing on her.

"How did your interviews go?" David's cheerful voice caught her off guard.

Relief washed over her. He hadn't heard. "They went well. I've signed up six plaintiffs," she said. "Dr. Nelson's cancer study reveals a clear association between cancer and living near petrochemical plants, as we had anticipated. She has ruled out other factors that account for only part of the excess."

"I'd expect nothing less than a solid investigation from her," David said. "Since your meeting at Mary Williams's house, several more locals have called our office to express interest in joining the lawsuit. People are dying. It sounds quite dire."

"Oh dear. I'll have to follow up." *Damn. What if Tori is indicted?* It would be disastrous for the plaintiffs' case if they lost their primary expert. Now was not the time to sign up more people.

Though she knew her timing was off, she took a deep breath and said, "I'd like to take a few personal days."

"Right now? Just when our case is heating up?" David's surprise was unmistakable, followed by a pause that stretched Jo's nerves. "But I guess you've earned some days off. But, then I'd like you to drive over to Oilton and talk with those additional folks."

Jo's grip tightened on the handset. *Tori better not be indicted.* No other medical expert could take her place. "I will," she promised, the words sounding hollow. She had a strong urge to tell him everything, but she swallowed it down. *Wait.*

"Thank you."

Tori knocked on the bedroom door.

"One minute," she called. "Just finishing a phone call."

"That's okay. We're finished for now," David said smoothly. "Keep me updated."

She hung up and opened the bedroom door.

"Sorry," Tori said. "I didn't realize you were on the phone."

"It's fine." Jo's tone was clipped. "Good timing. I'd rather not discuss your arrest with my senior partner until after the grand jury decision."

Tori's shoulders sagged. "Let's hope they decide in my favor," she muttered. "Just before you got on the phone, Rick called. He agreed to meet with the lawyer on Monday.

"Gallant of him," Jo said. The disdain in her tone wasn't subtle, and she didn't care if Tori noticed.

Later, as they tucked into tuna sandwiches, Jo couldn't shake Rick's comment, "She's asking for trouble." It teased her like a loose thread she couldn't stop pulling.

"It doesn't sound like Rick supported your cancer research."

Tori paused mid-bite, then set her sandwich down carefully, as if it might shatter. "No," she admitted. "He never asked about my study findings until recently. But he's always resented the time I spent on it, especially evenings and weekends."

Jo frowned, leaning forward. "What do you think he meant when he said you were 'asking for trouble'?"

"I'm not sure." Tori's brow furrowed, staring at her plate as though it held answers. "Rick has become so—I don't know—so conservative lately. Pro-business, anti-regulation, the whole package. My findings indicate that the region's petrochemical industry is causing harm that will be costly to rectify. Maybe he thinks I should back off, not threaten profits and jobs."

Jo didn't blink. "Does he work with the petrochemical industry at all?"

"I don't know." Tori's voice was tinged with exhaustion. "He has been secretive about his work over the past few months. I think he's embarrassed about his start-up failing and having to take contract IT jobs to make ends meet. He doesn't want to work for a salary again, but, well, he might not have a choice."

Jo took another bite of her sandwich, her mind running through possibilities. Could someone in the industry have pressured Rick to discourage Tori from pursuing her study? Or worse, could his bitterness over their impending divorce have driven him to tip off the FBI, claiming that Tori looked like the bank robber? The thought made her stomach churn.

As if reading her thoughts, Tori spoke. "Rick can be an asshole, and he's furious about the divorce," she said, "but I don't think he'd betray me or sabotage my work."

Jo wasn't so sure. She sighed and took another bite of her sandwich. Tori had always been blind when it came to Rick—too forgiving, too willing to see something redeemable in him that Jo never could.

After lunch, they moved to the couch with their coffees in hand. Orange Cat sprawled lazily between them. Jo broke the silence first.

"Why did you marry Rick?" she asked bluntly, unable to suppress the question any longer. Orange Cat lifted his head, amber eyes narrowing as if he also wanted an answer. Jo smiled briefly at the cat, then kept her gaze fixed on Tori, waiting for an explanation that might finally make sense—or confirm what Jo had always thought: Rick had never been good enough for her.

"You've met my parents," Tori said.

"Yes. I remember them well." How could she not? It had been one of those rare moments when she'd glimpsed what a "normal" family looked like, or at least what she imagined one to be. In college, Tori had invited her to spend Christmas at her parents' home in New Haven, Connecticut. The house was a modest bungalow on a quiet, tree-lined street, exuding comfort and stability. Tori's parents were older, her father worked for Winchester Repeating Arms, and her mother stayed home to care for Tori and her older brother.

Jo could still smell the chocolate-chip cookies Tori's mother had baked that day, pulling them from the oven just as the two of them arrived from university. It was such a small thing, but it stayed with Jo. She'd grown up with a single mom who came home late from work, too tired and irritable to fuss over her, let alone bake cookies. Watching Tori's mom beam as she handed over a plate of warm cookies made Jo's chest ache with envy. She'd wanted that kind of love, that kind of attention, and for a while, she thought she'd found it with Tori.

But then Rick happened.

Jo shifted uncomfortably on the couch as Tori spoke of him, her voice tinged with regret.

"Rick was different," Tori said, stroking Orange Cat absentmindedly. "My parents liked him—well, they liked his résumé more than anything. Upper-middle-class family, business and computer science degree, ambitious. My dad thought he was perfect." She gave a humorless laugh. "He probably thought Rick would keep me in line."

Jo nodded stiffly, trying to keep her expression neutral. She remembered Rick all too well—how he'd swept into their lives like some golden boy out of a rom-com. He'd once brought Tori roses and had even handed over another bunch for Jo, as if that would make up for how he'd monopolized Tori's time.

"And you?" Jo asked quietly. "What did you think of him?"

Tori shrugged. "At first? I guess I liked the attention. He came on strong—flowers, gifts, compliments—it was intoxicating in its own way." She paused, staring into her coffee cup. "But I never experienced that head-over-heels love my girlfriends talked about."

Jo stared into the middle distance, remembering that head-over-heels feeling. It had started with Tori. She shook herself. This was about Tori, not her.

"What changed?"

Tori sighed and leaned back against the couch as Orange Cat kneaded her thigh. Eventually, she said, "Texas changed everything. When Rick's company started struggling in Boston, one of his friends convinced him to move here for a job at another computer start-up. My grants were running out at Harvard, so I agreed to come with him."

Jo tilted her head, surprised. "No urge to stay in academia? You were on track to accomplish great things at Harvard."

Tori gave a small smile, but it didn't reach her eyes. "I thought so too—for a while," she admitted. "But academic politics wore me down. And Rick's salary wasn't enough to cover the lifestyle he wanted." Her voice hardened as she added, "So I took on more clinic hours to support us until his Texas start-up took off—which it didn't."

Jo glanced around the room, taking in the intricate millwork that framed the high ceilings and the ornate fireplace, which seemed plucked from a grand Victorian estate. "I guess you needed the extra income just to afford this place," she said.

"Exactly," Tori replied flatly. "And every time I worked

harder to make ends meet, Rick resented me more." She hesitated before adding, "He didn't care about my study. In fact, he urged me to drop it."

Jo frowned. "Did he give a reason?"

"Because they could be potential clients for his start-up," Tori said bitterly. "He said I was being naive, that those companies provided jobs and boosted the economy."

Jo couldn't hide her contempt. "Didn't you realize your values were completely out of sync?"

Tori looked away for a long moment before answering. "I grew up conservative too—staunchly Catholic parents who voted for Reagan." Then more quietly, she said, "Maybe I'm the one who has changed."

Jo gave her a look—one eyebrow lifted—but didn't ask, "How have you changed?" Instead, she said, "Have you told your parents about your arrest?"

"God, no. They'd flip out. My dad would probably have a heart attack right there on the spot—and then blame me for it."

Jo registered the raw vulnerability in Tori's voice. For all her strength and defiance, Tori was utterly alone in this fight.

"Tori," she said gently, locking eyes with her friend. "I'm with you on this. You're not alone."

CHAPTER 12

THE FOLLOWING MONDAY, Tori sat stiffly in the conference room of Brian's office, her hands folded tightly in her lap, trying to ignore the dull throb behind her eyes. She and Jo had been here for half an hour, growing more irritated by the minute. When Rick burst in, she frowned, offering only a curt greeting.

"Sorry, I had a meeting that ran over," Rick announced as he dropped into a chair with the grace of a collapsing bookcase.

His briefcase hit the table with a bang that made Tori jump. She caught Brian exchanging a look with Jo. Tori looked down at the table, focusing on the grain of the wood as if it might anchor her.

"Thank you for coming, Mr. Dynoski," Brian said smoothly, his lawyerly politeness firmly in place. "I'm Brian Kirkland, Dr. Nelson's legal counsel. We use first names here if that's okay with you."

"Fine." Rick leaned forward for a perfunctory handshake before slumping back in his chair, arms crossed like a petulant teenager.

Brian asked Rick standard introductory questions while

Tori's attention drifted. What did Rick really know about her or her current life? Most of his focus was on himself.

Brian jotted something on his legal pad. "Tori tells me you've separated and have your own apartment." He cocked his head, waiting for confirmation.

Tori's attention returned.

"That's right." Rick uncrossed his arms and bounced one knee.

"But you still see each other from time to time."

"Yeah." He fidgeted and looked away. "I keep some of my stuff at the house."

Tori kept her face neutral, but inside, she bristled. *Some of his stuff?* Half of their house looked like a storage unit for Rick's hobbies and failed projects.

"How did Tori seem to you before her arrest?" Brian asked.

Rick shrugged, his knee still bouncing like a jackhammer. "Okay. A little stressed. We didn't talk much, but that's not unusual."

Tori noticed Jo shift in her seat, and guessed they were thinking the same thing: *What's with this guy?* Irritated and nervous, but what did he have to be anxious about?

"How did you feel when your wife called you from jail?" Brian pressed.

Rick blew out a breath, impatient, as if this whole discussion were absurd. "Shocked, of course."

"Did you believe she'd robbed the bank?" Brian's tone sharpened.

Rick's manner changed subtly. He avoided Brian's eye. "I, um, I dunno. Why would they arrest her if she wasn't a suspect? The FBI doesn't just randomly arrest people. There's gotta be a reason."

He's avoiding looking at me. Tori clenched her fists under the table, nails digging into her palms.

Brian didn't let up. "Can you think of any reason for the FBI to consider your wife a suspect?"

Rick hesitated. "Um. I dunno. Before the separation, she was acting weird."

Tori froze. *Jesus, not this.* Her heart thudded against her ribs as Brian leaned forward.

"Acting weird? How?" he asked.

Rick glanced at Tori—furtive and quick—before looking away again. "She acted distracted and nervous. When she wasn't locked in her office working on her cancer study, she was on the phone with friends or out somewhere. She would often come home late. Sometimes she'd fall asleep at the dinner table." He paused, then added with an edge in his voice, "And the last few weeks, when I've talked to her, she seemed, well, wired."

Tori inwardly cringed. It was true. She had been a mess for the last few weeks. A glance at Jo revealed a tightening around her eyes. *Uh-oh.*

Brian didn't miss a beat. "Going out where?" he asked calmly.

"I don't know," Rick snapped. "And I don't care anymore."

The room went silent except for the creak of Rick's chair as he shifted and tugged at his tie.

"You seem angry with your wife," Brian observed.

Rick exploded, his voice rising as he pushed back from the table. "Am I on trial here? How are my feelings relevant? God only knows what Tori has gotten herself into, but it has nothing to do with me! I'm done with this." He rose, grabbed his briefcase, and strode from the conference room.

Tori froze, staring at the door, shaken by Rick's display of anger. Jo stared at Tori.

A very faint smile played around Brian's mouth, his demeanor completely relaxed.

"Well," he said, breaking the silence with deliberate calm. "I don't think your husband will make a very good witness."

He turned to Tori, and his voice softened. "So, is there any truth to what your husband said about your state of mind before the arrest?"

Tori shifted her gaze to Brian but didn't answer right away. Her throat tightened, and for once, she had no idea what to say or how much she dared to reveal. Her gaze flicked from Brian to Jo and back again as she drew deep breaths. The weight of her secrets pressed against her breast, demanding release—but she could only reveal part of the whole.

"I've been unhappy in my marriage for a long time—years, actually," she admitted, the words tumbling out. "We have little in common, and Rick has never seen the point of my research. Especially my cancer study."

She felt a familiar frustration rise as she recalled his dismissive comments. He treated her research as a frivolous hobby, something to be tolerated rather than respected.

"He said it required too much unpaid time and effort, and Big Oil would shoot it down, anyway."

An aching despair spread through her chest as she continued. "I've been under so much stress with my study, clinical work, setting up a lab, and the separation. I just wanted some time for myself with no responsibility. I didn't want to be around him anymore. So I went out in the evenings sometimes and didn't come home for dinner."

She fell silent.

"Go on," Brian prompted, his pen poised above his notepad.

Memories of their arguments surfaced, each one a fresh wound. "Rick's views on guns, politics, and women have become disturbingly conservative. He's concerned only with making money and achieving social status, although he's not doing well in either regard." Bitterness tinged her voice. "I don't enjoy interacting with his friends, and he doesn't like mine."

"Does Rick own a gun?" Brian's question was sharp and unexpected.

She shivered slightly, remembering the horror of touching the alien, black, cold metal in their bedroom drawer. "He owns a revolver," she confirmed. "We've had fights because I objected to him keeping it in the house. In the end, he took it away."

"Do you know where he keeps it?"

"No." The word came out sharper than she intended. "I didn't want to know."

She watched Brian scribble something in his notes.

"What about your late nights out? What were you doing?" His gaze was penetrating, searching for inconsistencies.

Her focus closed in, and she crossed her arms over her chest and hunched forward, head down. The question probed at secrets she wasn't ready to share, memories that belonged to her alone.

She looked up. "I was questioning my marriage and my life choices. I was trying to figure out who I really was," she said, each word carefully chosen. "I sought counsel from my women friends, not all of whom supported my desire to be happy." The judgment she'd seen in their eyes had stung. "We met for drinks, and the conversation lasted for hours. I didn't care about coming home to make dinner for my husband, nor did I want to explain where I'd been or with whom."

A silence followed. Tori fixed her gaze on a painting hanging on the wall. The abstract swirls of color mirrored the chaos of her thoughts. *They know I'm holding something back.*

Brian waited.

She tried deflection. "The number of women friends I have appears to have diminished further since the news of my arrest has gotten around." Her light laugh was brittle, and she felt she'd given something away.

"That reminds me," said Brian. "You haven't given me the name of the woman you were having lunch with on the day of the robbery."

Shit. I can't have Jude dragged into this mess.

"Oh, right." She sighed. "It won't help. She was a casual acquaintance. When she didn't show, I threw her number away."

"What was her name?" Brian pressed, his gaze unwavering.

A muscle clenched in her jaw. *Damn. I've got to give him something.* "Um . . .Jude, I think. I don't remember her last name."

The evasion felt flimsy. Jo was surely aware that she had a remarkable memory for names, faces, and details. They'd known each other long enough, and it was part of what made her a good doctor. But this was one truth she couldn't share. Not yet. Not with Jo. Not with anyone.

Brian's skepticism was apparent. He could probably spot a lying witness from fifty paces. "If you remember later, let me know. Just as a warning, I can't defend you adequately if you keep things from me."

He turned a page on his notepad. "Let's look at your bank statements," he said. He glanced at Jo. "Is it okay if Jo stays in the room?"

"Of course." Tori reached for her briefcase, grateful for the change of topic. "I also brought statements of my investments. They're in my name only."

She handed over the bank statements. Brian donned his reading glasses and began reviewing the documents with methodical precision.

After a while, he said, "You have had a direct deposit of $4,380 and three withdrawals over the past two weeks. What were these for?"

"The direct deposit is my salary from the clinic. The withdrawals are automatic payments for the total balance of our electricity and telephone bills."

"Do you receive a salary from the university?"

"No. I'm an adjunct associate professor. It's not a paid position." The irony wasn't lost on her—dedicating countless hours to research that brought her no financial reward, only the hope of a scientific breakthrough.

"I see you hold the checking account jointly with Rick. Are any of these earlier deposits his?"

She fought to keep resentment from her voice. "Yes. He still contributes to the mortgage on the house when he can, but not to any other expenses since he moved out."

"What is the outstanding balance on your mortgage?" Brian asked.

"About $250,000." The number hung in the air.

Brian's eyes widened. "Pretty hefty." He held out his hand. "May I see the statements for your investments?"

Tori handed him the statements for her mutual funds and money market account and watched as he flicked through them with practiced efficiency.

"There's a large withdrawal from your money market account of just over $25,000 two months ago," he observed. "What was that for?"

"I bought equipment for my laboratory," she explained, with a flicker of pride. "It's in the early stages, and I buy a little at a time."

Brian nodded, seemingly satisfied. "Your investments and bank balance total about $110,000. We can prove you're not a woman in dire financial straits."

He placed his notepad in his briefcase with a decisive snap.

"There is no financial motive, and if the FBI has no physical evidence, we will argue that your case is one of mistaken identity.

A smile spread across Tori's face. "Thank you."

"Don't thank me yet," Brian cautioned. "I have no control over what the grand jury decides next week."

CHAPTER 13

JO STEPPED OUT of the office building, and the Houston heat hit her like a wet, suffocating blanket. When they reached Tori's car, the door handle was too hot to touch. Sweat trickled down her temples and between her breasts. She swiped at her brow with a crumpled tissue.

"How can you stand living here?"

Tori shrugged as she slid behind the wheel of the Volvo, her movements unhurried despite the oppressive heat. "I barely tolerate it," she said. "But I've got to finish my work."

Jo flopped into the passenger seat and fanned herself with the notepad she'd taken from Brian's library. "That was intense. I thought Brian did a good job, but I'm whacked." She glanced at her friend's profile. Tori stared vacantly ahead. "Why don't we take it easy this afternoon? What do you like to do?"

Tori hesitated. "Go to the gym?"

Jo barely suppressed a groan. The last thing she wanted was more sweating, but the hopeful note in Tori's voice made it impossible to decline.

"Sure," she said with forced enthusiasm. "Let's eat first, though."

Tori smiled. "I can easily forget to eat, but you never do."

Jo studied her friend as they drove down the highway. Tori was thinner than she remembered—too thin—and there was tension in her shoulders that hadn't been there five years ago.

"Regular meals while I'm here will do you good," Jo said.

After lunch, Tori handed Jo a spare tank top and a pair of shorts that were a bit snug but serviceable. An hour later, they were side by side on treadmills in an air-conditioned gym that couldn't entirely banish the Houston heat. The gym smelled of sweat and socks, the air ringing with the rhythmic clank of machines. Jo gulped water between breaths, glancing over at Tori's toned arms and steady stride. This was routine for her. On the other hand, Jo might keel over at any second. Her twice-a-week gym habit wasn't cutting it today.

When they moved on to weights, and Jo's lungs finally stopped burning, she broached the topic that had been nagging at her since they'd left the lawyer's office.

"When you mentioned earlier that you were questioning your life choices, what did you mean?"

Tori froze mid-rep, then let the weights drop onto the rubber mat with a heavy thud. She pulled a handkerchief from her pocket and dabbed at her flushed face before answering.

"Oh, you know, midlife crisis stuff," she said lightly, though her tone didn't match the tension in her posture. "Wondering why I stayed with a man I could barely tolerate in a city I didn't even like. Why I didn't stay in academia instead of going it alone. Why I . . . " She trailed off and waved a hand dismissively before picking up the weights again. "Stuff like that."

Jo frowned. There was more Tori wasn't saying, but she didn't press as Tori powered through another set of reps.

Tori turned to Jo with an apologetic smile. "All I've done since you got here is talk about myself," she said, setting the weights down more carefully. "I want to hear what's going on in your life." Her smile turned playful. "After we get home, let's order pizza and open a bottle of wine. Then you can catch me up on your life—who you're dating, what's happening at your office, gossip about our old friends."

"Okay." Jo returned the smile and immediately bit her lip. What had Tori meant when she'd said in Brian's office that she was "trying to figure out who she really was"? And why had she been so vague about that woman she mentioned meeting for lunch? But something in Tori's tone warned her off for now.

"Sure," Jo repeated after a beat, forcing herself to match Tori's casual tone. There would be time later to dig deeper into what Tori wasn't saying. Pizza and wine didn't sound half bad.

"I'm going to get changed," said Tori. "Coming?"

Jo followed but felt something was missing. She looked around.

"I've left my water bottle somewhere. I'll come in a minute."

Tori went off to the locker room with a spring in her step. Jo, limping slightly, walked back to the weight rack, scanning for her water bottle. Her muscles still burned from the last set, but as she bent down and looked around the equipment, a new sensation prickled the nape of her neck. She glanced up.

In the far corner, on the chest press machine positioned at an angle away from where she and Tori had exercised, sat a hulking bald man. His arms bulged with every push, veins snaking across his glistening skin.

A memory stirred in the back of her mind. She got it! He'd been in the restaurant where they'd eaten Texas BBQ after the first meeting with Brian. Tori had thought he'd been staring at them because of the fuss about the bank robbery. Jo had thought he was staring at Tori because she was so beautiful.

She spotted her bottle by the treadmill between her and the hulking man. As she reached for it, she realized he'd had an unobstructed view of her as she'd exercised with Tori.

He caught her looking at him and returned her stare. His eyes locked onto hers, sharp and unwavering.

Her breath hitched. A stalker? Her pulse quickened as a dozen questions tangled in her mind. He looked like a body-builder, maybe a regular here. But how likely was it they'd encounter him at the gym *and* the restaurant?

The intensity in his eyes unnerved her. The word that came to mind was *threatening*. A chill rippled through her despite the heat of the gym. She moved away, aware that he was still watching her.

In the locker room, she mechanically changed into her street clothes. Tori was finishing up at the sink, oblivious to what Jo had seen. *Am I just being paranoid? Should I tell her?* She laced up her shoes while her mind ran in circles. Had the man simply taken a fancy to one of them? All he'd done was stare at her. But then, this was the second time she'd seen him.

She stood up and straightened her clothing, and as she did so, an even more worrying possibility hit her. Was Tori the target here? And if so, why?

She couldn't be sure he was interested in either of them. Instinct said *yes,* but her training told her she had no hard evidence. And Tori had enough on her plate without adding fear of this shadowy figure.

Jo swallowed her unease and said nothing, deciding instead to watch their backs from now on.

CHAPTER 14

THE SECOND GLASS of merlot had turned Tori's cheeks a faint shade of pink. She was a glass ahead of Jo, who swirled hers slowly and watched it catch the light. They sprawled on the couch, shoulders touching, feet propped lazily on the coffee table.

"Tori," Jo began, her voice casual but her mind sharp, "how public have you been about the health consequences of petrochemical companies' emissions?"

She saw a muscle tighten in Tori's cheek and felt slightly guilty for bringing the subject up while they were relaxing. But Tori seemed to pull herself together to answer.

"Well, earlier studies already show that some of the chemicals that refineries emit are carcinogens, both in animals and workers. I've written several letters to *The Houston Chronicle* about the potential hazards to the community."

The silence stretched as they both sipped their wine. Then Tori broke it, her voice soft. "About six months ago, I had this patient—a lifetime resident and a non-smoker—with metastatic lung cancer and chronic lung disease. She lived right behind the Oilton refinery. Practically in its shadow." Tori swallowed the last of her wine. "I called World Petrol to ask if they'd done any environmental monitoring for carcinogens beyond the fence line near her home."

Jo didn't need to hear the rest to guess how that story ended.

"They didn't even return my calls," Tori said. Her tone was flat. "However, it motivated me to study cancer rates in nearby communities. Plus, once my lab opens, I'll test for toxic substances in my patients' body fluids. That will provide us with hard evidence of individual exposures."

Jo leaned forward, her mind turning over possibilities like puzzle pieces she couldn't quite fit together yet. "Who knows about your study? About your new lab?"

"I've written to local health departments, the EPA, and the Texas Air Control Board and requested air monitoring data to correlate with the elevated cancer rates." Tori's lips pressed into a thin line. "No response."

"Who else?" Jo asked.

Tori ticked off names as if she were reciting a grocery list. "The university. The Cancer Registry. The physician organizing grand rounds at MD Anderson."

"And your preliminary results? Who knows about those?"

"A couple of faculty members in Epidemiology at UT and Harvard reviewed my methods and preliminary analysis before I present at the cancer center next month."

"Alarm bells must be ringing in the risk management departments of petrochemical companies. They've likely become aware of your study and laboratory."

"They've already faced one benzene lawsuit." Tori thoughtfully twirled the stem of her empty glass. "I'm not the first to raise concerns."

"No," Jo said, not hiding her admiration, "but you're the

most persistent and vocal, and you back up your concerns with solid science."

"Yes, I'm a real danger," Tori acknowledged with a wry smile.

She reached for the bottle and refilled Jo's glass. Jo stared into its depths as though it might hold answers—or warnings.

"I'm wondering . . . " But her words trailed off.

Tori's eyes narrowed, worry creasing her forehead again. "Wondering what?"

Jo hesitated, glancing at Tori before looking away, toward the window where shadows flickered in the night. The thought gnawing at her surfaced again: Was it no coincidence that the scary-looking guy was in the gym? Was he working for Big Oil? Was Big Oil tapping Tori's phone and keeping her under surveillance? And me, too?

She was making the discussion heavier than it needed to be tonight, and Tori had enough on her mind without adding further worries. She shook off her concerns and took a large mouthful of wine.

"Nothing important," she said, lightly, and forced a smile. "Let's talk about something more pleasant."

Tori's shoulders relaxed as if she'd been waiting for permission to move on. "Remember, you promised to tell me about your love life."

The sharp pivot caught Jo by surprise, but if that's where Tori wanted to steer the conversation, so be it.

"Ask away," she said, leaning back into the couch.

"What happened to that witty, stunning woman you were dating when I last saw you?" Tori asked, her eyes lighting up. "The lobbyist for the pharmaceutical industry. Remember? A few years ago. I met you both in DC at that fancy Italian restaurant while in town for a medical conference. She was a knockout."

Jo let out a short laugh. "Oh, yeah, her. She couldn't decide if she was straight or gay and kept nagging me to go into corporate law." She paused as uncomfortable memories surfaced. Time to deflect. "I think she's married now."

Tori tilted her head, undeterred. "And the British woman—the one you met in London. Are you still in touch with her?"

A sigh escaped Jo as she slouched into the cushions, tipping her head back to stare at the ceiling, remembering. "Yes. Lauren. Brilliant and lovely. She had it all. We could've had something incredible if it weren't for the damn ocean between us. Immigration barriers didn't help either." Her voice softened as she added, "We still write to each other sometimes, and there are occasional phone calls."

"What about now?" Tori asked in a quieter voice, but no less intent. "Who are you seeing?" She shifted closer, propping an elbow on the back of the couch as she studied Jo.

Jo met Tori's deep blue eyes. They stirred in her the familiar frisson—those eyes could still unravel her if she let them. She straightened abruptly, suddenly aware of how close they were sitting. She leaned forward to sip her drink.

"I'm surprised the pizza's taking so long," she said briskly. "I need something to soak up the wine. Let's grab some crackers." She headed for the kitchen.

"There are potato chips in the cupboard by the sink," Tori called from the couch.

When Jo returned, Tori hadn't forgotten her question.

"So?" Tori pressed, plucking a chip from the bag Jo offered but holding it idly between her fingers. "Who are you dating? Tell me."

Jo hesitated for a moment before answering.

"Well," she said, crunching on a chip to buy herself time, "I've been dating someone—her name is Kate—for seven months now. She's young, mid-twenties." She saw no judgment in Tori's expression, only curiosity, and continued. "She was a medic in the Navy and is now studying biology after her discharge. She's easy to be with—no drama—and often makes me laugh." Jo added, almost as an afterthought, "We have great chemistry in bed."

Tori shot her a curious look.

"Has she moved in? Is it serious?"

"Well, no U-Haul has shown up at my townhouse yet," Jo said with a chuckle before popping another chip into her mouth. "Not that I'm a good catch for anything long-term—I'm too much of a workaholic."

"Au contraire!" Tori exclaimed, leaning forward with sudden energy. "You're an excellent catch!"

Jo's smile faltered for just a second before she recovered. *I wish you'd thought so in college.* What she said aloud was, "Thanks. You're sweet."

Tori tilted her head. Her voice softened again as she asked, "What does Kate look like?"

"She's exquisite," she began, savoring the memory as she spoke. "Her mom was half-Cherokee; her dad was from Yugoslavia. High cheekbones, long, dark hair that falls to the middle of her back, and tawny-colored eyes. They're beautiful. Hard to describe." She chuckled, delighting in describing her lover. "She's an athlete too. Moves like a cat."

Tori's smile encouraged her to continue.

"A couple of months ago, she won a sailboard in a lottery and insisted we take it to a nearby lake. She pulled up the sail as if it were nothing and glided smoothly across the water." The admiration in Jo's expression turned suddenly to laughter. "When I tried? It took me forever to stand up on the thing. And then I fell right into someone's fishing line before I even got moving."

She expected Tori to join her amusement but noticed her expression had shifted—her face pensive, almost wistful.

"She sounds lovely," Tori said, her voice tinged with sadness. She turned her head away.

Jo frowned. *Have I been insensitive?* She set the bag of chips on the coffee table and let a few beats pass before saying, carefully, "I love Kate. But she's young and in a completely different phase of life." Her voice dropped lower as if she were admitting something aloud for the first time. "I'm giving it more time before making any commitments."

Something flickered across Tori's face—an emotion Jo couldn't quite name—and for a moment, it appeared she might say something more.

They jumped as the doorbell rang.

"Pizza!" cried Jo. Grateful for the interruption, she shot up from the couch as if it were on fire and headed for the door.

When she returned with the pizza, Jo forced herself into cheerful efficiency, setting the plates and napkins on the coffee table and refilling their drinks. As if sheer activity could erase whatever had just passed between them.

CHAPTER 15

THAT NIGHT, TORI awoke with a start as Orange Cat padded across her chest and curled up close against her ribs. Once disturbed, sleep refused to return, leaving her mind to wander through dangerous territory. Jo's face materialized in the darkness—that radiant smile, those expressive dark eyes that danced above high, elegant cheekbones. Jo, her protector. Jo, her rock. Jo, the woman who had unknowingly claimed a piece of her heart years ago.

A familiar ache spread through her. Her feelings for Jo had always transcended ordinary friendship, though she'd spent years pretending otherwise. Jo's closeness over the past few days reminded her of the pain of her loss.

For years, Tori had constructed her life around predictability and conformity. College had been particularly torturous, with Jo's constant presence igniting feelings Tori refused to acknowledge. The prospect of stepping beyond the carefully drawn lines of her existence paralyzed her. So, she'd buried those emotions deep, allowing them to surface only in fleeting moments—a lingering glance, a brush of fingers, a hug held a few seconds too long.

Her conservative upbringing loomed like a shadow, the specter of family rejection too terrifying to confront. Instead, she'd channeled her energy toward men, relationships that society deemed proper, but never ignited the same fire within her. Her marriage to Rick was the unfortunate result, a mistake that had wounded them both.

Tori's awareness of her attraction to women, which had begun with Jo, blossomed into an undeniable truth about herself. Now in her mid-thirties, Tori studied women at the gym with a new boldness. She admired the curve of a hip or the grace of movement—not out of envy, but with desire. Sometimes, she caught women returning her gaze with eyes that mirrored her own hidden hunger.

And then she met Jude at the country-western bar last spring. Jude, with her captivating green eyes, laughing, and tossing her auburn hair back, gazed at Tori over the rim of her wineglass.

The Lodge had become Tori's sanctuary when she first ventured there in early March, seeking refuge from the suffocating tension at home. She'd embraced line dancing, finding unexpected joy in the synchronous movement. A group of women always gathered near the wooden dance floor, their easy camaraderie and laughter drawing Tori's attention. They rarely partnered with men, preferring to dance the Texas two-step with each other.

Tori was astonished when one of them—a stocky blonde with mischievous eyes and an impish grin—approached her one evening, hand extended in invitation.

"Care to dance?" the woman had asked.

Alarm shot through her, quickly followed by excitement that made her spine tingle. She'd never dared to slow dance with a woman before, but something compelled her to accept. The woman—named Belinda, she learned later—led with confidence despite her shorter stature. After several stumbles, Tori moved in perfect harmony with her partner, swept up in the current of the dance.

"Why don't you join us?" Belinda had suggested afterwards. "I'll buy you a drink."

Grateful for the invitation, Tori followed her to a table where several women warmly welcomed her. That was when she first locked eyes with Jude—tall, lithe Jude, whose graceful movements on the dance floor had captivated her from afar.

Tori returned to The Lodge as often as possible, especially on weekends when Jude would most likely be there. She integrated herself into the women's group, learning new dances and occasionally partnering with one of the women at the table or a friendly man. Yet, while the group's lively chatter and shared laughter filled her evenings with joy, her focus always drifted to Jude—the quiet magnetism of her presence drawing her attention like no other.

The first time Jude asked her to dance, Tori nearly forgot how to breathe. Jude's hand pressed firmly against her back, drawing her close enough that she was certain Jude could feel her thundering heartbeat. She avoided those intense green eyes, afraid her legs might give way beneath her. Her cheeks flushed with embarrassment when she accidentally stumbled and stepped on Jude's foot.

Jude had pulled back, her lips curving into a smile. "Relax," she'd murmured, her voice low and intimate. "Just let me guide you and don't think about your feet."

Though her feet were the least of her concerns, Tori forced herself to take several deep breaths, willing her body to surrender to Jude's lead.

Many dances followed, but just as often, they sat out the music, lost in conversation. Jude possessed a sharp intellect and perceptiveness that matched her physical grace. Her Boston accent revealed her New England roots. She was pleased to learn Tori knew Boston from college days. They discovered they shared views on politics and environmental issues. Jude's irreverent humor often left Tori laughing until her sides ached.

Tori carefully avoided asking about Jude's profession or what had brought her to Houston, fearing she'd be asked the same questions in return. At The Lodge, she wanted to be just Tori, not Dr. Nelson with all the expectations and responsibilities that title carried. In this sanctuary of pulsing music and swirling bodies, she had found freedom she wasn't ready to compromise.

In the first few weeks, Tori moved through those evenings with ease, laughing, chatting, and bantering with the women in the group. She danced with others, but her awareness of Jude was constant, like a low hum in her chest. Jude's gaze lingered on her, and Tori felt it as surely as a touch. It thrilled her but also unsettled her in ways she was finally daring to name. By mid-April, the truth she'd been avoiding could no longer be ignored. She was wildly attracted to Jude. Her marriage to Rick was a hollow shell. She filed for divorce, and they separated.

Until then, she only saw Jude at The Lodge, where their chemistry had become impossible to hide. Others noticed, and one night, as Tori and Jude sat close, heads nearly touching in conversation, Belinda smirked at them from across the table. "Why don't you two go somewhere private and get on with it?" she teased before heading to the dance floor with the others.

When they were alone at the table, Jude leaned forward conspiratorially. "Shall we?"

The casual invitation sent Tori's heart into overdrive. She nearly choked on her beer but managed to nod. Her pulse raced as she followed Jude out to the lot where their cars were parked under the glow of a flickering streetlight. Jude stopped beside her camper van. "Would you like to follow me home? I'm just a mile from here."

Tori nodded again, words failing her. Jude stepped closer, lifting Tori's chin with gentle fingers before leaning in. The kiss was soft at first—tentative—but it ignited something deep within Tori. Her knees wobbled as she clung to Jude's neck and kissed her back with an urgency that startled her. When they finally pulled apart, breathless and flushed, Jude opened the camper van door and drew her inside.

Tori responded to Jude's kisses and touch with an intensity she hadn't known she possessed. A few minutes later, it took every ounce of willpower to pull herself away long enough to follow Jude's van home. But once there, the night unfolded in ways that left no room for doubt. She was head-over-heels in lust.

∽

The next morning, sunlight streamed through the kitchen window as Tori and Jude sat at an old wooden table sipping coffee. Tori felt weightless—dreamy—but eventually, she felt the tug of reality.

"There's something I have to tell you." She set her mug down and caught Jude's eye to be sure she was listening. "I didn't mention it before because it didn't matter. But," she ran her fingertip over the mug handle, "I'm married." She rushed on before Jude could react. "We've separated, and I've filed for divorce."

Jude's face broke into a slow grin. "Yeah," she said. "I kinda figured."

Tori blinked in surprise. "How?"

"You had a ring on when we first met," Jude said with a slight shrug. "Then later, you didn't."

Tori chuckled despite herself. "Of course."

"More coffee?" Jude picked up both mugs and poured refills at the counter.

Tori let her eyes run over her muscular back and down. Her attention was diverted by a pair of steel-toed boots by the wall and heavy-duty overalls hanging above them. She wondered who they belonged to.

Jude returned to the table.

"There's more," said Tori. "I'm also a medical doctor specializing in occupational and environmental medicine." She studied Jude's face for a reaction but found only curiosity. "At The Lodge," she continued, "I just wanted to be Tori. No titles."

Jude tilted her head. "Interesting," she said with a grin. "That explains why you have such strong opinions about the environment and health."

Tori regarded her over the rim of her coffee cup. "Now that I've shown you mine," she teased, "show me yours. What do you do? And whose are those steel-toed boots?"

Jude's eyes sparkled as she leaned forward with an impish grin. "Oh yeah, they're mine," she said. "I'm an industrial hygienist . . . for World Petrol."

Tori froze mid-sip. She barely avoided choking on her coffee.

Jude continued to smile. "Looks like we have quite a bit in common."

"From opposite ends of the spectrum," Tori murmured dryly.

Jude shrugged with the easy confidence that made Tori's heart skip.

"Maybe not," she said.

And just like that, Tori realized this was the beginning of something far more complicated and exciting than she'd ever imagined possible.

CHAPTER 16

TUESDAY MORNING, JO threw herself into work, tethered to the phone and fax machine as she wrangled with her office in DC. The federal appeals court had demanded more paperwork to justify her firm's appeal in a train spill case, and the back and forth with her paralegal had been relentless. When she was satisfied with the final draft, her head was pounding, and she was ready for a break. She leaned against the banister at the bottom of the stairs and called Tori, who was holed up in her office working on her MD Anderson presentation.

"Hey, Tori, it's time for lunch. Shall I whip up a salad?"

Tori appeared at the top of the stairs, her expression tight and drawn. Jo's stomach sank upon seeing those familiar worry lines on her face.

"What's wrong?" Jo asked.

Tori gripped the railing as though it might steady her. "I've been on the phone with the Texas Medical Board," she said. "They're allowing me to return to clinical practice for now—even though I was arrested for a federal crime—but they're launching their own investigation. They could suspend my medical license."

Jo frowned, her lawyer instincts kicking in. "But surely not if the grand jury fails to indict you. Let's not get ahead of ourselves. We'll know more later this week."

Tori didn't look convinced. "I don't know how I'll face everyone at the clinic or the university if I'm indicted," she admitted. "Only one or two colleagues have reached out in support. Most of them, nothing. Just silence."

"They're probably as stunned as I was," Jo said gently. She could only imagine what Tori was going through—her life unraveling piece by piece: a divorce, an arrest that defied logic, her career and research hanging by a thread. Tori needed something, anything, to pull her out of this spiral.

"Look," Jo said. "Stop worrying about what you can't control, right now. You can't predict your life beyond this week. Let's distract ourselves in the meantime with something fun."

Tori hesitated, then sighed. "I suppose you're right." She slowly descended the stairs, and together they headed to the kitchen to prepare lunch.

At the table, Tori lingered, fingering her napkin before glancing up at Jo, shyly. "Well," she began hesitantly, "I enjoy dancing."

Jo blinked. "Really?" She couldn't recall Tori being much of a dancer in college—unlike her, who used to live for Friday nights on crowded dance floors. "Where would you want to go?"

"There's this country-western bar downtown." Tori's face brightened, and her blue eyes sparkled. "It's in this old building with high ceilings and a massive wooden dance floor. They teach line dancing at seven before it gets too crowded."

Jo gave her a sidelong look. "You know I love to dance," she said cautiously, "but I don't go to straight bars and dance with men." She bit back a sigh. What was wrong with her? This wasn't about her. It should be what Tori wanted.

Tori gave a small laugh. "You don't have to," she assured her. "About every third dance is a line dance—no partners required—and nobody cares if two women dance together."

Jo tilted her head, studying Tori thoughtfully. Dance with Tori? The image sent an unexpected flicker of heat through her, but she shoved it aside. If dancing could make Tori smile again, then that's all that mattered.

"I've got an extra pair of cowboy boots that are too big for me," Tori added with a grin. "And a western shirt that might fit you."

Jo smiled, despite herself. "Well, then," she said lightly, "looks like I'm going line dancing tonight."

ॐ

Just before seven that evening, Jo pushed open the heavy wooden doors of The Lodge, her borrowed boots scuffing against the worn planks of the entryway. Tori followed right behind her. The place smelled of sawdust and spilled beer.

Jo glanced around at the rustic interior—the vast wooden dance floor gleaming under dim lights, clusters of tables surrounded by mismatched chairs, and two bars buzzing with activity. "Baby's Got Her Blue Jeans On" thumped through the surround-sound system, and Tori, vibrating with excitement, grabbed Jo's arm.

"Be right back!" Tori chirped before darting toward the dance floor. Jo lingered near the edge, unsure what to do with her hands. She shoved them into her jeans pockets and leaned against a post, watching Tori's fringed shirt swish as she danced. Jo smiled at how effortlessly Tori fit into this scene.

Her friend moved with a natural rhythm that Jo envied. She

was still admiring Tori when the song ended, and Tori walked toward her. A tall, butch-looking woman with auburn hair and striking green eyes appeared out of nowhere. She pulled Tori into a hug that lingered a few beats too long.

"It's so good to see you, Tori," the woman said, her low and intimate voice putting Jo on alert. "I've missed you."

Jo blinked. *Tori hangs out with . . . her?* She crossed her arms over her chest, feeling out of place in her borrowed boots and button-up shirt. The music shifted to another upbeat tune, drowning out whatever Tori said in response to the woman who squeezed Tori's shoulder and disappeared into the crowd.

Tori bounced over, all smiles. "I'll grab us some beers!" she said, brightly, before weaving through the throng toward the bar. Jo tracked her movements, noting how easily Tori greeted two men along the way, giving them big hugs and broad smiles. That was more like the Tori she knew.

When Tori returned with two frosty bottles in hand, Jo had barely opened her mouth to ask about Green Eyes when an announcer's voice boomed over the speakers. "Alright, folks, time for a line dance lesson! Everyone up!"

Tori didn't give Jo a chance to protest. "Come on!" she said, grabbing Jo's hand and tugging her toward the growing crowd on the dance floor.

The instructor, a wiry man with a sun-weathered face, clapped his hands. "We'll start with something easy: the Electric Slide! Y'all know this one."

Jo shot Tori a skeptical look, but got only an encouraging grin in return. "It's easy," Tori promised as "Electric Boogie" blasted overhead.

Tori was right. Halfway through the song, Jo moved in sync with everyone else, even managing a little hip swing that earned her an approving wink from Tori. Jo forgot about Green Eyes or any lingering awkwardness. This was fun.

The next dance was trickier—something called "Step That Step"—and Jo had to concentrate hard not to trip over herself. But she learned it well enough to stomp along in rhythm by their third run-through with music.

She caught Tori adding little flourishes to her steps—a spin here, an extra kick there that Jo marveled at. *When did Tori get so good at this?* The thought distracted her long enough to misstep and bump into a man beside her. She muttered an apology and refocused on her feet until the song ended.

As they left the floor, George Strait's "Fireman" started up, and Tori turned to her with an eager grin. "Dance with me."

Jo hesitated, scanning the room full of beer-swilling men in snap shirts and women with big, teased hair and tight jeans. "Uh, are you sure? In a straight bar?"

Tori laughed lightly and took Jo's hand. "Relax! Women dance together here all the time."

Still unsure but unwilling to disappoint her, Jo let herself be led back onto the floor. She naturally assumed the lead, placing one hand on Tori's waist and taking her hand with the other just as a man in a cowboy hat sauntered over, grinning widely.

"Hey there," he said, pushing his hat back, his leer revealing yellow teeth under a handlebar mustache.

Jo tightened her grip on Tori's hand and squared her shoulders. *Oh no, you don't.*

But Tori let go and stepped back.

The man's voice grated through the music. "Ah—a few of us fellas over yonder was talkin'. We was wondering if that lady doctor who robbed a bank last week was you."

Jo's spine snapped straight, and her pulse quickened, but she kept her face neutral, letting Tori handle it.

"No, it was not," Tori replied, her tone sharp. Her glare could have melted steel.

But the man wasn't deterred. He squinted at Tori and continued. "The TV said her name was Victoria, and the picture sure looked like you. Are you a doctor?"

Tori's jaw tightened. "You're mistaken. I've never robbed a bank," she said, each word clipped and deliberate.

Jo didn't wait for more. She grabbed Tori's hand and pushed past him, wrinkling her nose at his sweaty-man smell.

That was when she saw him, the bald guy from the gym and the BBQ restaurant, leaning against a lodgepole near the bar. Half hidden in shadows, a cigarette dangled from his lips, he stared at her, unblinking and cold.

Jo's chest tightened with a jolt of fear. *How long had he been there?*

She yanked Tori's arm harder than she meant to and veered sharply toward the opposite side of the room.

"Let's get out of here," she said under her breath, her voice low but urgent.

"Wait, Jo," Tori protested, stumbling to keep up. "That cowboy was just a jerk."

"It's not him," Jo hissed, scanning the room for exits as her heart hammered. Her eyes darted back to the lodgepole. The bald man had disappeared. *Uh-oh.*

"Is there a back door?"

"Uh—yeah, to the left, just before the restrooms." Tori seemed rattled now.

No surprise, given the way I'm acting.

But she didn't slow, carefully steering Tori across the crowded floor, weaving between dancers under the dim lights. Her grip on Tori's arm was protective but unyielding.

"Jo, what's going on?" Tori asked, her voice rising.

"I'll tell you in the car," Jo said tightly as they neared the door. Her senses were on high alert. Every sound was sharper, every shadow deeper. She didn't dare look back again. "Let's just go."

CHAPTER 17

TORI BARELY HAD time to process Jo's urgency before being shoved out the back door and into her Volvo. Jo slid behind the wheel without a word, her movements sharp and deliberate, as they tore out of the parking lot. The tires squealed as they hit the pavement, and Tori clutched the armrest, her pulse racing.

"Jo, please tell me what's going on," she demanded, her voice tight. Jo's eyes were fixed on the road, her jaw set. The silence grated on Tori's nerves, feeding a rising irritation. She hadn't even had a chance to talk to Jude again before Jo had whisked her away. And she missed her, despite the tangled knot of feelings she harbored for Jo.

Jo's hands gripped the wheel as she made random turns, her eyes darting to the rearview mirror. "I just want to make sure we're not being followed."

"Followed? By whom?" Tori's stomach tightened. "Who has you so spooked?"

Jo's voice was low and grim. "That big bald guy you pointed out at the restaurant. He was watching us at the bar. I think he followed us there."

Tori stiffened, unease sparking full-blown alarm. "I knew there was something off about him."

Jo nodded, her knuckles white on the wheel. "I didn't say anything earlier because you already have enough on your mind, but I saw him at the gym as well. At first, I thought it was just a coincidence. Guys stare at you all the time."

"And at you, too," Tori shot back.

Jo ignored the quip, her voice sharpening. "It can't be a coincidence. Not three places in the last couple of days. He's definitely following us. And he wants us to know it—like he's trying to intimidate us." She slowed to a stop as they approached a red light and turned to Tori. "Do you have any idea why someone might be stalking you? Or us?"

Tori swallowed hard, her thoughts spinning. *Is he connected to World Petrol? Have they discovered what Jude and I are up to?* The thought sent a chill down her spine. She debated how much to tell Jo. "Could it be the FBI?" she asked instead, stalling while she thought.

"No." The light turned green, and Jo stomped the gas pedal. "The FBI doesn't tail people out on bail for bank robbery unless they think you're about to bolt. Or, you're involved in something larger."

Tori heard the unspoken question. She sat rigidly in her seat, weighing her words. Her secrets felt like stones pressing down on her ribcage, heavy and suffocating. But this wasn't how she'd planned to tell Jo. And with that man hanging around The Lodge, she had to warn Jude.

"Take me back," she said abruptly.

"Back where?"

"Back to The Lodge."

"What?" Jo shot her an incredulous look before pulling over and killing the engine. "That's insane. I just got you out. Why?"

"I left my ID, my driver's license," Tori lied smoothly, though guilt twisted in her gut. "If that guy finds them, he'll discover where I live."

Jo rolled her eyes. "Where exactly did you leave it? Are you sure? Why don't we call the bar and have someone check?"

"No," Tori said, shaking her head. "We'd only get their answering machine this late." She was gripped by a sense of urgency and raised her voice. "We need to go back now."

Jo stared at her for a long moment, suspicion flickering across her face. Tori knew what she was thinking. *What aren't you telling me?*

Finally, Jo sighed and lifted her hands in surrender. "Fine." She started the car again and made a sharp U-turn back toward the bar.

The moment they pulled into the parking lot, Tori unbuckled her seatbelt and flung open the door. "Stay here with the engine running. I'll be right back," she called over her shoulder as she darted toward the entrance.

She didn't wait for Jo's response; every second seemed an eternity before she could reach Jude. The Lodge pulsed with energy, the bass thundering through the floorboards as boots stomped in rhythm. Tori pushed through the crowd, her gaze darting over heads and cowboy hats until she spotted Jude at their usual table, sitting alone. Relief flickered briefly, but her eyes continued to scan, searching for the hulking, bald figure. *No sign of him.* She exhaled sharply and made a beeline for Jude.

Jude's face lit up when she saw her. "You're back," she said, standing to greet her. "I couldn't resist hugging you earlier. Sorry if that was too much. But . . . what's wrong? You look like you've seen a ghost."

Tori's jaw tightened as she glanced around the bar again. She kept her voice down. "Someone's following me. Big guy. Bald.

Built like a linebacker." She leaned closer. "Be careful, Jude. Listen for unusual clicks on your phone. Lie low—no contact for a while. Please wait for me to call you. I shouldn't have come here tonight. I can't let you get dragged into my mess."

Jude's smile had vanished, and her brow furrowed. She gripped Tori's shoulders and looked her in the eye. "Tori, are you in danger? What's going on?"

Tori's nerves were frayed. "I don't know. Maybe I am," she said, keeping her voice low. "But I can't risk involving you."

Jude didn't let go, didn't look away. Her voice softened but stayed resolute. "You don't get to decide for me. I'm already involved. With you."

Tori's stomach dropped, and for a moment, she faltered under Jude's touch and steady gaze. But there was no time for this—not now, not with everything crumbling around her, and some thug watching her. She broke free from Jude's grip, eyes scanning the bar for the bald guy.

"Stay alert," she said firmly, her tone now all business. "Go about your normal routine at work. Don't do anything out of the ordinary. I'll call you when I find out if the grand jury decides to indict me."

"What. . . "

But Tori didn't wait for her to finish. "I have to go."

She turned on her heel and disappeared into the crowd. The pounding music faded as she slipped out the back door into the cool night air. Her eyes swept the parking lot—no sign of the stalker—but that didn't mean he wasn't lurking in the shadows. She climbed into the Volvo with a sharp breath.

"Did you find your driver's license?" Jo asked.

"No," Tori muttered, staring out the window, as if searching for an evasive answer in the darkness outside. "I might've left it at home." She glanced at Jo. The excuse sounded weak even to her own ears. Jo did not look convinced.

"Did you see him?" Jo asked after a beat.

"No."

Jo pulled out of the lot without saying another word, but their silence grew heavier with every mile they put between themselves and The Lodge. Finally, Jo slowed and pulled over as a loud truck roared past on the narrow road.

"Okay." Her tone cut through the tension like a blade. "What aren't you telling me?"

Tori slumped in her seat. *Jo deserves to hear at least part of the truth.*

"I'm working on something," Tori said, avoiding Jo's eyes. "Information that could blow your case wide open."

Jo's head snapped back, her eyes widening. "What? What kind of information? From someone at The Lodge?"

Tori placed a hand on Jo's arm. "Yes. But I can't tell you who or what yet," she said softly. "Just trust me on this—and don't bring it up on the phone."

Jo wasn't having it. Suspicion darkened her expression as she pressed further. "Who are you getting this information from? And how are you getting it?"

Tori stiffened at Jo's tone—an attorney's interrogation—and fought back the urge to spill everything. But no matter how much she wanted to confide in Jo, doing so could reduce the value of her discovery.

"That's the problem," Tori said, choosing each word carefully. "If I tell you everything now, you won't be able to use it in court."

Tori watched doubt flicker over Jo's face.

"It's illegal?" Jo's tone was sharp.

Tori didn't answer.

Jo leaned closer, lowering her voice. "Are you in danger?"

Tori let out a bitter laugh. "The FBI already arrested me for bank robbery and some goon is stalking me," she said dryly, meeting Jo's gaze with tired defiance. "How much worse can it get?"

CHAPTER 18

FRIDAY MORNING, JUNE 28th, Tori jolted awake, her breath catching in her throat and her heart hammering a steady drumbeat. The remnants of her dream clung to her, slippery and fleeting, but the heat of it lingered, a tangle of sensations she couldn't shake. Erotic flashes teased the edges of her memory, then vanished altogether. She threw off the covers and padded to the bathroom, her bare feet chilled by the floor. At the sink, she splashed cold water on her face, the shock grounding her. Reality settled in as she dabbed her cheeks dry with a towel.

The grand jury may have decided my fate.

Tori's premonition was prescient. Brian called them into his office just before noon.

The receptionist ushered them into the conference room, where they sat in tense silence. Jo appeared calm, but Tori's clammy hand probably gave her away. She gripped Jo's hand like a lifeline.

Mercifully, Brian did not keep them waiting. He strode in and sat next to Tori rather than at the head of the table.

Tori's gut told her what was coming.

Brian held her gaze as he spoke. "I wish I had better news, Tori. Based on the bank surveillance tape, the photos, and the three sworn eyewitness statements from bank employees, the grand jury decided there was sufficient evidence to indict you for armed bank robbery."

His words hit like a physical blow. Tori gasped and covered her face as if to block out the reality crashing down around her. Her heart pounded in her ears, drowning out all other sounds.

This can't be happening.

She couldn't speak as tears welled up, blurring the room. Jo put her arm around her, and Tori let out a muffled sob as she slumped against her shoulder.

Brian gave them a moment.

"I'm so sorry," he said. "But if all they have is eyewitness testimony and no motive or physical evidence, we'll have a good chance of arguing mistaken identity at trial."

Tori raised her tear-streaked face. "At trial? What about my work? My practice? The Texas Medical Board could suspend my license. How do I get through the next few months? Face my staff? My patients? The university? And my cancer study—what happens to that?"

Jo squeezed Tori's shoulder. "Don't jump ahead. Let's take this one step at a time."

Brian held her gaze. She saw concern and kindness in his dark eyes.

"Listen to me. We'll fight this. Come to my office tomorrow morning. The next step will be the arraignment, where the charges are read, and you will be asked to plead. Soon after, we will also find out who the judge will be and the trial date. I will work on getting a certified copy of the bank surveillance tape, hopefully this afternoon. Don't let yourself spiral into worst-case scenarios tonight."

He glanced at Jo meaningfully. "You'll stay with her?"

"Of course," Jo said, rubbing Tori's back in slow, circular motions.

Brian was halfway out of his chair when he turned to Jo. "How long are you in town?"

Jo hesitated. "I'm supposed to leave soon." Her eyes darted to Tori, who was blowing her nose quietly beside her. "But I'll stay with Tori at least through tomorrow."

Brian gave them a nod and a tight smile.

"Take good care tonight, both of you," he said over his shoulder as he headed out.

Jo turned to Tori. "Let's go," she said, linking arms with her as they rose, steering her toward the hallway. "We'll stop for lunch."

Tori moved mechanically beside her and murmured weakly, "I'm not hungry."

"I am. But we'll go home," Jo said. "I'll fix you something small, just enough to keep your strength up, and we can watch your Monty Python video."

Tori blinked, a flicker of confusion breaking through her daze. "Monty Python?"

"You know," Jo said brightly, apparently trying to inject some levity into the moment. "*The Life of Brian*." Especially that scene where condemned prisoners hang on crosses with dead bodies in the pit below, singing "Always Look on the Bright Side of Life". She whistled a few bars for effect.

A ghost of a smile tugged at Tori's lips. "You're daft," she muttered under her breath.

Jo grinned and squeezed Tori's arm as they walked out of the law office into the bright sunlight.

∽

When Jo lay in bed that night, her body felt heavy with exhaustion, but her mind refused to relent. She tossed and turned, the sheets tangling around her legs. All day, she'd fought to keep Tori's spirits afloat, throwing out lifelines of reassurance and distraction, but the results were dismal. She hadn't had a moment to untangle her own thoughts. What should have been a straightforward case of mistaken identity had mutated into a nightmare, threatening not just Tori's freedom but the integrity of their firm's lawsuit.

Eyewitness testimony was notoriously unreliable; every lawyer worth their salt knew that. Memories were fragile, easily warped by stress, media coverage, or casual conversations with other witnesses. And photo lineups? If the agents conducting them knew who they wanted witnesses to identify, bias was baked into the process.

Jo groaned and rolled onto her side, squinting at the glowing numbers on the clock: 2:00 a.m. The night stretched ahead of her like an endless void. She fought with the sheets to try to get comfortable.

Brian had better pull together an air-tight defense because this whole affair reeked from Day One. Tori's arrest hadn't made sense, and Jo's frustration was hardening into steely determination. Come hell or high water, she'd uncover the truth.

CHAPTER 20

SATURDAY MORNING, IN the conference room at Holmes, Kirkland, and Anderson, Jo sat across from Tori, waiting for Brian to appear. Tori looked as if she hadn't slept and was twisting a strand of blonde hair around her finger. In the drive over, Jo had absorbed Tori's tension and now was fidgeting, crossing and uncrossing her legs.

The door opened, and Brian appeared, striding to the head of the table and pulling a notepad from his briefcase.

"How are you holding up, Tori?"

"So, so." Tori's voice shook slightly.

"I understand. The grand jury's indictment wasn't a total shock," Brian said. "Despite the potential for error, the courts still rely on eyewitness testimony in bank robbery cases. But so far, they have not revealed any physical evidence to tie you to the robbery."

He took a VHS tape from his briefcase. "I was able to get a certified copy of the bank surveillance tape from the prosecutor's office. Shall we have a look?"

Tori's eyes widened, but she nodded.

Jo uncrossed her legs and sat up straight, her interest piqued as Brian pushed the tape into the VCR and turned on the television monitor.

The surveillance tape flickered to life, its grainy, soft focus making it almost useless. Almost. Jo narrowed her eyes to see the images better, and her pulse quickened as a woman approached the teller. She bore an uncanny resemblance to Tori—same height, same strong, elegant jawline, and hair color—but sunglasses obscured her eyes, and a rounded belly protruded under the oversized blue shirt.

This can't be Tori. She's slim. Jo wondered for a moment if she was relieved or protesting.

Tori sat in what appeared to be stunned silence as the tape came to an end.

"I know the facial resemblance is a bit of a shock," Brian said. "But this woman looks a bit heavier than Tori."

Jo shifted in her chair, rushing to Tori's defense, "Can we hire an FBI photo identification expert to examine the surveillance tape and photos? The woman on the tape looks like Tori superficially, but we all recognize that the robber doesn't have the same body type as Tori."

"Yes, we are thinking along the same lines," Brian said. "But since we're going to trial, I want to get more background today to ensure I haven't missed anything important."

He took out his pen and poised it over his notepad.

For the next half hour, Brian inquired about Tori's parents, her brother, her college and medical school education, her medical residencies, and her academic work and employment history.

Tori appeared still shaken by the video and answered mechanically.

"Have you ever had a drug problem?"

Tori looked away. "No."

Jo wondered what that glance away meant. She watched as Brian jotted a note.

"Do you have any active medical problems?" Brian asked.

Tori met Brian's eyes. "Not really," she said. "Migraine headaches, occasionally."

"Do you take any prescription medication?"

Tori hesitated, and, again, her eyes slid from Brian's momentarily.

"Um—I was taking an antidepressant, amitriptyline, for about six weeks, but it didn't agree with me, so I have tapered off it."

Jo sat back in her chair, crossing her arms, surprised to hear of Tori's depression for the first time.

"Are you seeing a psychiatrist?" Brian tipped his head.

"Yes. I was. Dr. Janet Novak. She prescribed the amitriptyline."

Brian straightened his reading glasses. "Tell me more about the depression."

Tori sighed. "My life was in upheaval—my husband and I have separated and will soon divorce. I'm questioning my life choices, and I hate living in Houston. But I'm staying because I have important work to do here. It was all getting on top of me."

"I see." Brian wrote on his legal pad. "Tell me again about your work?"

Jo watched the tension ease from Tori's face as she entered familiar territory and became more animated. "Every week, I see patients in my clinic suffering from chronic asthma, chronic obstructive lung disease, and various cancers that are likely caused by living near petrochemical plants that spew a toxic soup of respiratory irritants and carcinogens into the air, soil, and water. No one has systematically studied whether these medical conditions are associated with their environmental exposures, despite indirect evidence from animal and occupational studies suggesting a link."

Brian nodded. "Go on."

"I've nearly completed a study of cancer incidence in the neighborhoods surrounding the country's largest concentration of petrochemical plants. It confirms that cancer rates are elevated. Occupation, smoking, or stage of diagnosis can't explain the excess."

"Who's funding this effort?" Brian asked.

Tori's face fell. "No one, really. I received some funding from the University of Texas, which is allocated from the overhead of other grants, and I use their large computer for data analysis. However, my study is primarily self-funded through my clinical work."

"Have you published this study?" Brian asked.

"Not yet." Jo noticed Tori twisting her fingers in her lap. "I'm also setting up a toxicology laboratory. It's a small lab near the clinic, where I will test blood, urine, and tissue samples for toxic substances."

"Who are you testing?" Brian asked, his face showing curiosity.

"Initially, I'll test only my patients, with their consent," Tori said.

Brian made another note. "What's the cost of setting up the lab?"

"The analytical equipment is expensive. As you know, I've already bought some. However, I'll also need a gas chromatography-mass spectrometer, which costs approximately $50,000 to $75,000, along with other basic equipment such as refrigerators and fume hoods. Then, there are reagents, consumables, and rent for the laboratory space. Not to mention staffing, quality control, and accreditation."

Jo's eyebrows shot up. A glance at Brian revealed his surprise as well. She had no idea the lab was such a massive and expensive endeavor. She should have been more curious about the pressure it might be putting on her friend and delved into it further.

"Are you funding this on your own?" Brian said.

Tori scoffed. "I can't. I've secured the space and purchased some basic equipment. The setup will cost over $1 million. Then there's the ongoing maintenance and operating costs. It's a long-range project. I've applied for funding from various government agencies and even selected venture capitalists, but none have come through yet."

Brian jiggled his pen between his fingers and frowned. The silence hung heavily. Jo guessed he was thinking about how the prosecution would view this if it came out at trial. And then Tori brought it into the open.

"I'm seeking legitimate funding through grants," she said. "Not by robbing a bank. Anyway, how much money do you think the tellers have in their drawers?"

Brian regarded her, his expression inscrutable.

"Right." He snapped the lid on his pen. "Shall we take a brief break?"

In the restroom, Jo whispered to Tori, "I didn't know you were depressed."

"Yeah, well, I'm not as depressed as I was several months ago. That's ironic, isn't it? Plus, the medication didn't agree with me, and I'm completely off it now."

"But why didn't you tell me?"

A shadow crossed Tori's face. "I was in no shape to speak with anyone—even you," she said before ducking into a stall.

When they were washing their hands, Jo said, "You've taken on mammoth undertakings all by yourself: the cancer study, the new laboratory, and the divorce. No wonder you felt overwhelmed and depressed."

"Yes," Tori said. She met Jo's eyes in the mirror. "Not overwhelmed enough to rob a bank, though."

"No, of course not," Jo said. On impulse, she said, "We should tell Brian about that guy following us."

Tori turned to look Jo directly in the eye. "How can we be sure Brian's trustworthy?"

Jo's eyes widened. "I believe he is, but why do you ask?"

"He's a local Houston guy in a big law firm with other attorneys who might work for Big Oil."

"Yes, but he's your attorney and bound by attorney-client privilege."

She suddenly felt frustrated with Tori, frustrated by the need to defend the attorney who was trying to help her get out of this mess, and frustrated by Tori's reluctance to lay all her cards on the table. The shock of finding out about her depression and how much the lab would cost Tori still galled her.

"He'd have to disclose to you if he has a conflict of interest. And he can't effectively defend you if you don't tell him about being followed and your concern about your phone being tapped. It could be relevant to your defense. Surely, it's not only me thinking that you might have been framed for the bank robbery. And that your cancer study and whatever information you're getting that you can't tell me about threatens Big Oil because they're worried about being exposed as environmental criminals."

Tori sighed. She pulled down a towel and wiped her hands slowly. Then she met Jo's eyes.

"Yeah, okay. I'll tell him."

CHAPTER 21

BACK IN THE conference room, Brian continued his questions.

"Based on your statements, your finances appear in good shape. You've managed to save despite your investment in lab equipment and rent. What about your husband? You said he was working for a start-up, building personal computers. How are his finances?"

Tori shrugged. "I don't know now. He no longer shares his finances with me, and we have separate accounts, except for the joint one for household expenses and the mortgage. He told me a few weeks ago that he'd gotten a temporary contract job he hoped would turn into a salaried position."

"Have either of you ever declared bankruptcy?" Brian asked.

"I haven't, but Rick started the process of declaring it individually around the time of our separation, and I was notified. Our joint ownership of the house put me at risk, but my financial assets are in my name." Tori said. "Fortunately, he got this temporary IT contract job that apparently pays well, so he didn't go through with the bankruptcy."

Brian checked his notes, and in the pause, Jo thought it

might be a good time to allay Tori's concerns. She slipped her hand across the table to attract Brian's attention.

"Do any of the attorneys in your firm defend corporations accused of wrongdoing?"

Brian's head snapped up, and he looked taken aback. "Yes, we have two attorneys who specialize in corporate criminal defense. Why do you ask?"

"Will you please assure Tori that you will not share details of her case with your corporate defense attorney partners or associates?"

Understanding flickered in his eyes, and Brian turned to Tori. "I assure you that details of your case will remain confidential, and I'll only share them with my paralegal. The same attorney-client privilege also binds him. And I keep my files in locked file cabinets."

Tori stared at Brian as if deliberating. Then she nodded. "Okay, thanks."

"Tell him about the stalker," Jo urged.

Brian's face registered surprise.

"I'm being followed. A big, muscular, bald guy is watching me—watching both of us. In the last few days, he showed up at a restaurant, the gym, and a bar. He looks menacing and doesn't bother to hide that he's spying on us. Also, I'm sure my phone is being tapped."

Jo watched Brian's reaction. His eyes widened, his brow furrowed, and his lips pressed together. *Not the response of a man privy to a plot. Unless he is an excellent actor.*

"This is disturbing indeed," he said. "I'll look into whether the FBI might be tapping your phone, though I doubt they would have a reason to."

Jo stepped in.

"As Tori said, she's working on a study of cancer in

neighborhoods where petrochemical plants are concentrated and setting up a lab to test for toxins in the body fluids of some of those same people. What does this suggest to you?"

"Somebody hired by those companies is keeping an eye on her," Brian said.

"Right. We need to keep Tori safe. They may not just be watching. Do you remember the case of Karen Silkwood? She was killed on her way to report Kerr-McGee's environmental crimes."

Brian's expression was solemn. "Yes, I agree, we have to find out who this guy is working for. I can offer a private investigator. Though there'd be an additional charge."

Tori's eyes widened, and Jo wondered what she was thinking. Her expression looked very much like alarm.

"That won't be necessary," Tori said. "I may already have to take out a second mortgage on my house to pay your fees."

So that was it. Tori was naturally worried about paying even more legal fees. Just the same, Jo's suspicions were raised. She felt it was unreasonable not to take protective steps against a threat like the large, muscular stalker. Second mortgage? Or secrets? She clocked her friend's averted gaze, the tremor in her coffee cup.

"I'll be fine," Tori said. "I have friends to call if I feel unsafe."

Brian looked unconvinced but didn't press the issue. He was silent for a moment while he checked his notes.

"You said no one can vouch for your activities at the time of the bank robbery. Were you using your computer?"

"Yes, in my home office," Tori said.

"Can you check if there is a time stamp on any documents you worked on and saved during that time?" Brian said.

Tori nodded. "I'll check, but I've worked on the documents since then, so they will probably show only the latest one."

Brian was silent for a moment, apparently thinking, before he said, "The woman you were to meet for lunch on the day of the robbery. do you now recall her name?"

Jo noticed how Brian had abruptly changed the tone of his questioning. He was suddenly more intense, more determined to get a straight answer.

"Uh, no," Tori said, looking away.

"This is important, Tori. Did you remember her last name, where she worked, or how we might contact her?"

Tori's fingers pleated the hem of her blouse, and Jo recognized the nervous tic from when they'd crammed for finals in their cramped dorm room.

She hesitated before answering. "Like I told you, her first name is Jude. She's a casual acquaintance I met at a dance." There was a catch in her voice. "I don't have a way to contact her."

More words poured out, and Jo got the impression Tori was covering something by explaining too much.

"She suggested lunch, but as I said, I threw away the piece of paper on which she had written her name and phone number in a fit of pique when she didn't show."

What is Tori hiding about this woman?

Brian didn't let it drop. "I want details about your activities in the hours after the robbery to show that you were behaving normally. Let's go through it again."

They left Brian's office and headed into Houston's heat and humidity. As they approached the car, Jo said, "Do you trust Brian now?"

Tori unlocked the door. Her back was to Jo. "I'm not sure. Maybe."

"Do you trust me?"

Tori turned and held her gaze. "You're the only person I really trust, Jo."

As they drove through Houston's shimmering skyline, Jo was silent. She cataloged discrepancies: Tori's nervous pleating of her shirt fabric, the hitch in her voice when she'd said, "casual acquaintance". The way her eyes slid away when Brian asked if she took medication. Tori's life was no longer the open book it'd been when they were in college or when Tori lived in Boston, and they'd talked on the phone every few months.

Jo's stomach rumbled, demanding attention.

"How do you feel about Mexican food?" she asked.

Tori smiled. "Nothing gets in the way of your appetite."

They grabbed lunch at a Mexican restaurant so Jo could have the green corn tamales she craved. She savored every bite, washing it down with Dos Equis lager. When Tori finished her enchiladas verde, Jo decided to probe.

"Who is this woman you met at a party? Your lunch date on the day of the robbery?"

Tori played with her empty beer bottle, twisting it around, not meeting Jo's eyes. "I met her at The Lodge one night, dancing. She gave me her phone number and said we should meet for lunch. I called her, and we set up a lunch date. As I told Brian, she never showed."

"Why didn't you want to give Brian her full name?"

Tori lifted her beer bottle to drink, but, upon noticing it was empty, lowered it. Jo had the impression she was playing for time. She met Jo's gaze. "I don't want him to contact her and involve her in my legal problems."

Jo wanted to ask more, but the server came with their check, and Tori grabbed it to pay. The moment for tactful questioning was lost.

When the server left, Tori said, "I need to drop by my clinic before they close at 2:00 p.m. It's best if I tell the medical director in person that I've been indicted and that my case is going to trial. Of course, he knows of my arrest, but I haven't heard anything from him. I'll drop you off at home first so you can pack and call your office. Then we'll have a free evening on your last night."

Tori's face was strained, though she gave Jo a brave smile. A wave of empathy compelled Jo to say, "This is so hard, Tori, so unfair. I hope your director knows you'd never rob a bank."

Tori shrugged, looking despondent. "We'll see."

She'd look for a chance to ask about the mystery woman later. In the meantime, she needed to focus on the plaintiffs in her case. She had to decide whether to interview more potential plaintiffs in Oilton, as David had requested.

Would their lawsuits even be viable now that their prime medical expert was indicted for bank robbery?

CHAPTER 22

TORI BRACED HERSELF and entered the clinic, ignoring the receptionist's quick intake of breath. She turned her back on her and waited for the elevator to take her to the medical director's office on the fourth floor.

His medical assistant told her Dr. Jensen was finishing up with a patient and would be with her shortly. The air in the waiting room felt thick with judgment. Nurses' whispers prickled across her neck like spider legs while she counted ceiling tiles to avoid their stares. Her heart pounded, despite her efforts to practice diaphragmatic breathing.

Ten minutes later, Dr. Jensen walked out of an exam room, chart in hand, barking instructions to the medical assistant.

"Dr. Nelson," he said, walking toward her with a perfunctory smile. Somehow, his smile never reached his eyes, although suspecting what was to come, Tori was surprised he was trying to smile at all. "Come into my office."

He put a hand on her back as she rose—a power gesture that made her cringe. She resisted a strong temptation to shrug it off and instead increased her pace so that she walked ahead of him into his office. It smelled of leather polish and peppermint lozenges. The desk was scattered with files, the message clear: *I'm a busy man. Don't waste my time.*

Closing the door, he walked around his desk to sit in his high-backed leather chair. He steepled his fingers, his gray eyes cold. The question came like a scalpel sliding between ribs.

"What's this business I hear about you robbing a bank?"

Her chest and neck flushed red.

"I didn't rob a bank." At least her voice sounded strong and emphatic.

One white, bushy eyebrow crept toward his receding hairline. "Yet, I hear the FBI arrested you based on the photos that were circulated around the business district, including our clinic."

His eyes hadn't left her face, and his voice held a sharp edge.

Her tongue turned to clay, and the air conditioner's hum filled the uncomfortable silence. His accusatory tone tapped into how small and scared she'd felt as a kid when her father tore into her for disobeying him. "I . . . I . . . It's a mistake. It isn't me in those photos."

"Who do you think it is, then? A look-alike?" His voice kept its edge.

Tori struggled to control her breathing. *He assumes I'm guilty.*

"Apparently," she said. "There's no other evidence that I had anything to do with it. No motive, dye, money, or gun—nothing."

"So why, then, did the FBI arrest a gainfully employed medical doctor?"

"They got an anonymous tip that the bank robber looked like me," she said, struggling to keep her voice level. Her livelihood, if not her career, was at stake. "But it's a mistake. It isn't me."

His expression was mock quizzical. "So, they're dropping the charges?"

Heat rose to Tori's cheeks, and her heart pounded. Dr. Jensen—she could tell—smelled fear and was closing in.

"No. I've been indicted."

Her throat tightened as Dr. Jensen's face flushed crimson. He slammed his palm against his polished walnut desk and half-rose in his chair—another performance meant to shrink and intimidate her. She knew that was his intention, and unfortunately, it was effective.

"You've been indicted? You're actually going to trial?"

Her thumb worried the hem of her shirt sleeve. Twelve years since Dad's last outburst, yet here she sat, thirty-five years old, still flinching at the sound of a raised male voice.

"Yes."

"Oh dear. Oh dear." He shook his head, sat, and dropped his forehead into his hands. "This is the last straw."

He snapped his head up and glared at her.

"As I've told you, I'm already dealing with complaints from Dodge Chemical, World Petrol, and others, that you've been stirring up their workers, urging them to file claims against them."

"Every claim was medically substantiated." Her voice emerged steadier than she felt.

"I've told you repeatedly that is not our mission here." He slapped his hand on the desk for emphasis and Tori flinched.

"We're here to *treat* disease. As far as prevention is concerned, we urge people to change those things they have control over, like smoking, diet, and substance abuse. We're not rabble-rousers helping patients to gouge companies to pay for illnesses they didn't cause, nor are we here to promote new causes of old diseases like cancer."

Even if people are dying?

Ah, of course, she thought. *Local petrochemical companies contribute large sums to hospitals and clinics here.* There was no point in arguing with him. If he prioritized the clinic's income over patients' lives, they would never agree.

But he was on a roll. "I've told you I hired you to build an occupational medicine program catering to businesses' needs, to bring in an additional source of private pay income—medical surveillance, executive exams, drug testing—things like that. But no, that's not what you're doing. I hear you're even setting up your own laboratory to test toxic substances in body fluids, no doubt to create more claims for occupational injury. And more headaches for the companies we're here to serve."

Her lab. He'd found the very thing that gave her new strength in this battle. Her shoulders straightened as she pictured the centrifuge she had ordered last month, the toxicology manuals stacked beside the donated equipment.

"And what about the people—my patients? Aren't we here to serve them?"

Just as before, he didn't answer. Only glared. And that said it all.

She'd heard his complaints before, but this was the first time he'd pummeled her with such vehemence. Her earlier adrenaline rush ebbed, leaving her drained and immobilized. There was nothing for it now but to wait for the axe to fall.

"You've left me no choice. Effective immediately, Dr. Thomas will assume your duties."

The room seemed to close in, and the air conditioner's hum got louder—or was it the buzzing in her ears?

"Dr. Nelson. You no longer have a future here. We'll hand over your cases to Dr. Thomas. Please clear your office immediately."

He rose and picked up a medical chart. "Now, excuse me, I have patients to see before we close."

Tori rose and waited for her light-headedness to subside before following him out the door.

She filled a box with personal items from her desk and ignored the receptionist on her way out.

The June heat hit her like a wave as she stumbled to her car. Her head ached, but she paused before starting the engine to consider what this meant, especially for her patients. Dr. Thomas had neither the training nor the inclination to take on treatment for work-related illness. Her clinic work was her primary source of income. With mounting legal bills, her savings would vanish before her upcoming trial.

Oh, how I wish Jo weren't leaving tomorrow.

She released the brake and swung out of the clinic garage.

❦

As she prepared to turn onto the road, she glanced into her rearview mirror. A white van pulled into sight and followed her, a mere car's length behind. She took a second look and saw a hulking silhouette that dominated the driver's seat—broad shoulders, a skull smooth as river stone. Her throat tightened. Gripping the steering wheel, white-knuckled, she stepped hard on the gas, swerving at the last possible minute onto the freeway on-ramp. Horns blared, but the van clung like a parasite.

She kept her foot on the gas, though the freeway was crowded. Sixty. Seventy. Eighty. The speedometer needle trembled as she wove between vehicles. She'd left the turn signal on, being too busy keeping her car intact and her breath sawed in rhythm with it. Moments later, a glance at the mirror showed only the last truck she'd passed behind her.

She took a ragged breath. The van had disappeared. When

she was sure he was no longer chasing her, Tori drove onto an off-ramp and swerved into a grocery lot. All the while, her gaze flicked between rows of parked cars. *Still clear.*

She pulled into a parking space and opened the glove compartment. Pepper spray tumbled out, sticky with half-melted cherry ChapStick and old insurance papers. She tried several times to grasp it with trembling fingers, and once she had secured it, she dashed to a pay phone booth.

Jude's "Hello?" barely registered through the blood roaring in her ears. Footsteps approached, and a shopping cart rattled nearby. She spun, pepper spray raised, only to see an elderly couple unpacking their groceries.

"Jude. That big, bald thug watching Jo and me at the restaurant, the gym, and The Lodge just followed me from the clinic onto the freeway. He dropped back so maybe he just meant to spook me, but I'm concerned he might know what we're doing."

"This is scary, Tori. I'm worried about you. Is your friend still with you?"

"She's going back to DC tomorrow," Tori said.

"Do you want me to come over? I'm handy with a bat. I'll protect you."

Tori smiled briefly, visualizing Jude kneecapping the thug. "No, we can't call attention to our association. Have you noticed anyone like that following you?"

"No, I still haven't, but I'll be extra vigilant," Jude said.

"At work, has anyone questioned you when you're analyzing our samples?" Tori asked.

"No. But I'm cautious. My boss did comment on my long hours, but—"

This set off alarm bells for Tori, and she interrupted. "If he suspects anything—"

"Nah, he doesn't. If I keep up with the sampling and the

analysis he assigns me, and I'm not putting in for overtime, I don't think he gives a damn."

Jude was silent for a moment before she said, "Are you sure you're okay, Tori? I don't like this. He might be following you to find out where you live."

"He probably already knows that. Don't worry, I'll manage."

"Have you heard what the grand jury decided? Did they dismiss your case?"

Tori took a deep breath, pressing the receiver against her ear, as the stark reality hit her anew. "Unfortunately, no. I've been indicted for armed bank robbery."

"Oh, no! You're going to trial for bullshit charges? I can't believe it." Jude's voice rose with incredulity.

"It gets worse. The medical director at Novak just fired me." She could feel tears starting and steeled herself to suppress them.

"He fired you? The bastard! I want to punch his lights out."

Tori smiled at Jude's vehemence. "I know. It's bad news. But I'll have more time to work on my study. No one's going to stop me from publishing it. Unless I go to prison."

"You can't possibly go to prison. No way."

Jude had never asked Tori if she had robbed the bank, and she was profoundly grateful. They discussed the upcoming arraignment, the thug, and the firing for the next few minutes. Always the optimist, Jude ended with a pep talk and affectionate endearments.

But when Tori hung up, her pulse raced, and she had difficulty taking a deep breath. Her hands trembled, and she broke into a cold sweat as she contemplated her life spinning out of control. She craved the orange pills—a blanket to smother panic, but she had none. It took all her willpower to slow her breathing and stagger to her car.

CHAPTER 23

TORI'S CAR CRUNCHED on the gravel. Jo poured a glass of fresh iced tea with a slice of lemon and hurried to meet her at the door. When she opened it, Tori stumbled in. Her face told Jo all she needed to know about the meeting with the medical director. She took Tori's bag, set it down on the nearby table with the iced tea, and wrapped her arms around her.

Tori crumpled, her head resting on Jo's shoulder. Jo held her for a long moment, stroking her hair and resting her cheek on its softness. Tori shuddered and gripped her tighter.

"I gather it didn't go well," Jo said gently. She pulled back and lifted Tori's chin. "How about I switch out this iced tea for something stronger, and you tell me about it?"

Tori nodded and stumbled onto the living room couch, dropping into it like a rag doll. Jo hurried to the kitchen, rummaged for the bourbon and glasses, and poured each of them a finger. She handed the glass to Tori and sat beside her, shoulders and hips touching. Tori gave her a wan smile.

"Thanks." She took a sip of the bourbon. "That thug—I'm sure it was him—followed me in a white van when I left the clinic. I lost him on the freeway, but it freaked me out."

Jo's eyes widened, and she took a quick breath. "This is out-rageous! Freeway cat-and-mouse is dangerous. This has gone too far. Who is this guy? Who's he working for? And who's bugging your phone?" She turned to face Tori. "I'm willing to hire the PI for you."

Tori put down her drink. "You're a dear. I don't want you to pay for it. I'll take out a second mortgage if I have to."

"It's important, Tori. It must be done soon. Like tomorrow. I hate to leave you here alone."

"I'll be okay. If I feel scared, I can call my friend, Jan. She'd be willing to stay and loves Orange Cat. Besides, you'll be coming back after your interviews in Oilton, won't you?"

Jo inwardly winced. There had been a change of plan, but she hadn't wanted to discuss it with Tori just yet. "The office is working up my schedule. Now, tell me about your meeting at the clinic."

Tori's face fell. "Jensen, the medical director, was aware of the details of my arrest and probably already knew of my indict-ment. I suppose it's all over the press, and people will have been talking about it. He ranted about complaints from the com-panies he thinks I'm supposed to serve. To him, that's more important than serving the patients. Then he fired me."

An anxious look crossed her face. "My patients will think I've abandoned them."

"Oh, Tori, I'm so sorry." Ever the problem solver, she racked her brain for a solution. "Could you open a temporary office and . . . ?" She stopped when she saw Tori's dubious expression.

"I can't afford the overhead with my legal bills. The clinic owns the medical records, and I have no contact information for my patients to get them to sign releases."

"We could call Mary Williams and ask her to spread the word," Jo said, then bit her lip. She could see that Tori lacked enthusiasm. She remembered that Tori's MD Anderson presentation was scheduled for late July, that her study had yet to be published, and that her trial was looming, not to mention her divorce. Perhaps eliminating hours seeing patients was a blessing in disguise, despite the loss of income.

"No, Jo, I can't handle it now," Tori said with a note of finality.

Jo nodded to show she understood. They sipped their bourbon, both lost in their separate thoughts.

Impulsively, Jo broke the silence.

"Maybe you should get away from here for a while. Stay with me in DC after your talk at MD Anderson. I have a spare room. You can work on your study there."

The words had just slipped out, an impulsive offer she hadn't thoroughly considered.

Stupid, she chided herself. *Kate won't approve. Plus, she'd just assumed Tori would remain free before her trial.*

Tori's eyes found hers with such tender longing that Jo's breath caught in her throat. Tori's fingers brushed against Jo's cheek, making her heart speed up. *She's straight*, Jo reminded herself, even as Tori's thumb touched the corner of her mouth. *Married to a Rick, for God's sake.* There was a hitch in Tori's breathing, and her gaze dropped to Jo's lips.

Jo nearly stopped breathing.

Tori jerked her hand back as if she had been burned and swiped at her own cheek with the heel of her hand.

"I doubt the court would allow me to leave Texas."

Jo let out the breath she'd been holding. "Right, I wasn't thinking straight for a moment," she said, watching Tori retreat behind the familiar armor of pragmatism—talk of second mortgages, selling the house, the *I'll manage* refrain.

A wistful look crossed Tori's face, the same one Jo had seen the other night. "I wish you didn't have to leave for Oilton so soon."

She felt obligated to bring Tori up to date. "I had hoped the news of your arrest would stay local, and my law firm wouldn't hear about it until after your case was dismissed. Then, I'd tell the partners, if they asked, that your arrest was due to mistaken identity."

She wanted to crack open the floorboards and let this house swallow her whole before she admitted the truth. It had to be done now, though. She didn't have the luxury of choice.

"Unfortunately, they've already gotten wind of it and want me to fly back to DC tomorrow."

She looked back at Tori. "I'm sorry, but your arrest has put the future of our lawsuit and the plaintiffs' plight in Oilton in peril."

Tori squeezed her eyes shut and lowered her head.

"I've met many of those people, treated, and tried to help them. Believe me, I'm the one who's sorry."

CHAPTER 24

JO POPPED UP and dressed at six on Sunday morning, planning to slip out before Tori awoke. In the cool dawn, she loaded her bag and briefcase into the trunk, pushed the lid down, and got into the car. She was about to back out when the front door flew open, and Tori came flying down the porch stairs to the car, her crimson robe billowing behind her like a distress flag.

"Christ," Jo muttered. She put on the brakes and rolled down the window.

"Please don't let your partners talk you out of continuing with the lawsuit," Tori said, almost breathless in her rush. "I'm getting information that will break the case wide open."

Jo's brow furrowed. "What information? From whom?"

Tori bit her lip. She was clearly weighing something. Suddenly, she seemed to make up her mind.

"I know an industrial hygienist who works for World Petrol. She has access to years of air-monitoring data that show the company has been exceeding government standards for worker exposure to various toxins. She's also been testing the air for carcinogens beyond the fence line. The readings for benzene, for example, are high—very high."

Jo drummed her fingers on the steering wheel. *Damn. Tori is a party to corporate espionage. And now she's told me, I can't walk away from it.*

Tori placed her hands on the car's roof and leaned in. "Assuming the industrial hygienist can get this air monitoring data to me safely. This data—in combination with my findings of excess cancer in the surrounding communities—is the evidence you and the plaintiffs need. We will hold this huge multinational company accountable for the harm it has caused."

"You're working with the industrial hygienist to obtain this data without the company's knowledge?"

Tori didn't answer.

So not just espionage, but also theft?

Jo's stomach churned. It might have been last night's bourbon, or maybe it was the way Tori's eyes glittered with reckless conviction. It was her eyes that spurred Jo to make the connection.

"So this industrial hygienist . . . it's Jude. The mystery woman you were to have lunch with on the day of the robbery."

"Yes."

"Right, Tori. We never had this conversation. You are likely aware that illegally obtained data is generally inadmissible at trial in Texas. Plus, you put yourself in further danger of being accused of another crime."

Jo paused to think. "But there might be another way." She checked her watch. "I need to go, or I'll miss my flight. I'll call you when I get home."

"Let me call you. Remember, someone may be tapping my phone."

"Right, I keep forgetting."

Jo's head throbbed. She hated the feeling that things were

happening out of her control. But it was about to get so much more confusing.

Tori leaned through the window and pulled Jo's face toward her, the press of her fingertips on Jo's jaw commanding. Her kiss carried the scent of jasmine shampoo and the taste of toothpaste, her lips as soft as rose petals.

Then, just as suddenly, she pulled away.

Stunned, Jo released the brake and waved as she backed out. She was barely fit to drive, experiencing the dizzying realization that her friend had just handed her a smoking gun, a potential ethics violation, and then—*what the fuck?*—sealed it with a kiss.

୶

The plane's recycled air carried the aroma of stale coffee. Jo shifted, trying to find a comfortable position for her long legs, her seatback tray trembling with each jolt of turbulence. The most compelling thing on her mind was Tori's kiss. Remembering it made her stomach flutter. *Straight women sometimes kiss each other that way, but Tori knows I'm a lesbian.* Was she teasing her? Sending her a message?

Jo sighed, leaned back, and closed her eyes. She had to stop thinking about Tori's kiss and focus instead on her revelation about Jude and obtaining monitoring data from World Petrol.

The lawsuit would be strengthened by proof that World Petrol habitually violated government-mandated health and safety standards and air pollution regulations. But could a physician, a target of the industry's ire, safely get such damning information into the hands of responsible government agencies without being accused of another crime?

The threatening leer of the thug at the bar loomed in her mind. Had he been hired to prevent that from happening? Her chest tightened as she thought of the risks Tori was taking.

A flight attendant's cart rattled past. Jo declined drinks and continued her musing.

Whistleblower protection was discussed as a matter of federal law that needed to be addressed; however, the various vested interests remained powerful influences in the debate. Jo wasn't sure what the position in Texas was without researching it properly. There was a chance that if Tori's industrial hygienist friend gave the monitoring data directly to a government agency, such as the EPA's Office of Compliance, it could be used legally. But the industrial hygienist would likely suffer in the process.

Jo had to accept she didn't have all the answers yet. She surrendered to the steady hum of the plane's engines and dozed.

The taxi dropped Jo off in front of her townhouse complex, and she let herself in through the gate, rolling her bag and briefcase behind her. She unlocked the door. No Doberman bounded over to jump up and lick her face, and no girlfriend wrapped her arms around her. Kate was in her own apartment, studying for an important test on Monday. She had Sam with her, of course. She'd be back on Monday evening.

Jo set her bags down and opened the refrigerator. A few slices of deli ham and stale bread made for a quick sandwich before heading out to the grocery store and other errands.

That evening, she collapsed onto the couch. The afternoon had been filled with lengthy phone calls with Tom, her paralegal, who worked overtime on the weekend to update her. Jo's restless fingers drummed against the leather. The absences gnawed at her—Sam's warm weight missing from her feet, the air devoid of Kate's laughter.

Her longing for comfort increased to the point of forcing

her off the couch. She grabbed her car keys. *I'll spend only 10 minutes with Kate and pick up Sam.*

When Kate's doorbell chimed, Sam's happy yelp was enough to unravel the tension knot between Jo's shoulder blades. Through the mail slot, she glimpsed a hurricane of dark fur.

"There's my best boy!" she crooned, laughing as his wet nose sniffed and licked her fingertips, before he scrabbled at the door.

Kate ordered him to sit and opened it, her lips spreading into a wide smile. She held Sam's collar, but his whole body wriggled joyfully as he strained to get to Jo. She kneeled to receive his enthusiastic kisses, as she kneaded his ruff, delighting in the warm welcome.

Kate's outstretched hand hovered between them. Jo pressed her lips to the fluttering pulse at Kate's wrist before surging upward to hug her, burying her face in her neck. Kate's long, silky hair tickled her cheek as she inhaled the fresh, citrusy smell of her. Then she tilted Kate's chin up and kissed her, lingering in the sweet softness.

"Missed me, counselor?" Kate murmured against her jaw, backing up until they toppled onto the couch, their bodies entwined in the cushions. Sam wedged between their knees, nostrils flaring as he investigated Jo's pant leg. Smelling the cat, he let out a disgusted snort.

"Oh, I know, old boy, I've been consorting with the devil. Orange Cat, to be exact. You'd like him. He's like a dog." Sam cocked his head to the side and gazed up at her. She rubbed his ears before lying back against Kate, who wrapped her arms around her, nuzzling her ear. Jo sighed with pleasure.

"Keep that up, and you won't get any studying done tonight."

"Hmm," Kate murmured, still nuzzling and sliding her palms under Jo's shirt, "That might be my reward for being so diligent all weekend. How was your trip?"

The reminder of Oilton and Houston jerked her from more pleasurable thoughts. "Heart-wrenching. Disappointing. Dark. Tori's been indicted for bank robbery, and her case is going to trial. Some big, muscular thug is stalking her. To top it off, the senior partners want to drop our toxic tort case. That'll leave the people I interviewed without recourse."

"Gosh, I'm sorry."

Jo pulled herself up with reluctance. She'd love to vent with Kate. And to indulge in the erotic reunion she craved. But if she succumbed to her desire, then hours from now, when she came to her senses, she'd regret distracting Kate from her studies.

"You've got important work to do of your own."

Kate tossed dark hair over one shoulder and smiled up at her, an invitation in her eyes.

"Stay. I won't be reading another word knowing you're back in town."

Early Monday morning, in sheets tangled by impulsive decisions and smelling of lavender, Jo watched as dawn gilded Kate's shoulders.

Sam's leash landed with a jingle on her stomach. She looked over the edge of the bed into his dark, pleading eyes.

Kate rolled over to face her. "It appears Sam has forgiven you for leaving him and consorting with cats. But not for sleeping through walk-time."

They lingered for a few minutes of cuddling before rising together and dressing.

Jo fastened Sam's leash and grabbed his food bag and bowls. Kate walked her to the door, and Jo dropped everything to kiss her again, swept up in the moment.

A crunching sound interrupted them. Sam's nose was in his food bag.

Jo laughed and picked up his leash and clutter. "I'm off. Good luck with your test. I expect you'll ace it."

CHAPTER 25

LATER THAN MORNING on the Metro, Jo ruminated on how to convince David and Colin, the two senior partners, not to drop the lawsuit because of Tori's pending trial. In the office elevator, she ran into Tom, who followed her into her office and displayed a torrent of paperwork on the train spill appeal and other matters.

"Hold on, Tom," she said. "Let me catch my breath and update the senior partners about my trip before I dive in."

His face fell. "Okay. I organized everything we discussed yesterday, here, in order of priority."

"You're a peach."

David and Colin kept her waiting all morning. Jo's nerves hummed like live wires as she glanced at her watch for the millionth time. 1:58 p.m. Their laughter echoed down the hall, increasing her irritation.

When they finally beckoned her into the conference room, David's snow-white hair glowed under the recessed lights, his crinkled smile starkly contrasting with Colin's starched Oxford shirt and glacial posture. She'd always found David the warmer partner, the kind of man who'd ask about her weekend and bring homemade carrot cake to a meeting. Colin was a product of an English boarding school and was much more reserved. David's "Welcome back, Jo" rang genuine.

Her fingers tightened around her notepad as she walked into the room. She declined coffee; she was already buzzing with nervous energy as she joined them around the mahogany conference table.

David leaned back and steepled his hands. "So, we have much to discuss. The arrest of our key medical expert certainly puts a spanner in the works of our lawsuit."

Jo's pulse spiked. *Here we go.* She launched into her rehearsed defense of Dr. Nelson—no motive, likely no physical evidence, mistaken identity—but Colin's frosty stare cut through her words until she got to the crunch point.

"So did the grand jury indict her?"

"Yes."

David jiggled his pen. "And you found this out when?"

Jo cleared her throat. "Friday."

The word hung in the air like smoke.

Colin's voice turned arctic. "Our key expert witness indicted for bank robbery absolutely undermines our case."

"Yes, I know. I suspect World Petrol is aware of that as well." Jo's chair creaked as she leaned forward. "World Petrol, perhaps in cahoots with others, is likely behind this. The FBI's 'anonymous tip' reeks. Since when do they arrest and indict someone based on a facial look-alike? I've seen the videotape. The robber's body looks different."

David's eyebrow arched.

"She could have disguised her body," Colin retorted.

David ignored Colin's remark. "You think she was framed?"

"Possibly. You're familiar with her impeccable medical credentials and reputation as a physician and epidemiologist. You've met her in person. Can you imagine her risking her career and reputation to rob a bank?"

Colin frowned and, swiveling on his chair, stared out the window.

"It seems unlikely," David admitted. "But maybe she did. While she was high on drugs? Or having a financial crisis?"

She met David's gaze. "She was my roommate in college, and we've been friends ever since. I've never seen her smoke even one joint. She drinks a glass or two of wine, but I've only seen her drunk once. I've never known her to act impulsively. She's a respected and hardworking medical doctor with substantial savings. Where's the motive?"

Colin, still frowning, turned to stare at her. They sat in silence for a moment. Her heart pounded as she considered her next move.

"A huge muscular thug has been tailing Dr. Nelson, watching her in a restaurant, gym, and bar. Not bothering to be discreet. I was there. I saw him. He even followed her from the clinic and chased her on the freeway. I'm pretty sure someone hired him to intimidate her. Big Oil is number one on my list."

Colin snorted. "So Big Oil hired a look-alike and staged a robbery to frame Dr. Nelson and then hired a thug to tail and intimidate her? That's conspiracy theory drivel."

Jo's nails dug into her palms, remembering the thug's sinister stare at the gym, his ominous leer at the bar. "The oil companies are terrified of her research. She's setting up her own laboratory. What happens if she proves their toxins are in patients' blood and tissues?"

David rubbed his cheek, looking thoughtful. "Yes, she's clearly a pain in the ass to the petrochemical industry. But to

the point of framing her for bank robbery? It implies cooperation from law enforcement—even the government."

Colin slapped his palm on the table.

Jo startled, the sound reverberating in her ribs.

"And the judiciary?" Colin snapped. "You expect us to
believe they're in World Petrol's pocket too?"

She took a deep breath and slowly exhaled. "Yes, it's possible." The words came out quieter than she'd intended. She
straightened, meeting his glare. "They could have bribed the
eyewitnesses. And they've bought politicians for decades."

She didn't care for Colin. He loomed over discussions like
a dark cloud, dissecting her arguments with surgical precision.

David sighed. "Even if you're right, proving it will be nearly
impossible."

"We dig." Jo's voice didn't waver. "Find out the identity of
the thug and who he's working for. Subpoena World Petrol's
security contracts."

She hesitated, taking another deep breath to steady herself,
still undecided about what to reveal. Both David and Colin
were eyeing her. She knew she was on thin ice. But she had one
more card to play.

"Dr. Nelson may have access to evidence of criminal negli-
gence that will strengthen our case against World Petrol."

Colin brought his palm to his forehead and mock-banged it
against his head.

"Bloody hell, this sounds like a British crime novel." He
raised his eyes and glared at Jo. "How did she get this information? Hopefully, not illegally. If so, we can't use it in Texas, no
matter how damaging it is."

"I agree." David shifted in his chair and ran his hand through
his hair, a telltale sign of brewing disapproval. "How involved

are you in this, Jo? It sounds like you've been spending a lot of time with her."

"I helped her get a good defense attorney, Brian Kirkland. I met with him and Tori a couple of times."

She saw Colin purse his lips as if sipping spoiled milk. Her fingers dug into her thighs. *They're not listening.* She had one more point to make.

"Karen Silkwood died ten years ago because she threatened to expose Kerr-McGee's flagrant violations of health and safety to *The New York Times.* World Petrol might be playing the same game."

Colin scoffed. "Should we expect Meryl Streep to star in a movie playing Dr. Victoria Nelson?"

Heat crawled up Jo's neck, prickling like a rash, but she'd had enough. She lowered her voice, removing all traces of defensiveness. Each sentence came out like a bullet.

"Silkwood's body was found in a ditch, Colin. Mega companies are capable of acts of sabotage or even violence to protect their profits and interests. Why are you even questioning this possibility?"

Colin was ready for her. "What evidence," he spat, "proves they framed her?"

David's pen stilled, waiting.

"If we continue to gather plaintiffs for our lawsuit and hire our own private investigator, we'll find it." She made sure to catch each man's eye. "Can you imagine what a case we'd have if we found that one or more petrochemical companies framed a physician for bank robbery? To prevent her from revealing they had persistently and knowingly harmed not only their workers but also surrounding communities?"

"Fantasy." Colin dumped his notepad in his briefcase and snapped it shut. "This kills our hopes for a toxic tort case."

David's sigh, she knew, was a death knell to her argument.

"You're too close, Jo. What if she's guilty?"

They've already written the obituary for this case, she thought, *abandoning Tori and the people of Oilton.* If the petrochemical companies did have something to do with her arrest, this was precisely the outcome they'd want.

Why couldn't they understand that?

"I've been friends with Dr. Nelson for years." She could hear the pleading tone in her voice. "She just couldn't have robbed the bank."

David's expression softened. "So you've said. I understand your loyalty. But sometimes people change." He smirked and glanced at Colin. "Several of my former Vietnam War protestor comrades are now Reagan supporters."

"This isn't politics," she insisted. "People don't change their basic moral fiber that easily. Besides, where's the motive?"

"Who knows?" Colin said. "Regardless, we can't have her legal troubles associated with our law firm. File the notes of your interviews."

"What about the plaintiffs I've already signed up? Maureen is probably dying."

"Write to them. Say there has been a development preventing us from proceeding," Colin said.

She glanced at David.

"I agree," he said.

My case is toast. Her appetite for fight drained away, leaving only the sour aftertaste of defeat.

CHAPTER 26

LATER THAT EVENING, Jo's fingers drummed against the steering wheel as David's remarks coiled around her thoughts—what if Tori *had* robbed the bank?

The highway lights blurred into streaks as she replayed Tori's confession that she'd been on amitriptyline for depression. Could such medication have altered her judgment, perhaps making her agitated and impulsive? Rick said she'd been acting weird and seemed nervous, even wired, in the weeks before the robbery. But Rick was a jerk and angry about the divorce. Plus, Tori was a physician, and if she were experiencing unusual side effects, she'd surely have consulted her psychiatrist and stopped or changed her meds.

She spotted the sign for her local drugstore. On impulse, she swerved into the parking lot, tires scraping the curb. Inside, a pharmacist with owl-eyed glasses was lecturing a bewildered retiree about pill schedules. Jo hovered by the allergy relief display, counting the minutes. The old woman's cane finally tapped away, and Jo stepped to the window.

"Hi there." Jo slid a business card across the counter, its embossed "Attorney at Law" catching the fluorescent light.

"Can you tell me about amitriptyline's potential behavioral side effects?"

The pharmacist returned with a package insert. Jo unfolded it and narrowed her eyes to read the tiny print.

Patients may experience changes in behavior such as anxiety, panic, aggression, impulsivity, severe restlessness, and hyperactivity.

"Does that give you what you need?"

"Yes, thank you."

Could impulsively robbing a bank really be a side effect of medication for depression? It seemed unlikely.

The pharmacist tilted her head quizzically.

"Are you researching a case? What's it about?"

Jo kept her expression neutral and her manner distantly polite.

"Will you please make a copy for me?"

The pharmacist hovered for a moment, hoping Jo would say more, before turning away to comply.

Jo plucked the frozen dinner from the microwave, her mind racing. She settled at the counter, a wine glass in hand, missing Kate. With her nurturing ways, Kate always knew how to ground her, to pull her from the spiral of her obsessive thoughts. Jo's childhood, marked by a stressed single mother's inconsistent care, had left her craving the stability Kate offered. But tonight, Kate was absent, in her own apartment, studying.

Jo grimaced at the still-cold potatoes and shoved the tray back into the microwave. As the appliance hummed, her mind drifted to the conversation with her law professor.

A small subset of women who rob banks do so to seek control amidst chaos.

Tori's life certainly had been challenging before her

arrest—the stress of research, clinical work, and an impending divorce. Her recent escapades at the country-western bar and cryptic comments about figuring out who she really was suddenly took on new meaning.

Jo's brow furrowed. Had Tori's moral compass shifted? Accessing sensitive information illegally, even by proxy, was troubling enough. Could it be a gateway to more serious transgressions?

Tori's need for lab funding also concerned her. Surely Tori couldn't believe a bank teller would hand over that much cash? It seemed absurdly naive. But had she gone so far over the edge as to think it would work?

She abandoned her half-eaten meal, dropping the tray to the floor for an eager Sam, and retreated to the couch. She thought about Rick. His lack of support and blame-shifting grated on her. Tori had denied the possibility, but could he have been the anonymous tipster? Would he truly be that vindictive?

Jo rose to refill her glass and tried to shake off the troubling hypothetical scenarios. Regardless of her guilt or innocence, Tori needed help. Perhaps her life had unraveled more than Jo realized. The mysterious thug following Tori added another layer of urgency. Despite her senior partners' warnings, Jo couldn't abandon her friend.

"Oh, Sam boy, what am I going to do? My friend is in deep shit, and my lawsuit never got off the ground. And I must tell those poor, suffering people who trusted me to bring them justice that we're not going forward with their case."

Sam cocked his ears and looked soulfully into her eyes.

"I know." She fondled his dark, sleek head. "You think a walk solves all problems."

He gave her a dog smile, panted, and waggled his tail stump.

"Okay then. Let's go."

CHAPTER 27

TORI WORRIED THAT news of her arrest would reach the physician in charge of grand rounds at MD Anderson, and it had. He called her home on Monday, July 15th.

"What's this I hear about you being arrested for robbing a bank?" He sounded more curious than accusatory.

"I was arrested." Tori kept her voice clear and confident. "But I didn't do it. It's a case of mistaken identity. The FBI found no motive and no physical evidence. Their eyewitness testimony is fallible. I expect to be acquitted at trial."

"I see," he said, then paused for an excruciatingly long moment. "Do you still want to present your study? I'm sure you have a lot to deal with right now."

Her stomach tightened. *Don't you betray me, too.* She took a steadying breath.

"I want to go ahead." Listening intently for any signs of doubt, she added, "If you still want me to."

"From what you've shared, your study sounds relevant and important. So, if you're up to it, we'll proceed. As the moderator, I won't allow any questions about your arrest."

Relief flooded her chest. "Thank you," she said.

⨘

For the rest of the day, Tori poured everything into preparing for the presentation. Each slide had to be precise and compelling enough to make these cancer specialists see what she saw: a future where their work wasn't just about fighting cancer, but also about recognizing and preventing environmental contributors.

Her mind drifted back to her days at Massachusetts General, where she'd watched patients endure invasive procedures that offered little more than borrowed time—weeks or days at best. Sometimes those treatments hastened the very deaths they were meant to delay. That wasn't why she became a doctor. She wanted to stop suffering before it started, discovering what caused disease and preventing it.

Around dinnertime, Orange Cat jumped onto her lap and walked across her keyboard. Through eyefuls of tail fur, her computer screen went wild. Orange Cat turned and sat deliberately on the keyboard. His amber eyes were wide and penetrating.

"Okay, you win." She shut down the computer. "I'm sorry, Orange Thingy, but I'm clean out of cat food. I'll have to run to the store."

She grabbed her purse and car keys. Orange Cat followed her downstairs and rubbed against her legs. A mess of tawny fur transferred itself onto her black slacks.

"You guard the house while I get dinner for both of us."

Orange Cat meowed, sat on the lowest stairs, and tucked himself into a boxy rectangle. Tori closed the door, and the lock clicked behind her.

She glanced across the street and her heart leaped into her throat. A white van was parked in front of her neighbor's house with a man sitting in the driver's seat. Even from a distance, she thought she recognized the thug who followed her from the clinic.

Sweat beaded on her forehead. What was he doing here? Should she go back inside and call the police? But they hadn't been her friends lately. What would she say? *There's a van parked on the road. Yes, legally. Has the driver threatened you? No.* It was hopeless. There was no law against stalking women.

She walked swiftly to her car as if she hadn't seen him and jumped in and locked the doors. Her fingers trembled on the steering wheel.

I won't let him intimidate me. She reached into her glove box for the pepper spray, just in case. Then she popped the car into gear and backed out. Her breath caught in her throat when, in the rearview mirror, she confirmed the driver was indeed Van Guy. She squinted to make out the front license plate, but it was covered in dirt.

As she drove away, the van stayed where it was. Tori kept glancing in the mirror but saw no sign of him following her. Her pulse slowed, but her mind continued to race. *What if he knows about Jude and what we're up to?* He might have been outside her house to intimidate her, so she'd be fearful of presenting her findings to MD Anderson physicians.

She clenched her jaw. *Nope. He's not stopping me.*

She tried to think of what to do.

There'll be a phone booth at the grocery store. I'll call Jude. Maybe he's following her now.

She parked her car in a crowded area, making sure it was visible from the phone booth. Climbing out of the car, she glanced around to ensure the van and driver were nowhere to be seen and dialed Jude's number. It rang and rang. *Jude, pick up. Please.* Finally, Jude's answering machine clicked on, and Jude's upbeat, perky voice told her to leave a message.

"Jude, where are you? I'm scared. That thug I told you about is parked in front of my house. I'll try you again later."

Leaving the booth, she cast furtive glances around the parking lot. There was no sign of the van or driver. She returned to her car and turned on the ignition, only to remember that she hadn't bought Orange Cat's food and her shopping.

Wow, this stalker is messing up my head.

While she was checking out her groceries, she asked for a phone card and put fifteen dollars on it to save the hassle of lugging coins around. When she emerged from the store, she glanced around for Van Guy. Not there. She placed her groceries in the car and darted into the phone booth to try Jude again.

This time, she picked up.

"Jude, I'm so glad I reached you. The thug I told you about has been following me and was parked outside my house when I left—the same guy. I think he's trying to intimidate me from sharing my study findings at MD Anderson. Have you seen him? In a white van? I'm worried he might be on to us."

"I haven't seen him. But this is scary, Tori. He knows where you live. I'm worried about you. I'm coming over."

"No, Jude. Absolutely not. If he suspects something, it will confirm that we're in cahoots together and put all our efforts at risk."

Jude was silent for a beat before she said, "Your safety is far more important to me than what we're doing."

Warmth filled Tori's chest, and she smiled. "I'll be okay. I'll call the police if he approaches or threatens me."

"I worry about you, Tori. I've never met anyone like you. You take such risks for something you believe in. Somehow, knowing you has made me a better person."

"Thanks, Jude. I think it goes both ways," she said, and replaced the receiver.

She sighed, her conscience pricking her. She wished she could tell Jude everything.

CHAPTER 28

BACK HOME, TORI pulled into her driveway, eyes darting across the street. No white van. She struggled out of the car, carrying two heavy grocery bags. She nearly tripped over Orange Cat, who shot out of the shrubbery, his fur ruffled, meowing in distress.

"What are you doing outside? I thought I left you inside to guard the house."

Wary, she set the grocery bags on the front porch to unlock the door.

It was unlocked and slightly ajar.

The hair on the back of her neck stood up, and her pulse quickened as she pushed the door open. The view from the hallway revealed nothing out of the ordinary. She glided into the living room, careful not to make a sound. Light poured from the kitchen.

I didn't leave the light on.

Her senses heightened, and every creak and shadow posed a potential threat. Casting nervous glances around the living room, she picked up the iron poker from the fireplace. The silence was broken only by the ticking clock and her heart thudding in her ears. She startled when Orange Cat brushed by her and squeezed under the couch.

She crept toward the kitchen, peering around the corner. A half-empty water glass and a discarded ham packet on the counter spoke of an uninvited guest.

Could it be Rick?

Given creepy Van Guy had been lurking outside earlier, she wasn't taking any chances. She advanced down the hallway with the fire poker at the ready. There was nothing in the rooms downstairs.

Tori crept up the stairs, stopping to listen when a stair creaked. When she heard nothing, she continued. At the top, she hesitated, scanning the landing. Her office door stood half open, and she detected the faint odor of cigarette smoke.

Rick doesn't smoke.

Her muscles tensed further, and her fingers tightened around the fire poker. She crept along the hallway and poked the office door fully open with the iron bar, flattening her back against the wall. Nothing moved. The cigarette smoke smell intensified. Whoever was responsible had only just left.

Or is still here. Tori held her breath and raised the poker. *Now!*

She whirled into the room, ready for battle. And then stopped dead in her tracks. The chaos in her office hit her like a physical blow. Her research folders lay scattered and empty. Her computer was missing—all her hard work ripped away. She nearly choked.

Clutching her weapon, she crept down the hall to the bedrooms, checking behind doors, in the closets, and under the beds. All clear.

She returned to her office and sank into her old, familiar

chair. The adrenaline was ebbing, leaving her trembling and spent. The reality of the situation began to sink in.

So, Van Guy is trying to keep me from presenting and publishing my study findings.

Suddenly, she remembered the slides for her talk. A jolt of alarm propelled her upright. With trembling fingers and a brain fogged with shock, she opened the bottom drawer of her desk. Empty!

She flicked through the files on her desk and in her chair, looking for her MD Anderson presentation notes, but they were gone too.

She dropped into her chair again. When she'd arrived, the front door was unlocked and ajar, yet she was sure she'd locked it. And there had been no sign of forced entry. Had Van Guy picked the lock? And helped himself to a glass of water and ham slices? The only other person with a key to the front door was Rick. Her heart sank. The thought that Rick might have helped Van Guy enter her house added another layer of betrayal.

She remembered she needed to feed Orange Cat and descended the stairs on shaky legs.

"All clear, now," she called to Orange Cat. He only squeezed himself out from under the couch after she opened his food with the electric can opener. On automatic pilot, she dumped the smelly fish concoction into his bowl. He sniffed it and walked away.

"Not hungry? I know. I've lost my appetite, too."

She unpacked the refrigerated groceries and considered calling the police. Closing the freezer door, she sighed and leaned against it. She badly needed to talk to someone. *Not just someone, Jo.* She grabbed her car keys and left the house to drive to the nearest payphone. Her eyes constantly scanned for Van Guy.

An unfamiliar voice answered Jo's phone. *Perhaps Kate?* Tori introduced herself and asked for Jo. She heard the woman whisper, "It's your friend Tori. She sounds upset."

"Hi Tori, what's up?" Jo asked. "We just finished dinner. I tried your sweet potato fish taco recipe."

"Van Guy was lurking across the street when I left for the grocery store. And while I was out, someone broke in."

"Oh, my God, Tori, are you okay?" Jo said.

Jo's concern enveloped her like a comforting embrace. "Yes. He was gone when I returned. I checked the entire house. The door was unlocked, but I'm sure I locked it. I smelled his cigarette smoke. He stole my computer, my MD Anderson presentation slides, and notes. I'm guessing he was hired by someone who didn't want my cancer study made public."

"Holy shit. We knew it! All your data and hard work! Bastard!"

Tori found herself clinging to the sound of her friend's voice, a lifeline in chaos and loss that had become her evening.

"Right." She swallowed the lump in her throat. "He even helped himself to a glass of water and slices of deli ham and had a smoke. As if he were taunting me."

"What?" Jo said. She paused. "Does Rick still have a key? Could he have helped him?"

Tori ran a hand through her hair. "Yes, but Rick wouldn't do this."

"Hmm," Jo said. "I hope you're right."

Torn with uncertainty, Tori wanted to dismiss the possibility of Rick's involvement outright, but the thought stuck. *I should change the locks.*

"Should I call the police?" Tori asked.

"Yes, call them. To document the break-in." She hesitated. "But—"

Tori finished her sentence. "But the police may be in on it?"

Jo paused, and Tori could imagine her biting her lip as she thought.

"No, that would be absurd. Really, I doubt it. But if we could prove someone hired by World Petrol stole your data to suppress your study, that might strengthen your case at trial."

Tori sighed. "Okay, I'll call the police for whatever good that will do."

"Even if they don't find out who broke in, it will be recorded in their files."

Tori twisted a strand of hair around her forefinger. "You're right. But I don't know who to trust anymore."

"I can understand." Jo was silent for a moment, then said, "Do you have an off-site backup of your study data?"

A flood of relief filled Tori. "Yes! I was so flustered before, I nearly forgot!" A month ago, she'd thought of protecting her precious findings, and so she had done just that. It had seemed prudent to store a backup away from her home in case of fire. She felt a glimmer of hope. But as quickly as it came, it was replaced by a new worry. "Oh my God. I hope it's still there."

"At the university?"

"No. In my locker at the gym."

"Where he's also been watching you."

She frowned, thinking. She couldn't imagine how a guy like that could inconspicuously enter the women's locker room and break into her locker.

"I'll have to wait until morning to find out if it's all still there."

"Have you spoken with Brian about hiring a private investigator yet?"

"No. But I agree, it's time. I'll call him tomorrow." She and Jude had little in-person contact now, anyway.

"Okay. Can you call someone to stay with you tonight?"

"No. Not at this hour. But I'll be okay. I'll call the police. And don't worry. Van Guy got my study data. I assume that's all he wanted."

"Probably. But call me later. And let me know if your backup is still at the gym, okay?"

"Will do."

As Tori replaced the handset, a sense of loneliness gnawed at her gut. The thought of spending the night alone in her violated home filled her with dread. But she steeled herself, determined not to let it consume her.

≪

Tori had one more call to make. To warn Jude.

When Jude answered, Tori told her about the break-in.

"Oh Jesus, Tori, all your data? But thank God you weren't home and you're okay. I knew I should have come over."

Jude's genuine concern touched her. "I'm fine, and I have backup discs and magnetic tape of my data files. *If* they are still in my gym locker. But this heightens my worry about you and what we're doing. Van Guy could be someone hired by your employer. If World Petrol finds out, who knows what they'll do to you."

She shivered, imagining the thug physically harming Jude.

"I can't quit now." Jude's voice was firm. "I've got lots of incriminating measurements. Plus, it's important for your study."

Tori wondered if it was all worth it, if she shouldn't ask Jude to stop. Recent events—her arrest, the stalker, and now this break-in—had shifted the balance of their risky endeavor.

"Are you doing this just to help me, because we—"

Jude interrupted. "No, Tori. The more sampling I do, the more it confirms what I've often thought. The refinery is poisoning the surrounding neighborhood. It's like a sacrificial zone. Why should innocent people have to get sick or die so that oil companies can make huge profits, and we can buy cheap gas for our cars that pollute the air for all of us?"

"Good point. You'd do it anyway, even if we weren't lovers?"

"Yes, Tori, I would. Plus, I've done some research. If I submit this data to the EPA's Office of Compliance, we might have a chance not only to use it in your study but also to force the company to clean up its act."

Tori wasn't convinced, but she was too upset to analyze it just then.

"Okay, as I mentioned earlier, we need to maintain a low profile. No contact."

Jude sighed. "I miss you."

Tori said, "I miss you too." She surprised herself, feeling the intensity behind her words. As she hung up, Tori was left grappling with her feelings—guilt, affection, and a growing sense of dread.

CHAPTER 29

THE HOUSTON POLICE arrived ninety minutes after Tori phoned. Two officers: one burly and red-faced, the other shorter with a permanently dour expression. She explained that her call was delayed because she had to search the house and was still in shock.

"Can you describe the van?" the burly officer asked.

"Solid white, like a delivery van, but without lettering on the side. The license plate wasn't visible in front," Tori said.

"Did you see the driver?"

"He was middle-aged, with muscular shoulders, bald, and wearing a black T-shirt. This guy has been stalking me, showing up at restaurants, the gym, and following me from my clinic."

"Why do you think he's tailing you?" the dour officer asked, his pen poised over a notepad.

Tori sighed. "I believe he is trying to intimidate me. He only stole my cancer study data, slides, and notes. Someone must not want my study to see the light of day."

He looked quizzical. "Why not?"

A wave of exhaustion and frustration overtook her. "It's a cancer study implicating Big Oil's pollution as a significant contributing factor. They have their reasons for not wanting me to publish it."

"Do you have thoughts on who *they* might be?"

She certainly did. World Petrol or someone they hired. But these local officers probably wouldn't buy it. "I have no idea. There are many petrochemical companies in the study area."

He looked hard at her, then shrugged. "Okay."

The officers walked around the house, took pictures of Tori's office, and requested an inventory of the missing items. They dusted for fingerprints, and the entire investigation, including their interview, took only an hour.

When the police left, Tori closed the front door and sagged against it. Orange Cat appeared from wherever he'd been hiding and rubbed against her legs.

She took her camera from the shelf in her office and snapped pictures of the mess before methodically placing the files and any remaining contents back in order. Halfway through, fatigue overtook her.

"Come on, Orange Cat. We've had quite a shock. Let's get some sleep."

The following morning, Tori stood outside the gym at 6:50 a.m., waiting for it to open at seven. When a blurry-eyed young man unlocked the door, she rushed to the locker room, her heart racing. *Please let the backup be here.* Her hands shook as she fumbled with the combination lock and swung open the door. She shoved aside a pile of sweaty gym clothes she'd meant to take home to wash and pulled out the shoe box where she'd kept the backup data. Tearing off the lid, she peered inside.

They're here!

Three magnetic tape drives and eight floppy discs. Tori hugged the box to her chest.

Placing the tape drives and discs into her gym bag, she shut the door and refastened the combination lock just as three twenty-something women entered, laughing and bantering with each other.

Gripping the strap of her gym bag, she walked briskly to her car and drove home. When she entered her study, the blinking red light on her answering machine beckoned her—a message from a colleague at the university.

"Hi, Dr. Nelson. Some guy came around this morning asking questions about your study. He didn't look like a researcher. No one we knew. He wanted to know if you had an office here. I didn't like his looks, so I told him nothing. I just wanted to give you a heads-up."

So, he's looking for backup copies of my study.

She sank onto the couch to think. It was time to face reality. She could no longer be the sole keeper of the study data. What if the guy who stole her computer tried to steal it again? Or assaulted her? There was her pending trial. If a jury found her guilty, her credibility as the study's author would be ruined. Her patients would be left without a medical advocate, and her medical license would be suspended.

She dropped her forehead onto her hand. She shouldn't have taken on a study of this magnitude alone. But that was all in the past. What she needed now was co-authors—one or more people of stellar reputation—who could publish without her if the need arose.

Who can I ask?

She got up and paced around the room. She had solicited peer reviews of early study drafts from two former colleagues at the Harvard School of Public Health. Perhaps one or both would collaborate and help her integrate Jude's environmental monitoring data, if she ever got it. But she had little time, especially if she wanted it done before the trial.

She reached for her purse, and then a thought struck her. Where should she leave the box of discs? For a moment, she panicked until she reasoned that Van Guy had already searched her home and gotten what he'd come for.

Just the same, she took the backup into her bedroom and pulled out a drawer. It was the lowest in the chest, and underneath was a hidden compartment between the floor and the drawer's underside. She slipped in the discs and drives and pushed the drawer back into place.

Flipping through her Rolodex, she found what she needed and drove to a payphone. *Having to drive somewhere to make a phone call is getting old.*

She rang Dr. Ellen Grenoble, an epidemiologist at the Harvard School of Public Health. She and Ellen had been coauthors on other papers during her time at Harvard and had become friends. Ellen came from a wealthy family and didn't rely on government or industry grants or her meager salary to survive. Tori had enormous respect for her. Ellen was her top choice, but first she needed to gauge Ellen's level of interest.

"I thought your study was coming along nicely when I looked at it earlier," Ellen said. "Have you completed it?"

"I've nearly finished, but I'd like to reanalyze the findings and hope to incorporate important environmental monitoring data. To compare cancer rates with emission data and distance from the plants." Tori began. "But it's getting too much for me, and I'd love you to work with me on it."

She waited, shoulders tensed, for Ellen's answer.

Ellen took her time. "Possibly. I don't start teaching again until the second quarter. But you've done so much work on your own. Why do you need me?"

It appeared that Ellen had not yet learned of her arrest. Tori took a deep breath. "In mid-June, I was arrested for bank robbery. A grand jury has indicted me, and my case will be going to trial." She bit her lip, hoping this wasn't a deal breaker.

Ellen took a quick breath. "Oh dear." A long silence followed. Tori's heart sank.

"I understand if you don't want to be associated with me," Tori said.

"Did you do it?" Ellen asked.

"Of course not," Tori said. "It's a case of mistaken identity. I resemble the bank robber. That's all."

"You're going to trial, you say?"

"Yup." Tori's shoulders hunched further.

"And you want us to collaborate before your trial?"

"Yes." She held her breath.

"We'd best get to work then," Ellen said.

Tori let her breath out. But it wasn't a sure thing yet. "Umm." She changed the phone receiver to her other ear. "There is something else."

"Oh, dear God, please don't tell me you're charged with murder too," Ellen said.

"No. No." Tori forced a laugh. "But I don't yet have any environmental monitoring data. There is a possibility that I may not receive it or be able to use it."

"Okay," Ellen said. "It would certainly strengthen the study, though. Anything else?"

"Yes. Someone broke into my house and stole my computer, which had all my study data. Fortunately, I had a backup. But I would keep our collaboration under wraps for now."

"Are you thinking the petrochemical companies don't want you to publish?"

"Something like that."

"You are courageous to do this research, Tori."

I can't blame her if she doesn't want to get involved.

Ellen's voice came through, steady and clear. "A colleague in Louisiana has made me aware of how Big Oil is embedded in universities, providing funds to achieve research outcomes favorable to their interests. Much like tobacco companies did in decades past." There was another pause. "Of course, I will collaborate with you."

Tori closed her eyes, her knees weak with relief.

"Thank you so much, Ellen. I'll make a copy of the data and FedEx it to you with my study draft, first thing tomorrow."

It was an enormous relief to have one collaborator, but it wouldn't hurt to ask another. Tori put a call in to another former colleague, Dr. Jeff Townsend, now a professor of industrial hygiene and toxicology. He could help her integrate whatever data Jude managed to hand over to the EPA.

He was happy enough to collaborate on her paper, but when she told him about her arrest, the call went downhill.

"You did what?" His yell was piercing. Tori jerked the receiver away from her ear. She could still make out his squeak. "You robbed a bank?"

When the phone went silent, she said calmly, "I didn't rob the bank. I was accused of robbing a bank. A case of mistaken identity that should be resolved at trial."

"Seriously? I don't know, Tori. I'll have to run it by the Institutional Review Board. Harvard will probably not want my name associated with a potential felon."

Ouch.

"Dr. Ellen Grenoble has agreed to collaborate with me on this paper."

"Oh, yeah? Did she run it by the Institutional Review Board?"

"No, she didn't mention it. And I'm not a convicted felon."

Not yet.

But she was frustrated with Jeff. Even if she were convicted, collaborating with her on the cancer study would not violate research ethics or regulations. She sighed. There was no point in telling him about the illegally obtained monitoring data now.

"I don't think I can get an answer from the IRB very soon," Jeff said.

Tori's chest tightened. "Will you just look at it for now? Like I said, I haven't been convicted of a felony, and my lawyer thinks I have a good chance of being found not guilty at trial. Your input will be crucial if I can obtain toxic emission data to correlate with excess cancer rates."

"Really? You might get environmental monitoring data? Okay, send me what you have so far," Jeff said. "But I make no promises."

"Thanks, Jeff." Tori hung up.

She rubbed her eyes and leaned against the side of the phone booth, staring vacantly at the passing traffic. She'd have to reconstruct her MD Anderson talk from memory and use overheads instead of slides. *At least my study data will be safe with Ellen and Jeff in Boston.*

She had one more call to make.

CHAPTER 30

FORTUNATELY, JO WAS in when Tori rang her.

"My backup discs and magnetic tape drives were in the locker," Tori said.

"Oh, I'm so relieved! I didn't sleep much last night, worrying," Jo said.

"And I called the police. They took pictures and dusted for fingerprints. I took my own photos as well."

"Good. That was smart. At least the crime is documented," Jo said. "Did you call Brian to tell him about the break-in?"

"Not yet. I'll drop by his office later. And listen, Jo. Someone was nosing around the Department of Epidemiology at the university, asking about my study—probably the thug who stole my data."

"Oh, Jesus."

"I need to keep the data safe in case they try to steal it again. So, I called a colleague, Dr. Ellen Grenoble, at the Harvard School of Public Health and asked her to collaborate with me. Thank God she agreed. I'm sending her a copy of my study data tomorrow. I'm also sending a copy to another colleague who, unfortunately, was reluctant to work with a potential felon." She inhaled deeply. "If I am convicted, I'll remove my name from the paper, and Ellen can publish it under her name alone."

She scrubbed her hand over her face. It hurt to think she'd not get credit for all she'd risked.

"Good plan, although I sincerely hope it doesn't come to that," Jo said. After a pause, she added, "Unless the judicial system is corrupt and in the pocket of Big Oil, I just can't imagine you'd actually be convicted."

"Yeah, well. This work is of great importance to the people in those neighborhoods, and your lawsuit. It must be published. If I am convicted, it will cause unnecessary problems if my name is on the paper."

"You're my hero," Jo paused, and Tori tensed, sensing she had more to say.

"I'm sorry, but I have some bad news."

Unconsciously, Tori flung her free arm across her chest and gripped her shoulder, bracing herself for news she didn't want to hear.

Jo said, "I told you the senior partners heard about your arrest and were upset. Then, when I informed them that your case was going to trial, they decided not to pursue the class action lawsuit."

"Oh, no. What about the people you signed up? Are you going to leave them hanging?"

"I haven't contacted them yet. But you're our key expert—"

Tori interrupted, "I know, I know. If I'm convicted, my testimony and my study would be useless if my name is on the publication. But if my colleague, Ellen, is the lead author, maybe—"

"Right, I get it. I will bring this up with the senior partners." Jo cleared her throat. "They flipped out when I told them about my involvement in your legal problems. They want me to back off."

Tori nearly choked. *Is she going to abandon me?*

"This means you should stop calling me at the office. And unless the partners change their mind, I won't return to enlist other plaintiffs."

Tori slumped against the side of the phone booth.

"But I won't abandon you, Tori. You're my dear friend. But from now on, please call me at home."

Tori's knees nearly buckled. "Thank you," she managed. Her eyes pricked with tears.

"Of course," Jo said softly, "I'd love to be present when you talk to Brian. Do you think we can schedule a conference call for early evening? It's an hour later here, so I could make it home by 5:30 p.m. your time."

"Okay, if he agrees, I'll leave a message on your answering machine at home."

∽

When Tori arrived at Brian's office late that afternoon, he met her at reception and ushered her into his surprisingly small office. She was briefly distracted by pictures of his beautiful, smiling wife and two dark-haired teenage daughters. She sat across from his desk, and he sat in the chair beside her. "The judge has been assigned, and we have a trial date. September 3rd, right after Labor Day."

A cold wave of fear passed through her. "So soon?

"Yes. It's unusual to proceed to trial so quickly."

"But why is this happening?" Her mind was shutting out this news, unable to process it amid recent events.

"I don't know," Brian admitted. "We'll certainly have to work hard over the summer."

"I'm already upset. Someone broke into my house and stole my computer and files. Plus, someone is tapping my phone."

Brian's eyebrows shot up and drew together as he hunched forward, his face settling into an expression of deep concern, as she told him what happened.

"Can we include Jo in this conversation?" Tori said abruptly." She's waiting for our call."

"Of course."

He dialed Jo and put the call on the speakerphone.

"Tori has told me about the theft of her study, which she suspects was committed by the same guy who has been following her. It's certainly alarming."

"Right," Jo said. "He stole only her data, as well as the slides and notes of a presentation she was to give to the medical staff at MD Anderson. Don't you think this lends more credence to our theory that Big Oil wants to put Tori out of commission?"

"It does," Brian said. "Once again, I recommend we hire a private investigator to find out who this guy is working for."

Tori bit her lip. "I agree. Let's do it." She was finally committed.

"Great," Brian said, sounding relieved. "I have an excellent PI in mind, and I'll call her as soon as we're off the phone. She's very sought after, so I hope she's available."

"What about asking the PI to look into the possibility that not only did World Petrol, and maybe other petrochemical companies, steal Tori's study data, but they also framed her for the robbery?" Jo said.

"You mean by bribing the FBI, the judge, or the eyewitnesses? That seems unlikely."

"But if they're willing to break into Tori's house and steal her study data, they're obviously motivated to stop her from publishing any way they can," Jo insisted. "Shouldn't we look into it?"

Brian frowned. "Let's focus on finding out who this goon is working for first. If it is a petrochemical company, we can use that to plant reasonable doubt in the minds of at least a few jurors. We want them to think the same outfit might be behind her arrest. Some people know that these large multinational companies have excessive influence in this region and don't like it. I'll be picky when it's time for jury selection."

"Thank you," Tori said, relief in her voice.

"Tori, tell me more about what the police did?"

"The cops took photos, a list of the missing items, and dusted for fingerprints, although they said the burglar might have worn gloves. I also took photos of the mess in the office and kept an inventory of everything missing."

"Okay. Please send me your inventory and photos. Then we'll ask the PI to collect information to plant reasonable doubt in the jury."

"I'd also love to discover who the anonymous tipster was who told the FBI the bank robber looked like Tori," Jo said.

"You and me both," Brian said.

CHAPTER 31

A WEEK LATER, when she'd caught up on her cases, Jo sat twiddling her pen between thumb and forefinger, gazing out her office window at the clouds forming on the horizon. *Rain is coming.*

When Tori told her, her case was going to trial in early September, Jo bristled. Was it too far-fetched to imagine Big Oil would stage a bank robbery to implicate a troublesome physician? And could the oil companies really put pressure on a federal judge to conduct a swift trial to convict and discredit her before she could publish her study? She hated not being able to openly investigate the possibilities.

She dropped a notepad into her briefcase and rose to leave. She almost collided with Tom.

"Perfect timing." She thrust a document at him. "I've finished writing the factum for the train spill appeal. Please make sure there are no typos. I'm heading to the public library to do some research."

∽

Jo enlisted the librarian's help in finding articles that examined worker illness or mortality in the petrochemical industry. Most articles from industry scientists showed no increase or a decrease in cancer and respiratory diseases, such as asthma.

In contrast, she discovered academic cohort studies of oil refinery workers that showed an excess of lung, blood, kidney, and brain cancer. Letters from World Petrol scientists to the editor of the same medical journals attempted to poke holes in these authors' methods and conclusions.

She found only one industry-funded cohort study of a rural population living downwind from a natural gas refinery. It found no excess of cancer when residents were matched with age and sex-adjusted controls.

Of course, it wouldn't.

This was what Tori was up against. Jo's library search demonstrated that Tori's study of excess cancer in communities surrounding petrochemical plants was sentinel and groundbreaking work. It would motivate public discussion of stricter air quality standards, industrial hygiene, and engineering controls that could cost companies tens of millions, not to mention potentially fomenting toxic tort lawsuits and federal fines.

No wonder they want to squelch it.

She perused other articles and editorial pieces related to World Petrol. Climate models developed by academic and government scientists predicted catastrophic global warming by 2030, primarily due to continued reliance on fossil fuels. Their studies predicted sea-level rise, ice-sheet melting, and rapid, unpredictable climate shifts that, if left unchecked, would become irreversible.

Yet these massive oil companies had used their vast resources to debunk these studies. They published their own analysis, which overemphasized uncertainties and denigrated government climate models by promoting the myth of global cooling and questioning the discernibility of human-caused warming. They proclaimed that the planet was warming due to natural climate variability, rather than the burning of fossil fuels and human activity.

She rolled her eyes and read on, learning more about their tactics. World Petrol's scientists evoked sunspots, Earth's wobble, and the cooling effect of aerosols—anything but fossil fuel consumption. They stated that the cause of the warming trend was still uncertain. The vehemence and scope of their efforts to stir controversy led Jo to suspect that World Petrol knew very well that burning fossil fuels would cause catastrophic planetary warming. Yet acknowledging it would threaten their vast profits.

It made her blood boil. But it was a fight for another day.

When Jo returned to the office, Tom caught up with her in the hallway. "We just got the notice. The appellate court will hear our appeal in the train spill case next week."

"Okay. I'm on it," she said. But first, she needed to talk with David. She found him in the coffee room, chatting with an associate attorney. She loitered nearby until they finished and asked to see David in private. He motioned her into his office, and they stood facing each other.

"Someone has been following Dr. Nelson. They broke into her house and stole her computer, which contained her study data and the slides and notes for her MD Anderson talk," Jo said.

David's eyes widened and his mouth dropped open. "Sit

down. Tell me the details." He took a seat behind his mahogany desk. She sat opposite him and told him all she knew.

"Thank goodness she had an off-site backup copy." David scratched his head. "This break-in lends more credence to your concern that the petrochemical companies are actively trying to prevent her from publishing her study."

"That seems obvious." She hesitated to mention the unlocked front door and her suspicion that Tori's estranged husband may have facilitated the break-in. To hit Tori where he knew it would hurt—her precious research.

She said, "Is it still so far-fetched to imagine Big Oil implicating a physician who threatens their profits as a suspect in a bank robbery and putting pressure on prosecutors and judges to ensure her conviction?"

David leaned back in his chair. "Maybe not. But the federal judge is appointed, not elected. Do the police have leads in the break-in?"

"Not that they're telling her. Her attorney is hiring a private investigator to find out who the stalker, who's also the thief, works for."

David sighed, his eyes narrowing. "If World Petrol and other companies are involved in her arrest, her attorney will need solid evidence. Framing a physician-scientist for bank robbery and breaking into her house to steal her research data would raise their treachery to a whole new level. Currently, there's only inference."

"Remember the Karen Silkwood case. She was forced off the road and murdered on her way to reveal damaging violations of worker safety to *The New York Times*."

David nodded. "Yes. I'm sorry about Colin's sarcasm. He shouldn't have made light of that."

"I'd like to keep on top of this," Jo said. "If we find evidence to corroborate our suspicions, it may help us to revive and rebuild our lawsuit. Also, Dr. Nelson has found a physician at the Harvard School of Public Health to collaborate on her study and possibly become the lead author."

"Interesting. That changes the landscape," David said. "I'll talk with Colin. Find out what you can. However, remember that you aren't retained as your friend's defense attorney. Don't encroach on—who was it—Kirkland's territory."

CHAPTER 32

ON FRIDAY, JULY 26th, as Tori left the tranquil tree-lined streets of Houston Heights, she buzzed with excitement. Her destination was the Texas Medical Center, one of the world's premier cancer-treatment and research facilities, and she was about to deliver her talk. The city's skyline loomed ahead, a testament to Houston's rapid growth and the petrochemical industry's dominance. As she drove south on I-45, her mind whirled with anticipation.

The familiar landmarks of the medical complex came into view, and she navigated through the network of streets and buildings with ease. Parking her car, she took a deep breath. It helped her nerves to envision the attentive audience of medical professionals she hoped to inspire.

A distinguished-looking older physician in a long white coat introduced her in the lecture hall, highlighting her impressive background and training. As she approached the lectern with her notes, Tori's palms began to sweat, and her mouth felt dry. She scanned the hall. The audience of at least fifty physicians was impressive for late July. Using an old public-speaking trick she'd learned in college, she quickly selected a friendly-looking face in the audience. Her gaze settled on a woman physician in the second row, whose pleasant, interested expression calmed her.

Tori projected her first overhead onto the screen, displaying the title of her study: "Cancer Rates in Communities Surrounding Petrochemical Plants on the Texas Gulf Coast."

"This table shows the incidence of all cancers along a fifty-mile stretch of the Houston Ship Channel. It's much higher overall than in the rest of Texas and the US."

She quickly got into her stride. As her confidence built, she displayed and explained more tables showing rates of various cancers broken down by age, sex, occupation, smoking, and socioeconomic status. When she'd completed her talk with ten minutes to spare, the audience peppered her with questions.

"Dr. Nelson, were you able to get exposure data at the individual level?" a distinguished-looking older physician asked.

"Not as this time," she answered. *Not until I get Jude's monitoring data and my lab up and running.*

Another physician raised his hand—a middle-aged man wearing heavy, dark-framed glasses. He cleared his throat. "Of course, a typical weakness of population-based cancer incidence studies is that they might show that cancer is on the high side in a group of people, but they can't tell you why. You have only crude measures of confounding factors, such as access to health-care and socioeconomic status. What about the duration of residence near the petrochemical companies or the influence of previous residential exposures?"

"I can attempt to get residence duration from census or voter registration data, but it's challenging and often incomplete," she said. "And the stage of diagnosis *is* a measure of access to medical care."

She steered the discussion toward established knowledge.

"You are correct that we can't draw firm conclusions as to the causes of excess cancer in these communities, but we do have other corroborating data from animal and occupational studies that the toxins emitted by these companies cause cancer."

Glasses Man persisted. "Yes, yes, but we can't say living near a petrochemical plant caused an individual patient's cancer."

She guessed Glasses Man was a petrochemical company plant. Just as she was about to respond, a young physician intervened to address Glasses Man.

"We know that excessive childhood sun exposure increases the risk of melanoma. Even if we can't prove it caused an individual's melanoma, we have a solid basis to say it probably did."

Tori noticed a nod of agreement from the woman physician.

"Yes, that's a good point," Tori said, grateful for the support.

"Yeah, but what about smoking, alcohol consumption, exposure to radiation, and other known carcinogens?" Glasses Man retorted. "These carcinogens may be responsible for the excess cancer you describe."

"As you probably know," Tori said, "tumor registries don't routinely gather data on smoking or alcohol consumption, though I got smoking data from other sources. If I get more funding, I will attempt to collect information on exposure to other carcinogens."

What she didn't say was that obtaining that data was unlikely, particularly without the necessary resources or time to manage the complex process of gathering patient information. Maybe one day, if she weren't in prison, she'd join the full-time faculty of a School of Public Health. Then, she could apply for an NIH grant to do a nested case-control study of cancer patients from the area and control for genetic and lifestyle factors known to cause cancer.

She continued, her voice firm. "I realize the limitations of this type of population-based study. But when my study is published, other studies of different designs will follow."

"I focus on known cancer risk factors in my patients, such as lifestyle," Glasses Man said. "No point in chasing after iffy risk factors they can't control, anyway."

He's definitely a plant.

"But," Tori argued, "if pollution from the petrochemical plants is causing cancer in the workplace and surrounding communities, wouldn't you want to know? Patients may be unable to control the air they breathe, but environmental agencies and local public health departments can. If they have the data to implement regulations."

"Too much government regulation as it is," Glasses Man grumbled.

The moderator recognized that the discussion was turning into a two-person argument and ended it. "Thank you, Dr. Nelson, for a provocative presentation."

On her way out, the young physician who spoke about sunlight and melanoma followed her.

"Dr. Nelson? Hello, I'm Dr. Worsham. I'm caring for a patient in the ICU who worked at an oil refinery for years. He's dying of acute myelogenous leukemia. I plan to support his workers' compensation and disability claim. What specific questions should I ask regarding his work history?"

"If he's lucid, find out if he worked around seals, pipework, or storage tanks with exposure to leaks of volatile organic compounds."

"I will. Are there any books or papers you recommend I read to learn more about occupational and environmental medicine?"

She gave him an approving smile. "Of course. The best place to start is *Environmental and Occupational Medicine.* It's by William N. Rom and others."

Her mood, dampened by Glasses Man, lightened after encountering the young doctor. If she'd inspired just one physician to consider the environmental causes of cancer, her talk would have been worthwhile.

The physician moderator caught up with her.

"Nice job, Dr. Nelson," he said. "It appears that you've at least a few physicians considering occupational and environmental exposure when evaluating their patients."

"I hope so," she said. "Too bad they don't get any teaching about it in medical school."

When she settled in her car, she smiled at herself in the rearview mirror. *World Petrol didn't prevent me from presenting my findings to these cancer specialists after all.*

A moment later, her smile faded. Glasses Man had foretold the problem of assessing causality for individual patients. Getting Jude's air monitoring data was essential. But was it worth the risk?

CHAPTER 33

THE FOLLOWING EVENING, Tori paced her living room, sipping a glass of chardonnay. She was wrestling with what to do about Jude. Orange Cat, lounging on the back of the couch, watched her through narrow eyes.

What worried her most right now was how honest she'd been with Jude. Was she entirely sure she hadn't taken advantage of Jude's crush on her? She'd been anxious to gather damning environmental monitoring data to reinforce her cancer study and show the world the company's habitual disregard of environmental standards. But was she being fair to Jude, who was taking the most risk?

"When did I become such an environmental activist?" she inquired of Orange Cat.

He stood up, yawned, and stretched his back. *Like forever,* he seemed to say.

"I guess it all started when I was twelve, and we tried to save those oil-soaked birds and baby seals on the beach in Cape Cod," she told him.

Yet she had always considered herself an objective scientist, adhering to scientific methods and refraining from drawing conclusions that exceeded the evidence. Though she'd advocated for her patients who deserved workers' compensation for work-related conditions, she didn't claim causality for illnesses that didn't meet the test of "more probably than not."

Orange Cat leaped from the couch to the floor, rolling around on his back. It was a well-known signal: she was required to dangle a feathered toy over him while he batted at it with a lazy paw. But she was not tempted to play today as she continued to wrestle with her conscience.

Jude was only in her late twenties. She'd risk her career as an industrial hygienist by handing over company documents and conducting surreptitious environmental monitoring. Retribution could be harsh, especially given the uncertainty surrounding whistleblower protection. Could she believe Jude's assurances that she wasn't motivated solely by her crush?

And then there was Jo. This was an added complication. Tori's feelings for Jo had resurfaced and remained unresolved. Could she truly be in love with two women at the same time?

"Oh, Orange Cat, what am I going to do? I care for Jude, but I can't get Jo out of my mind."

Orange Cat rolled upright, pounced on the feathered toy, and laid it at her feet.

Tori made up her mind. She had to talk to Jude.

"Not now." She gave Orange Cat a hasty stroke and grabbed her car keys.

⌘

Jude picked up on the third ring and greeted Tori warmly.

"I have good news." Jude's voice was excited.

"Oh Jude, I hope you haven't done anything to draw attention to yourself. I worry —"

Jude interrupted. "Hear me out. I've conducted passive and

active air sampling for volatile organic and sulfide compounds beyond the fence line. It was tricky getting into the lab to use the gas chromatograph and mass spectrometer to analyze them without my boss noticing. But he went on vacation for a week, and I analyzed all my back samples. I also used some direct reading instruments around the neighborhood. Wow, we were right. The levels are significantly above the EPA limits. Especially during flares and process malfunctions."

A surge of excitement made Tori's resolve waver. "Just as we thought."

"I've downloaded the results on floppy discs. When can we meet so I can give them to you?"

Tori's excitement faded. "This is dangerous, Jude. You risk your entire career."

"We've been through this, Tori. I'm doing this for myself as well as you."

Tori frowned as she reassessed the situation. She'd love to get her hands on that monitoring data even before Jude handed it over to the EPA.

"When can we meet?" Jude pressed.

Tori gave in. "Tomorrow night?" She couldn't keep the excitement out of her voice, not just because of getting the data. She hadn't seen Jude for weeks, and she missed her. "Meet me at 9:00 p.m. in Woodland Park. In the parking lot off Houston Avenue."

The following night, at 9:00 p.m., Tori drummed her fingers against the steering wheel of her car—the only one in the parking lot. A cop car cruised by and slowed. Tori held her breath. No doubt her solitary car looked suspicious. She breathed out

when the cops moved on. She drove to a spot just outside the
park entrance to avoid further scrutiny.

Forty-five minutes later, she was still waiting. She hugged
herself, rubbing her hands up and down her upper arms, as her
mind churned with dark possibilities. *Where's Jude? Has something happened? Has she been caught? Is Van Guy on to her?*

Finally, restless and worried, she jumped out of the car to
pace the sidewalk, keeping within range of the car and anxiously watching every approaching headlight. Then she stopped
abruptly.

An ominous orange glow had begun to spread into the night
sky to the east. Her heart leaped into her throat as she stared
with her mouth agape.

CHAPTER 34

TORI DROVE TO a nearby pay phone, her fingers trembling as she dialed Jude's number. Not even Jude's voice sounded on the answering machine. She tried again after fifteen minutes, but still, no answer. A cold dread seeped into her bones. *Something has happened to her.*

Tori covered her face with her hands, taking slow, deliberate breaths to calm her racing thoughts. Then she started the car and headed toward Jude's apartment. Tori needed to be there, to see and touch her when she returned. She wouldn't rest until she knew Jude was safe.

As she drove, she flipped through the radio stations for local news. At last, she heard, "A fire and explosion have ravaged the World Petrol refinery in Oilton. Firefighters are battling the blaze, but it's only 10 percent contained. Residents are advised to stay indoors with doors and windows sealed."

Her breath hitched. *Oh Jude.* Had they discovered what she was doing and put her in harm's way?

Tori pulled over. She took rapid, shallow breaths. Her head was spinning. Her fingers and lips tingled.

It's my fault.

But after a few agonizing minutes, Tori forced herself to

slow her breathing. She was catastrophizing. Jude was likely responding to the emergency, distributing protective gear, and monitoring toxins. With renewed resolve, she continued driving to Jude's home.

She parked on the curb in front of Jude's apartment and waited, reclining the car seat. The orange glow in the east grew larger. The radio reported that the fire was only 25 percent contained. *Please let Jude be safe.* She also worried about the workers and firefighters.

Eventually, her breathing slowed, and she drifted off to sleep.

In the gray light of dawn, she awoke coughing. A smoky haze hung in the air, filling it with an unfamiliar, pungent stench that made her eyes water.

She knocked on Jude's door in case she'd slipped in without seeing Tori's car out front, but there was no answer. Flicking on the car radio, she searched for local news.

"The fire at the World Petrol refinery in Oilton has claimed the lives of three workers. It is still only 50 percent contained, and public health officials are urging residents to remain indoors with doors and windows closed."

She brought her hands to her face. "Oh no, no, no," she moaned. Who could she call to find out about Jude? And three deaths? She doubted anyone at the refinery would pick up, and it was too early for the press to release the names of the deceased. Her anxiety was almost unbearable. Oh, how she wished she still had those little orange pills.

Stiff as the Tin Man, she had to pee. She started the car and drove to a nearby donut shop. After attending to her basic needs, she found a payphone and called Jo, guessing she wouldn't have left for work yet.

"I hope I didn't wake you. Something terrible has happened. There's been a fire and an explosion at the World Petrol refinery.

Three workers were killed. I'm worried sick for my friend—the industrial hygienist I told you about."

"I saw it on the morning news. It looks horrendous. It's a shame there were deaths. I hope your friend is okay. She's an IH, not a process worker, so hopefully she wasn't injured in the explosion."

"But I'm sure she's in the thick of it. I'm concerned too about the workers and residents. This explosion likely released a load of toxins into the air. And I have nowhere to see those who are ill or injured."

"What about one of the independent pulmonary specialists? Could you possibly use an extra exam room temporarily?"

"Possibly. That's a good idea. I'll ask. I just haven't been able to think straight."

Should I tell her what Jude really means to me?

"Some good news, Tori. I spoke with my senior partner about your break-in. He agrees that Big Oil may be behind it. I've had work on my other cases over the last week or so, but this is now a priority. I'm coming to Houston."

Tori's anxiety drained from her body like water from a bathtub. Her knees nearly buckled. "Oh, I'm so glad, Jo."

"Where are you calling me from?"

She looked around. "I don't know, somewhere near Jude's apartment. I went to talk with her, but she never came home. I slept in my car waiting for her."

Jo was silent.

That probably gave me away.

"Jesus, Tori. Go home. Take a shower. Call around for a place to see patients. I'll be there soon."

She could only gulp, "Okay." Tears welled in her eyes.

"And don't worry about your friend," she said, her tone gentle. "If she's an IH, she knows how to protect herself. She'll probably get in touch when the emergency is over."

CHAPTER 35

EARLIER THAT MONDAY morning, after calling David to brief him about the refinery explosion and fire, Jo had strolled into the kitchen and put her arms around Kate from behind. She inhaled the smell of maple bacon frying as she nuzzled her ear.

"How did I get so lucky to have a beautiful woman in the kitchen making me blueberry pancakes after a night of dynamite lovemaking?" she whispered low into Kate's ear.

"Must be your sexy voice and magical touch," Kate said, turning around for a kiss. They pulled apart only when the pancake began to smoke.

When they sat down to their stack of pancakes and crisp bacon, dousing the lot with Vermont maple syrup, Jo said, "I talked to David about the refinery explosion we saw on the news this morning."

"It looks bad. I know you saw some of the people who live nearby. It must be awful for them.

Kate's expression remained somber as Jo continued, "I spoke with David, and he and Colin are now open to adding plaintiffs to our lawsuit. Also, the families of the workers who died in the explosion may separately want to file wrongful death claims."

Kate's eyes widened slightly. "Uh-oh, I feel a trip coming on."

Jo nodded. "I'm going to try to get a flight this afternoon."

Kate's brow furrowed. "Will you wear a mask if you're outside? Protect yourself from the smoke and toxic air?"

Jo smiled. "Yes, of course."

Kate ate her pancakes in silence for a few minutes, her expression pensive.

"What's up, sweetheart?" Jo said, though she had an idea.

Kate looked up, her voice tinged with vulnerability. "Will you stay with your old girlfriend again?"

One thing Jo loved about Kate was that she expressed her feelings and concerns openly, so they did not come across as passive-aggressive or indirect.

"Probably at some point, but she was never my lover. We're just dear friends. I'll spend most of my time in Oilton talking with plaintiffs."

Kate avoided looking at her, and Jo reached across the table to take her hand.

"Kate, look at me."

As Kate's eyes met hers, they welled with tears.

"I told you I once had a major crush on Tori in college," Jo said gently. "But that was years ago. Life moves on. Since then, I've had relationships with other women. I'm well over my infatuation with her. You're the woman I want. You, and only you." She continued to hold Kate's gaze.

Kate still looked solemn. "What if she makes a move on you?"

The kiss momentarily flashed through Jo's mind. With a quick huff, she dismissed it and squeezed Kate's hand. "Oh my

God, please don't keep yourself up at night with such fantasies. I'm a big girl, remember? Also, I'm sure she has much more to worry about now than her love life."

Kate finally smiled, the tension gone. "Okay," she said. "Would you like me to give you a ride to the airport?"

Jo grinned. "That would be lovely."

∽

Later that morning, after speaking with Tori, Jo contacted Mary Williams. "How are you, Mary? Is the smoke affecting you?"

"The fire is mostly under control now, and the smoke is not as bad as it was. I'm okay if I stay in the house with the windows and doors closed and the air conditioner on. But I've had to change the filter twice," Mary said.

"I'm glad you're okay. I'm flying to Houston this afternoon and hope to talk with you and the others in person tomorrow. Would you let them know?"

"Yes, I will. But Maureen, the gal with leukemia, is in the hospital. The doctors don't expect her to survive."

Jo sighed and closed her eyes. "Oh no, I'm so sorry."

"And Georgia, with the asthmatic kids, has just packed up and left for New Mexico to live with her sister. The refinery fire was the last straw."

Jo understood the difficult choice. "It makes sense that her children's health took priority, but it's a shame she had to choose between her marriage and their health."

"There's gonna be many more people wanting to talk to you. That awful explosion tipped the scales for them. I'll spread the word," Mary said.

"Thanks, Mary." Jo's thoughts turned to those most affected by the fire. "Do you know the families of those killed?"

"I know one family very well. They're just down the street. Mark Evans leaves behind three little 'uns. It's tragic."

Jo's heart went out to the grieving family. "I'm sure his wife is in shock. When you think it's appropriate, can you let her know I'm here for her if she eventually wants to file a wrongful death lawsuit? It can't compensate for the loss of her husband, but it might help her care for her children."

"I will," Mary said with firm determination. "I best get to work, letting people know you're a comin'."

∽

When Jo's plane descended into Houston in the early evening, a smoky haze covered the greater Houston area. She drove south into Houston through the gray haze that irritated her eyes. The fiery red sun bathed the west in an orange glow as it dipped low on the horizon.

"This happens occasionally," the rental car agent had said. "You get used to it."

You shouldn't have to. She could never get used to it.

When she rang the doorbell at Tori's, she heard the thump, thump, thump of her footsteps as she descended the stairs. Tori opened the door and flung herself into Jo's arms.

"Oh, Jo, I'm so glad you're here!" she said, breathlessly.

Jo pulled back and examined her friend. Tori looked even thinner and more exhausted than when Jo last saw her.

"Have you heard from the industrial hygienist?" Jo asked with genuine concern.

"No, and I'm so worried. I've been calling her house every hour." Tori grabbed Jo's carry-on bag and pulled her by the arm into the house.

"As I said, she'll probably be all right. Have you had dinner?"

"No, I'm not hungry."

"You must keep up your strength, doctor," Jo insisted, striding to the kitchen and opening the refrigerator. "I'm making a salad. Do you have any protein?"

Tori appeared frazzled and distraught all evening, far from the cool, confident physician in a crisis Jo thought she knew. Tori barely managed to choke down her salad, and two glasses of wine did nothing to calm her. She sprang from the couch and paced, calling her friend several times from the house phone, apparently unconcerned that it might be tapped.

Orange Cat had picked up her tension and kept zooming across the living room with no visible provocation, his claws clattering and rucking up the rug.

Was it her friendship with the industrial hygienist or the possible loss of access to World Petrol's monitoring data that caused Tori such distress? Either way, the intensity of Tori's agitated worry surprised her. So far, Jo's efforts to distract her had failed.

"Did you contact any physician colleagues to see if they have space you might use to see patients from the refinery?"

"Not yet, but I will first thing tomorrow morning," Tori said, continuing to pace.

Worn out, Jo eventually gave up. "Go to bed, Tori. You can't do anything tonight. You need your sleep. Do whatever you normally do to calm yourself."

She hugged Tori and retired to the guest room to read herself to sleep. Half an hour later, she heard Tori's footsteps come up the stairs and cross the landing. They paused at her door. She lowered her book and waited. A few moments later, the footsteps continued down the hall, and Tori's bedroom door clicked shut.

CHAPTER 36

AS THE MORNING sun leaked through the blinds, Tori sprang into action to secure a consulting office. She made several calls until Jo's stirring in the kitchen signaled it was time to join her downstairs.

Tori hugged Jo good morning and announced, "Right away, I found an allergy office willing to rent me space to see patients three days a week. The arrangement is almost too good to be true—no need to set up my own scheduling and billing system. It'll fit right into theirs."

"That's wonderful, Tori. When can you start?"

"As early as this Thursday. In only two days."

"Fantastic!" Jo said. She raised her palm for a high five.

Tori's excitement was muted. She still couldn't contact Jude. Jo handed her a plate of scrambled eggs and toast, her expression somber. "I spoke with Mary Williams yesterday. She knew one of the workers who was killed. Mark Evans. He leaves behind a wife and three young children."

Tori nearly dropped the plate. "Oh, no. I know him. He's one of my patients. He was toxic from exposure to volatile organics, but he didn't want to piss off the company and file a workers' comp claim."

She sank into the kitchen chair and rubbed her forehead. "And now he's dead. His poor family."

"I'm so sorry." Jo touched her arm. "I can help his wife bring a wrongful death claim." She took her hand away. "Small comfort, I know."

Jo remained standing. "I've already eaten, and I must be off. I told Mary I'd be there by ten this morning."

✤

When Jo left for her meeting, Tori remained seated, her gaze drifting blankly over her plate of untouched breakfast. The silence was oppressive, filled with thoughts of Mark and the other workers who had lost their lives.

And Jude. Where is she? The uncertainty was unbearable. She left her breakfast and grabbed her car keys.

Tori headed to Jude's apartment, praying she'd finally be there. As she pulled up to the curb, Jude emerged from around the corner, her work clothes covered in soot, and her eyes red-rimmed. Her face was grimy around where she'd worn a respirator, and strands of sweaty auburn hair clung to her forehead. When she saw Tori, she dropped her hard hat and stood still, eyes wide.

Tori's heart leaped for joy. She jumped out of the car and rushed toward her. She threw her arms around Jude, who slumped against her. Tori buried her face in Jude's hair, ignoring the reek of smoke. She held on tight, tears pricking her eyes.

"Oh, Jude," she breathed. "I've been so worried."

Jude coughed a dry, racking cough.

Alarm shot through Tori, and she pulled away. "You're not well. Let's get you inside."

She helped Jude up the stairs and fumbled in Jude's pack for the keys. Inside, Jude collapsed onto the couch with another fit of coughing. She brought Jude a glass of water, helped her out of her filthy overalls, and covered her with a blanket.

"Thank you," Jude rasped. "I was okay until I got home. Then I just hit a wall."

Tori hugged her. "Stay sitting up. I'll go downstairs and get my medical bag."

Tori was relieved to find that her stethoscope and medical bag were still in the trunk, untouched since her firing from the clinic. Upstairs, she pressed her stethoscope to Jude's chest. *Loud wheezes.*

Jude coughed up a wad of black mucus, a testimony to inadequate respiratory protection.

"Eurgh," she croaked.

Tori went to the sink and filled a glass, her hands shaking. "Here, drink more water."

Jude drank and coughed some more. Then she slumped backward on the couch.

Tori brushed strands of hair from her forehead. "Do you feel strong enough for a bath?"

Jude gave her a wan smile. "Yes, I'll be fine. I just inhaled a lot of smoke despite using a respirator. I had to give all the good ones to the guys fighting the fire."

Tori filled the bath and helped her to undress and get in the tub. She perched on the edge as Jude sank to her chin in the warm, soapy water. She gently washed the grime from Jude's face.

"We'll wash your hair in the shower when you're done." She squeezed Jude's shoulder. "I can't begin to tell you how relieved I am you're relatively okay. We'll have to keep an eye on that cough, though, so it doesn't become chronic."

"Yes, ma'am," Jude said, smiling for the first time.

With clean hair and body, a chicken sandwich, and hot broth in her belly, Jude lay on her bed and instantly fell asleep.

Tori sat by the window in the hazy sunshine. A deep sense of concern weighed on her. Her feelings for Jude had grown stronger than she'd previously admitted to herself. She had drawn Jude into a perilous venture, and the thought of causing her harm was unbearable. She resolved to stop putting Jude in danger. The risks were too great—physical danger, legal trouble, and professional blackballing—if she were caught stealing data. Tori's ambivalence had vanished; she knew what she had to do.

"We need to stop," she murmured, the words slipping out before she realized she had spoken aloud.

Jude's small voice startled her. "Stop what?"

Tori rose and sat on Jude's bed, her eyes locking onto hers. "Stop the monitoring. Stop everything. Destroy the data. It's too risky. I couldn't bear it if anything happened to you." The anxiety that had gripped her when Jude didn't show the other night still roiled her stomach.

Jude sighed and rolled onto her side. "Look, Tori, I'm not a child. I understand what I'm doing is risky. When we make this data public, I'll lose my job. Do you think I want to work for these shitheads forever? They just killed three guys. Guys I saw almost every day and liked. I'm ready to move on."

"I know you're not a child. But I'm bad news. Trouble follows me, and I've dragged you into it." She bit her lip, fighting to keep her emotions in check. "I couldn't bear it if something happened to you."

"Let me make my own decisions," Jude said. "The stuff I was going to bring you is in the red bag over by the dresser."

Tori was torn. "No, I can't take it. Please get rid of it."

"I can't, Tori. But I'm too tired to argue," Jude said, turning over onto her back and changing the subject. "A lot of people need your help after the fire."

Tori's mind jumped to the tasks ahead. "I know. An allergy office offered me a clinical space three days a week, and I'll start seeing workers and residents starting Thursday. And I now have a colleague collaborating with me on my cancer study."

Jude's eyes lit up, a slight smile forming. "Are you always this driven?"

"Yes, this is me. How I've always been," Tori said.

"Give me the clinic info, and I'll refer people to you."

Tori jotted the clinic location and phone number on a nearby notepad. "I need to leave now. Think about what I said. And please take care of that cough. Drink lots of water. I'll stop by a pharmacy to pick up a nebulizer, a steroid inhaler, and an expectorant for you, then drop them off before I head home. If your cough doesn't improve within a week or so, please schedule an appointment with me in my new office."

"Yes, ma'am," Jude said with a playful grin. "I'll come to see you, regardless. So you can examine me. Thoroughly."

CHAPTER 37

JO SURVEYED THE lingering haze that shrouded Oilton, a ghostly reminder of the recent catastrophe. As she exited her rental car at the gas station, her nostrils flared at the acrid odor that hung in the air. Despite the town having officially emerged from shelter-in-place orders, it was unsettling how residents milled around in the streets, carrying on with their usual business as if a disaster hadn't just struck.

Mary's house came into view, and Jo was surprised to find both sides of the street lined with parked cars, forcing her to continue two blocks further before finding a space. Wheeling her file case along the fractured sidewalk, Jo spotted Mary emerging from her home. The woman's flower-print dress and flip-flops provided a splash of normalcy against the somber backdrop. Behind Mary trailed four unfamiliar faces, their expressions a mixture of concern and hope.

"You're here!" Mary's voice rang out with unexpected cheer. "I've got a crowd of people clamoring to talk to you, and I'm plum out of lemonade."

Jo's professional demeanor softened as she wrapped her arms around the woman. "It's good to see you, Mary," she said. The introductions followed: Nina Jerrard from the street behind, Neal Brown with his expertise as a retired refinery engineer, Laura Trombley, who lived in the shadow of the refinery, and Fred Burns, uncle of one of the workers killed, each represented different facets of the community's suffering.

Jo's voice lowered with sincerity when she shook Fred's hand, his bearded face shadowed beneath his Astros cap. "I'm so sorry for your loss."

His silent nod and downcast eyes spoke of grief too fresh for words.

The living room, which awaited Jo, resembled more a town hall than a home. Bodies occupied every available surface—the couch, the edges, the chairs—people gathered through Mary's remarkable community connections in under a day. The buzzing conversation died instantly as Jo entered, all eyes turning to her with an intensity that spoke of their collective concern.

"I see a few familiar faces here," Jo acknowledged, naming those she recognized, and the room's energy shifted. She could sense their desperation, their need for someone to champion their cause. "The recent explosion, fire, and tragic loss of life have clearly heightened your concerns, and ours too, about the dangers of working in and living near the oil refinery complex."

A murmur of affirmation rippled through the crowd.

Jo scanned the room deliberately, making eye contact with as many people as possible, silently promising each of them her attention. She explained her role as an environmental attorney with practiced precision, but beneath her professional exterior, the magnitude of their suffering wasn't lost on her. These weren't just potential plaintiffs; they were real people whose lives had been irreversibly altered.

"I realize money never brings back a loved one's loss of health or life. It only lessens the financial impact. However, we hope a substantial monetary award to our plaintiffs will motivate the corporations to modify their practices and prevent similar harm to others."

Fred Burns broke the momentary silence, his voice carrying the raw edge of grief. "Will you help my family sue World Petrol for the death of my nephew? His wife has three little kids under ten to care for alone."

"Yes, I will help your family. Let's speak afterwards."

Laura Trombley, a middle-aged woman crowned with big, teased hair, spoke. "I've always worried about the pollution from the plant overlooking my backyard wall. It often smells like rotten eggs, making my eyes and nose burn and run like crazy. But the fire worsened it. Even with the doors and windows closed, it seeped through the cracks, making me feel sick. I've lived here for twenty-two years. I'm glad my kids have grown and gone. With the price of real estate and rent these days, I can't afford to live anywhere else. And who would buy my house anyway with that stench from the refinery?"

"I understand. I've heard similar complaints from many of you. Our class action lawsuit will contend that World Petrol's emissions have caused cancer, upper and lower respiratory illness, heart disease, and other health problems in your community."

"That's for damn sure," a frail elder spoke up. "I worked in the crude oil distillation unit at that refinery. The gases coming offa that made me stupid and dizzy. They contain benzene, and I heard it causes leukemia. I ain't sick yet, but I know one guy I worked with for years got some kinda blood problem. I'm for damn sure that explosion and fire let loose a ton of benzene and other nasty stuff."

Neal Brown, the retired process engineer, said. "Of course it did. And the workers breathed the worst of it. But as I look around the room, I don't see anyone currently working in the refinery who is attending this meeting."

"No, they're all too scared World Petrol will fire them if they get involved with any lawyer out to sue the company that pays their wages," another man said. "I'm sure World Petrol's heard you've been nosing around here and are none too happy."

"Mary tells us that the lady doctor over in Houston is willing to see any of us who are sick from the smoke," said a woman in a raspy voice.

"Absolutely," Jo said. "I'll leave her details with Mary. And any workers from the refinery who have become ill or injured, although that's more in the domain of workers' compensation."

Jo's eyes scanned the room again, meeting the faces of those gathered. She'd developed a deep connection to their stories, each one unique and intricately linked to the refinery's impact on their health and lives.

"I want to speak to you individually, hear your stories, and we'll decide together if joining our lawsuit is right for you," she said.

"When do ya' wanna get started?" Mary asked.

"As soon as I've answered all your questions," she said. "Everyone needn't stick around. We'll schedule interviews at intervals, and I'll be here tomorrow and through the weekend if necessary."

"Y'all're welcome to use my dinin' table. I'll keep outta y'all's way, so your interviews will be private," Mary said.

"You're very generous, Mary," Jo said, flashing her a brief smile.

"It's the most hopeful thing that's happened 'round here in years," Mary said. "I'll set up a schedule."

Fred Burns leaned against the wall, his arms crossed, looking drawn and miserable.

Poor man. He's suffering. Jo walked over to him. "Mr. Burns," she said gently, meeting his sad eyes. "If you can stay, I'll start with you."

CHAPTER 38

FRED SETTLED BESIDE Jo at the pine dining table, his Astro cap resting on his lap. His fingers worked nervously, cracking his knuckles in the sudden quiet.

Jo studied the grieving uncle, noting the tension in his shoulders. Spotting an opportunity, Jo nodded toward the cap. "Was Mark an Astro fan too?"

Fred's expression softened. "Oh, yeah, big time. He rarely missed a game. We'd often go together, have a brewski or two, and let off steam at the players."

"It sounds like you were close," Jo observed.

"We were. I kinda stepped in when my sister's husband took off." Fred's voice grew heavier. "I asked her to come with me today, but she's a mess. Mark was her only son." He looked away, clearing his throat as emotion threatened to overwhelm him.

Jo's heart ached for his loss. "I'm so sorry," she said softly, giving him time to compose himself.

Fred continued after a moment. "I've never liked Mark working at the refinery. He was a smart boy. He could've gone to college. But he married young, and his wife kept popping out the kids." His hands tightened around the cap. "He needed the money for his growing family, and the pay was good." A heavy sigh escaped him. "Not that I begrudge the little ones. They're great kids, and he was a devoted father."

For the first time, a genuine smile crossed Fred's face. "I was there only last week when his three-year-old daughter burst into tears because her older brother had snatched her stuffed giraffe. Mark pretended to be a horse, hoisted his daughter onto his back, and galloped around the house after her brother until she stopped crying and giggled. Then he gently convinced the older brother to apologize and return the giraffe."

This family's loss hit Jo even more acutely. "He sounds like a wonderful guy," she said.

"He was. His family came first. That's why he stuck with that dangerous job in the catalytic cracking unit."

Jo steered the conversation toward the case. "What do you know about the explosion?"

Fred's expression darkened. "I only hear rumors. One former employee believes a faulty value allowed hydrocarbon gases to flow into the electrostatic precipitators, causing them to ignite."

"Are you familiar with the company's maintenance and safety practices in the catalytic cracking unit?" Jo pressed gently.

"No," Fred said, his voice hardening. "But they obviously weren't good." His lips compressed into a thin line as he cracked his knuckles again.

Jo explained the legal process with practiced calm. "To file a wrongful death suit, we need to get accident reports, eyewitness statements, maintenance records, and so on. It's best if Mark's wife files the suit. The sooner, the better, before the company covers its tracks."

Fred's eyes flashed with grim determination. "Then let's start. I'll talk to her tonight and get her here tomorrow. If she's willing."

"Do you know the other workers killed?" Jo asked.

"No, but I met the families. The company asked us all into the main office to tell us our loved ones had died in the explosion." Pain washed over his features as he looked away.

"Please let the others know I'm here for them if they also wish to file a wrongful death case."

"I'll talk with them. What else can I do?" Fred fingered his cap.

Jo considered their options. "Do you know anyone currently working in the catalytic cracking unit whom we can ask about the company's work practices and safety?"

"No, but the others might. One man they killed had a cousin working there." Fred frowned. "But the guys probably won't talk to an attorney suing their employer for fear of losing their jobs."

"They might talk to you. It's a start," Jo encouraged.

"Okay, I'll get on it." Fred's shoulders slumped as he stared down at his hands, twisting his ball cap. His voice broke as he said. "Nothing I do will bring that boy back to his wife, to those poor kids. I hear the little ones asking their mama why Daddy isn't coming home. They don't understand death." His voice dropped to a whisper. "I don't understand Mark's death. Why didn't the company protect him and the others?"

Jo searched for words of comfort but found none. She reached out and laid a hand on his forearm, bearing silent witness to his pain.

Mary arrived with burgers and fries. Fred thanked her but said he wasn't hungry.

When Fred left, Jo managed to eat three bites of her burger before Rhonda Mills, a middle-aged cashier at a local convenience store, arrived. She was thin and pale with short gray hair, looking older than her forty-seven years.

"Last year, I was so tired. I got bruises on my arms and legs and couldn't climb a flight of stairs without panting." She coughed into a handkerchief. "I got one cold after another and couldn't fight them off. Finally, my doctor did blood tests, and then another doctor stuck a needle in my bone marrow."

Jo winced. "Ouch."

"Oh, yeah. No fun," Rhonda said. "They diagnosed a blood pre-cancer, myelo something."

"Myelodysplastic syndrome?" Jo said.

"Yeah, that's it," Rhonda said.

"How long have you lived near the refinery?" Jo asked.

"Just about all my life. My family moved here when I was three. My daddy worked for the company that owned the oil refining facility before World Petrol bought and expanded it. He died of mesothelioma from asbestos exposure."

"I'm sorry. You probably know that's a well-known hazard of refinery work. Did you ever work there?" she asked.

"Yeah. I worked in the personnel office for about five years before having my kids. Doing clerical work. I never worked in any dangerous areas, but I've breathed plenty of bad shit going in and out of the refinery and living right next to it."

Jo continued the interviews into the early evening. She invited Mary out to dine at a local diner that Mary enjoyed. As they ate their BBQ beef, beans, and cornbread, they discussed the day's events and the interviews planned for the next day. Jo marveled at Mary's efficiency in contacting many people on short notice and arranging the interviews. On first impression, Mary could easily be underestimated. But she was invaluable to their lawsuit.

As they left the restaurant, Jo turned to her, "You know what?"

"What?" Mary said.

Jo smiled. "You would've made a fine business administrator."

Mary smiled back, her eyes sparkling with amusement. "Why, thank ya. I'll try to remember that for my next life."

CHAPTER 39

REFINERY WORKERS AND nearby residents with acute respiratory, skin, and eye symptoms caused by the refinery fire filled Tori's days in the allergy office. For many, cold symptoms and bronchitis followed their initial exposures. Some patients had underlying chronic illnesses unrelated to their exposures but worsened by the fire. And sometimes, she had to inform her patient that the fire was unlikely to have caused their symptoms.

Rick called twice to ask if he could collect some belongings, and she suggested he come by later. That evening, she found his car parked outside her house. The changed locks had been her small victory, but now she was forced to play gatekeeper whenever he wanted something.

"Hi, Tori," Rick chirped with unnerving cheerfulness as he bounded from his car. His voice carried the false brightness of someone with a hidden agenda. "I want to pick up more summer clothes and tell you my news."

She unlocked the door, looking in dismay as he barreled past her and dropped his duffel with the territorial confidence of someone who still believed he belonged there. He disappeared into the guest room closet, emerging moments later with an armful of shirts and pants that he stuffed unceremoniously into his bag.

He strode to the refrigerator with the entitlement of a co-owner, helping himself to her chardonnay.

"I wanted to share my news with you in person."

Orange Cat crouched nearby, his ruff bristling like a warning flag, his tail twitching.

"Okay," Tori said, eyeing Rick warily. "Shoot."

"Next week, I'll be moving out completely. I've bought a house."

Tori remained speechless as the announcement hung in the air. While Rick's permanent departure was welcome news, alarm bells rang in Tori's mind. *How can he possibly afford to buy property?* Their divorce proceedings remained in limbo, and financial entanglements continued to bind them. The prospect of being saddled with another mortgage if Rick defaulted made her wince.

She frowned. "Jesus, Rick, are you out of your mind? You've been complaining about the cost of my legal fees, and you almost went bankrupt. Buying a house now? It's crazy. You've barely been able to contribute to the mortgage we have."

Rick's face transformed into a smug expression, making Tori's skin crawl. "Ah, things are looking up for me. I had a temporary contract job but now, I have a permanent position. With a large, guaranteed salary. I can afford my own place."

Tori stared at him, processing this unexpected development. Rick with a stable, salaried job? This could work in her favor. A judge would be less likely to award him alimony if he were financially independent.

"What kind of job?" she probed, suspicion coloring her voice.

Rick lifted his chin with newfound confidence. "It's an IT position."

"With whom? You've never told me who you're working for," she pressed, sensing his evasiveness. "Why not?"

"All you need to know is that it's a large corporation that can afford to pay me very well. I'm setting up computer systems and networks to support their operations."

"In Houston?" The question carried her hope that he might be relocating far away.

"Yup," Rick confirmed, dashing that small hope.

"Tell me more," Tori urged, her instinct for diagnosis detecting something off in his story.

"I don't have time. I just needed to share my news, grab a few items, and let you know that the movers are coming on Wednesday morning to take care of the rest."

He drained his wine with a flourish of finality. "I made a list of the furniture I'll take. Please review it, and then we can discuss it over the phone." He thrust the list toward her.

From the corner of her eye, Tori noticed Orange Cat backing deliberately into Rick's duffel. Up went his tail and his back legs trod the ground like an athlete warming up.

Rick's secretiveness about his employer annoyed her. Scanning the furniture list, her irritation flared further. But she wasn't prepared for a property battle tonight. Instead, she shifted topics.

"Someone broke in a few weeks ago and stole my computer and cancer study files."

Rick's face remained neutral. "Oh, yeah?" he responded, his tone suspiciously indifferent.

Tori's body tensed. "Was it you?"

Rick offered a noncommittal shrug. "Why would I steal your study files?"

She fixed him with a penetrating stare. "To get back at me? You were never a fan."

"You're right, I wasn't." Rick's gaze slid away as he bent to retrieve his duffel. His expression suddenly contorted in disgust, and he dropped the bag as if it had transformed into something venomous. "Shit! Your fucking cat sprayed my stuff!"

Tori fought to suppress a smile. *Way to go, Orange Cat.*

"Now I'll have to wash everything," Rick complained, tearing off a paper towel to handle the contaminated bag.

As he turned to leave, Tori stepped deliberately into his path. "Did you let someone in to steal my study files and computer? The door was unlocked, and I locked it before I left."

Orange Cat arched his back.

"You're too much," Rick snapped, his facade cracking. "Things are starting to shape up for me. Believe it or not, I'm not as angry about our divorce and am trying to look at things differently. But you don't care how I'm doing. You and your damn study and your fucking cat. That's all you care about."

He pushed past her, his bag reeking of cat urine. "You don't need to be home on Wednesday. Leave a key."

"Oh, I think I do," Tori countered before the front door slammed behind him.

As Rick's car disappeared around the corner, Tori's mind churned with suspicions about his mysterious new employment. His refusal to deny stealing her study data also troubled her.

Jesus, do I have to suspect even my husband of foul play?

This unsettling thought led her to certainty. It was time to accelerate their divorce rather than wait until after the trial.

CHAPTER 40

ON TUESDAY, AUGUST 6th, Tori's morning was disrupted by an unexpected call from Brian's office requesting her presence at noon. Despite her patient appointments, she managed to carve out forty-five minutes from her busy schedule.

When she arrived, she was still simmering with anger from her confrontation with Rick. "I'd like to speed up my divorce."

Brian looked surprised.

"I'm not asking you to act for me, of course. I'm just letting you know."

"In the unlikely event that you're convicted, Rick will have the upper hand in any property dispute," Brian said. "However, if the divorce is finalized before your trial, Rick no longer has spousal immunity, and the prosecutor could call him as a witness."

Tori sighed. "Right. I'd still rather get it done."

Brian regarded her for a moment before he pulled his notepad from his briefcase. "First, I have some good news concerning our pre-trial discovery. The government has confirmed that the FBI investigation revealed no physical evidence to tie you to the robbery in your home, car, or clinic office. They'll not be bringing up any new evidence at trial."

"That's not surprising. I couldn't imagine that they would. Unless, of course, someone planted evidence."

Brian nodded and cleared his throat. He tapped his fingers on the table, a gesture that Tori recognized as his tell for bad news.

"What else?" she asked, bracing herself.

"When we met with your husband after your arrest, his attitude surprised me. He seemed angry, even hostile. I asked our private investigator to examine his background and recent activities."

He paused, clearing his throat again, and the tension in the room thickened.

"And?" Tori pressed.

"It may be relevant to your arrest or the break-in."

"It may also be relevant to my divorce," she urged, leaning forward.

Brian held her gaze with an intensity that made her stomach tighten.

"Your husband works in the IT Department of World Petrol."

The revelation hit Tori like a punch, knocking her off balance.

"Oh, fuck," she gasped, the pieces suddenly falling into place. No wonder Rick had been so secretive about his new employer and had discouraged her from pursuing her cancer study. He probably also knew it was central to Jo's lawsuit against World Petrol. Her hands trembled with anger as she reached for her water glass, taking a small sip to compose herself.

"I asked him yesterday," she said, "if he was involved in the break-in and theft of my study data since the front door had been unlocked. He wouldn't answer me directly."

Brian pursed his lips thoughtfully. "Hmm."

"What else did the PI find out?" Tori asked, still reeling.

"The man following you, and who likely broke into your house, works for a private security firm. His name is James Hogarth. We notified the police, who took fingerprints at your home, and suggested they follow up."

Tori sat up straight, her mind racing. "Who hired him?"

"That we don't know. The security firm rigidly guards the confidentiality of its clients."

Her shoulders slumped. "So, there's nothing concrete to link World Petrol or any other company to my arrest or the break-in."

Brian rubbed his chin, his expression thoughtful as he considered.

"No. From what we have now, it's implied and circumstantial. Until we determine who hired the security firm, I doubt this judge will even allow us to raise the issue."

"But we still have the mistaken-identity defense, don't we?" Tori asked, clinging to this thread of hope. "You told me last week that the FBI photo expert will testify that the woman in the videotape of the robbery has significant differences from me."

Brian nodded. "Right. And one more thing. The FBI and local law enforcement are definitely not tapping your phone."

"Well, somebody is," Tori stated with certainty.

"The PI suspects it's the security firm."

Tori considered trusting Brian with another piece of the puzzle as he had consistently proven himself to be her advocate.

"There's more you need to know."

One eyebrow edged up. "Okay."

Tori steeled herself. "Jude, the woman I was to meet for lunch on the day of the robbery. She works as an industrial hygienist for World Petrol."

Brian straightened. "Somehow, all roads lead back to World Petrol. Go on."

"She was collecting environmental monitoring data for me. World Petrol has been exceeding government-mandated air quality standards for years."

Brian's brow furrowed, and he scribbled on his notepad.

"After the break-in and her injury in the fire, I asked her to stop," Tori continued. "I didn't want her to get caught. World Petrol could blacklist her from the industry and ruin her career—or worse." She shuddered. "I don't want our association to become public knowledge. She's at risk for the surreptitious monitoring she's already done."

"Okay," Brian said, rubbing his chin thoughtfully. His gaze sharpened. "Why are you telling me this now?"

"If World Petrol suspects a mole is handing me damning environmental data, they have an even greater reason to want to put me out of commission. And her too."

"You don't want this to come out at trial?"

"Absolutely not," Tori insisted firmly. The words *because we're also lovers* caught in her throat. "However, I thought you should be aware so that you can object if the prosecution brings up my friendship with her."

"How would they know about it? And it might help your case if we're allowed to bring up the conspiracy theory," Brian said, holding her gaze.

"Believe me, it won't," Tori said with finality. "But I worry the guy who's following me might share whatever he knows with the prosecutor."

Brian's mouth opened, then shut. Finally, he said, "Gosh, you do have a complicated situation, Tori. We'll need to sort this all out before the trial."

CHAPTER 41

AS TORI SAT in her allergy office at day's end, her mind seethed with anger and a sense of betrayal. The revelation that Rick had taken a job with World Petrol was upsetting enough. But what really fueled her fury was the suspicion that he might have played a role in trying to sabotage her cancer study. Could he have been involved in stealing her data or even orchestrating her arrest? She shuddered. Rick's conservative and pro-business views had always been a source of tension, but she could hardly imagine him stooping that low.

When she called Jo from her office to share the news, her friend's reaction was explosive.

"Oh, my God. The bastard."

"He's coming tomorrow to move out. I have to cancel my patients to accommodate him, but he doesn't care. I'm not letting him take half the stuff he feels entitled to. I'll confront him about going to work for the dark side."

"It sounds risky. Do you want me to come back for the day? I can reschedule my interviews."

Yes, I would, but . . .

"I don't want you to feel you must drop everything and rescue me whenever I have a minor problem."

"None of your problems have been minor, Tori," Jo said. "You don't need to confront him alone. I'm coming."

Tori leaned back in her chair and let her eyelids close.

"Okay, thank you. See you tomorrow."

≫

Jo arrived early Wednesday morning. She strode through the door with purpose, slung her arm over Tori's shoulders, and hugged her.

"I want to see Rick's face when you confront him," she said with gleeful anticipation.

Tori smiled. "Rick has always been a bit afraid of you."

Jo tipped her head to the side, feigning innocence. "Whatever for?"

"Your warrior energy and your height. A woman looking him directly in the eye on the same level makes him twitchy."

They had just finished lunch when the moving van arrived. She secured Orange Cat in the TV room. A minute later, Rick drove up in a new Audi Coupe GT.

Tori huffed, *"He didn't waste any time spending his blood money."*

Rick jumped out and directed the van to back up the driveway with an air of self-importance. When Tori opened the door, Rick's eyes locked on Jo standing behind her. His face fell.

"What are you doing here?" he demanded, without any pretense of politeness.

"Hello, Rick. It's nice to see you, too," Jo replied coolly.

Tori suppressed a smile, savoring the discomfort that flashed across his face.

Avoiding Jo's gaze, Rick addressed Tori, "Did you review the list? Empty out the drawers of the oak desk and the bureau in the bedroom?"

"No, I *did not*," she said, handing him a revised list. "This morning, you may take only the items that I marked as yours."

Confusion clouded Rick's features as he scanned the paper.

"Also, we've passed the mandatory sixty-day cooling-off period," Tori continued. "I would like to finalize our divorce next week."

Rick frowned. "You said we'd wait until after your trial because you didn't want to deal with it."

"That was before I discovered what an untrustworthy sleaze you are," she said.

"What do you mean?" Rick asked, his eyes darting nervously from her to Jo.

Tori took a deliberate step toward him. "You didn't tell me you're working for World Petrol."

A flush spread over Rick's face as he blinked rapidly, caught like a deer in the headlights. He began to stammer. "It . . . it was none of your business. I knew you would disapprove."

"It's absolutely my business, which is why you didn't want me to know. Did your new job also require you to steal my study data and computer?"

Rick's eyelids continued to flutter. "I told you. I had nothing to do with that."

Tori exchanged a knowing glance with Jo.

"No, you *didn't* tell me," she said.

Rick shook his head and appeared to gather himself. "This is unbelievable. I'm taking my stuff and getting out of here." He brushed past her.

Jo stepped directly in front of him, blocking his path. They nearly collided.

"Were you involved in framing Tori for the bank robbery?" Jo demanded, standing firm.

He looked as if she'd struck him. "What? No! Why are you asking me that?"

Jo didn't blink. "Were you involved?"

"No. I wasn't. You must be crazy to think I . . . You can't be serious." He turned to Tori with a pleading look.

"I don't know what you're capable of these days," Tori muttered, studying his reaction.

"Not *that*. I'd never do *that*. How could I?" he said, spreading his arms.

"Did your employer frame her?" Jo asked, holding his gaze.

"No. I mean—how would *I* know?" He addressed Tori. "Can we speak privately, please?"

Tori regarded him carefully. His shock appeared genuine. Perhaps they were wrong about his involvement.

"Okay, come up to my office."

Once inside her office, Tori shut the door behind them. Rick held out his arms with palms up.

"Look, Tori, I know I've been a prick lately," he began. "I was hurting when my start-up failed, and you were unavailable, either working on your cancer study or out with your friends. Like you didn't care about me anymore. Then, when you asked for separation and divorce, my hurt turned to anger." He dropped his arms, and his voice softened. "But I'm getting back on my feet now. And I'm dating again. I'm not as angry anymore, and in retrospect, I could see how we'd grown apart."

Wow. He has revealed more of himself than he did in eight weeks of couples therapy.

"I'm happy that you're recovering," she said sincerely.

He smiled. "Thanks."

"Why didn't you want me to know who you work for?" she asked, returning to the core issue.

"Because I know how you feel about multinational oil companies."

"We think World Petrol, perhaps in cahoots with other petrochemical companies, hired someone to break into the house and steal my cancer study data to keep me from publishing. Then, I find out you're working for them."

"Yeah, I know. I should have been upfront about that," Rick said, appearing genuinely contrite. "I understand how important it is for you to publish that study. But I'm disappointed you think I'd help them break in . . . *if* World Petrol is involved."

"You never showed any support for my research."

"It wasn't your research so much, although I thought you were asking for trouble. But I resented your intense focus on it. You shut me out completely."

Tori studied him with curiosity. *He's never shown so much insight before. Is he doing individual therapy?*

"But hey, you know I work in IT," Rick continued. "I'm in and out of offices all over the company, working on computers. I can keep my eyes and ears open. Maybe find something out for you."

His offer caught her off guard, dissolving her remaining skepticism. Her tone softened. "Thanks, Rick," she said. "I'm being followed, my phone is tapped, and someone broke into my home to steal my study data. You can see how I might be a little paranoid."

CHAPTER 42

WEDNESDAY EVENING, THEY had dinner at Jo's favorite Mexican restaurant and discussed Rick's apparent turnaround. Afterwards, they lounged on Tori's couch, sipping Tia Maria from crystal cordial glasses.

"What an intense few days," Jo said. "I needed a day off from hearing so many heartbreaking stories."

She kicked off her heels and put her stockinged feet up on the coffee table, the couch cushions folded around her, welcoming and soft.

"I know how you feel."

Jo said, "You mentioned you had news from Brian."

"Yes, the private investigator discovered Van Guy works for a private security firm, and his name is James Hogarth. They are very cagey about who hired the firm—they insist on client confidentiality—so he doesn't know yet. And the FBI is not tapping my phone, so maybe it's the security company or whoever they hired."

"There must be a way to determine who hired them. Maybe Brian can subpoena their records." Jo said. She took a sip of her drink. "Has he heard anything from the FBI photo expert?"

"That's the good news. The expert said the video and photos of the bank robber differ in subtle but significant ways from the photo of me."

Jo sat up and hugged Tori. "Wow, that's *excellent* news!"

Tori held on longer than she should have. When she pulled away, tears pricked her eyes. Since her arrest, Jo's physical presence in her home had triggered feelings she'd long tried to suppress. Despite her genuine feelings for Jude, she still fantasized about what might have been with Jo. It was time to tell her what she couldn't tell her years ago.

"What's wrong?" Jo said, "That's good news, isn't it?"

Tori's heart pounded in her throat. She took some deep breaths. *Should I tell her?* She needed relief from the weight of her feelings. To take the power from them by laying them on the table.

Am I really going to do this?

"What is it?" Jo's brow furrowed.

She's taken. I lost my chance years ago. I'm with Jude now. Stop.

Jo took her hand in both of hers. "Tell me. You said before that you trusted me."

The tears spilled over. "I want to." Her voice shook. "It's too late. I shouldn't. I'm not sure. . . "

"Whatever it is, Tori, I won't judge you. You can tell me anything." Jo let go of her hand and reached for the napkin under her cordial glass. She dabbed at Tori's tears, then took her hand again.

The dam broke, and Tori couldn't stop herself, though her voice choked.

"I love you."

Jo's face softened. "I love you, too, Tori. You know that."

"No . . . I mean . . . I know you do. It's just that . . . It's different. I've always loved you. Since college. The same way you loved me."

Jo's eyes widened. "Oh . . . I see."

A jolt of fear shot through Tori. *I shouldn't have told her. What did I expect?*

"I've upset you," she said, pulling her hand away. "I'm sorry. You're with Kate now. It's my fault that I didn't tell you in college. I was a coward."

"No, no, I'm not upset," Jo said, shaking her head. "Just surprised. I didn't see this coming."

"It's just that you're here now. I can't stop thinking about it. Things have become clear to me in the past year." She took out a handkerchief and blew her nose. "I'd always thought my wanting you was unique because of how close we were—and still are."

She searched Jo's eyes for understanding.

"And it's not?" Jo's voice was gentle.

"No. It's who I am. It was at the root of my marital problems."

"You're sure? Women often form close emotional bonds with one another. Sexuality exists on a spectrum and . . ."

"Yes, I'm sure. I've had sex with a woman—well, not just sex. Jude, the industrial hygienist. And I love her, too. In the same way." Tori took a deep breath.

Jo's shoulders relaxed. "Oh, dear. Why did you wait so long?"

"I know. We could have been together," she said, unable to suppress the longing in her voice.

Jo gave her a warm smile. "Yes, we could have. And it would've been wildly exciting at the time. You were my first love. It was the reason I came out to myself as a lesbian." She reached for her cordial glass and swallowed the rest of her Tia Maria in one gulp.

She regarded Tori thoughtfully, "But do you think two

ambitious, driven, workaholic women would make compatible partners in the long run?"

Tori sighed. "I don't know." *But I'd have loved to have tried.*

"However, we do make wonderful friends. We're a fantastic team." Jo said.

"We are," she agreed. *But I always wanted . . . more.*

"So, Jude—the one you were to have lunch with and whose giving you environmental data—you wanted to keep her identity a secret, not only because of what she was doing at World Petrol but also because you're romantically involved with her?"

"Well, yeah. Wouldn't it tarnish my image for a Texas jury if they knew I was a lesbian, hanging out in bars, and hooking up with women for sex?"

Jo's eyes widened again. "Women?"

Tori smiled. "Just one woman."

Jo blew out her breath. "Phew. I'm not sure how I'd handle the news that you're sleeping around."

"I have my standards," she said, managing to smile.

But do I really? Declaring my love for a woman who's taken? And when I'm also in love with Jude?

"Once we started talking about my work, she began gathering environmental monitoring data, some of which is alarming. I've asked her to stop, though. My arrest, the guy following me, the break-in—the stakes are too high. If the company finds out, I don't want her personally or professionally harmed."

Jo was studying her with a curious expression.

"It's not like I was trading sexual favors for information," Tori said, suddenly defensive.

"No, I can't imagine you would," Jo said, smiling.

"I've done some checking since you first mentioned the possibility of getting this data. You can have her report World Petrol's excessive toxic emissions to the Hotline at the

Environmental Protection Agency, Office of Inspector General, or the EPA's Office of Enforcement and Compliance Assurance. Then, we can request that information through the Freedom of Information Act. That way, neither of us will have acquired it illegally. You can use it in your study, and I can use it to bolster our lawsuit. It remains unclear whether she will have whistle-blower protection, though. We should assume she won't."

"I thought so. World Petrol could very well make her life miserable."

"Right. They could," Jo conceded. She was quiet, apparently thinking. "You say you've asked her to stop, but what does she say?"

"That's the problem. She's stubborn," Tori said, tipping up her glass to swallow the rest of her drink.

Jo smiled. "Not unlike someone else I know."

CHAPTER 43

JO'S CALM RESPONSE to Tori's confession reduced the power of her long-held fantasies. It was time to let go. Retreating to her bed, Tori allowed herself the cathartic release of tears, clutching her pillow tightly as she buried her face to stifle the sound. When her sobs finally subsided, she lay on her back, her gaze drifting upward to the ceiling. Something had shifted. Her grief over lost opportunities and years of suppressed emotions began to lift, clearing her mind and heart. She fell asleep, longing to see Jude.

In the guest room, Jo lay awake, her mind replaying Tori's revelation like a persistent melody. She admired Tori's courage in overcoming societal norms and embracing her true self. On her recent visit to Houston, Jo had caught glimpses of this new side of Tori, but she had dismissed them, remembering Tori's past declarations of being straight and her marriage to Rick. Now, she reevaluated those subtle touches and glances—especially the kiss—realizing they'd meant more than she'd realized.

But Jo was no longer a besotted young adult. As she'd told

Kate, much more experience with women had given her a better idea of what worked for her. Not intensity and drama but comfort and ease. That's what Kate offered, and Jo, in turn, tried to give Kate the love and stability she needed.

She sighed and rolled over, her thoughts turning to her eventual reunion with Kate: the simple joys of grocery shopping, cooking, and strolling through Rock Creek Park together. They would savor intimate moments, relish excellent coffee, and read *The New York Times* in bed on Sunday mornings. Just what she needed to ground herself and take her mind off the suffering of others and the environmental crimes of profit-hungry petrochemical companies.

The sound of Jo stirring downstairs instantly put Tori on alert, despite the early hour. A wave of anxiety flooded over her as she remembered the previous evening. *Will it be awkward between us now?* The question echoed in her mind, bringing the anguish of uncertainty. Without giving herself time to overthink, she pulled on a pair of jeans and a T-shirt, then hurried downstairs barefoot.

The aroma of fresh coffee greeted her before she even reached the kitchen. Jo stood there, looking completely at ease as she poured a cup and extended it toward Tori.

"Good morning," Jo said with her usual warmth. "I was going to slip out without waking you since we had a late night."

Tori studied Jo's face, searching for any sign of discomfort or regret, but found none. Jo's manner and attitude remained unchanged as if their late-night conversation had only strengthened rather than complicated their friendship. The tight knot of worry in Tori's chest began to loosen.

"No chance I'd let you do that," Tori replied, accepting the coffee with relief and gratitude. "I want to see you off."

Jo leaned against the counter, her eyes reflecting concern. "You'll have your hands full now with clinical work, writing up your study, and preparing for trial. It's coming up so fast. Just weeks away."

With the reminder, Tori's shoulders sagged. "I know." She sighed, the weight of her responsibilities suddenly pressing. "It's overwhelming."

Jo tilted her head. "What about your lab? Are you keeping the space?"

The question touched a raw nerve. "I don't know. I can't fund it on my own. Especially now." Her voice lowered, the admission painful. "I'll have to sell the equipment to cover my defense costs."

Jo clicked her tongue, her expression softening. "That's a shame."

Not wanting to dwell on things she couldn't change, Tori took a quick gulp of her coffee, the hot liquid burning a path down her throat. "Do you want me to fix you some eggs and toast? Oatmeal?" she offered, shifting to something practical, something she could control.

"No. Must dash. I'll pick something up on the way to Oilton. But thank you."

Jo paused. In the silence, her eyes sought Tori's and held her gaze. Tori was unable to look away, even as her heart pounded against her ribs like a trapped bird.

At last, Jo said, "I'm pleased you shared what you did last night." Her voice was gentle but firm. "I know you've got things to sort out within yourself and with the woman you've been dating. Our friendship won't change. It's as strong as ever."

The simple reassurance broke something open inside Tori.

Tears welled up in her eyes, blurring Jo's face. Her legs suddenly felt too weak to support her as she stepped into Jo's open arms. Jo held her close, stroking her hair with a tenderness that made Tori wish she wouldn't stop. Then, she let go.

"Okay, get to work. I'm off," Jo said, her tone brisk but kind.

Tori pulled herself together, wiping her eyes and straightening her shoulders.

"When will you return?" The question came out with more vulnerability than she'd intended.

"When I finish in Oilton, I'll fly home. I've tentatively booked an evening flight on Sunday." Jo's eyes softened again. "Depending on how things develop, I'll return for your trial, if not before. I'm not keeping my distance—Colin be damned."

She drained the last of her coffee, bent to give Orange Cat an affectionate pat, and headed for the door where her bag awaited.

Tori followed her, a hollowness spreading in her chest.

"Thank you, Jo. For everything." Inadequate words to express all she wanted to say.

Jo turned, her face illuminated by a warm smile that could have melted butter.

"Of course," she said.

And then she was gone, leaving Tori standing in the doorway. The morning suddenly seemed quieter and emptier than it had just moments before.

CHAPTER 44

WHEN JO'S FLIGHT arrived at Washington National Airport Sunday evening, Kate and Sam were waiting in the baggage claim area. Sam saw her first and nearly yanked Kate off her feet as he strained his leash to get to her. He leaped up, paws on her shoulders, to plant wet dog kisses on Jo's upturned chin. She laughed, pushed his shoulders down, kneeled, and allowed him to snuffle her ear.

"Did you miss your human? Was that other lady not good to you?"

Kate laughed. "That other lady fed him his favorite this morning. Eggs and sausage."

"Oooh, not bad," Jo cooed. "Bet you wish I'd go away more often."

She stood up and took Kate in her arms. "Hello, sweetheart. It's good to be back."

"I missed you," Kate said, nestling her face into Jo's shoulder and hugging her tight.

↭

Later that night, as they lay in bed, Jo continued to fill Kate in on the details of her trip, leaving out one crucial interaction. But when the discussion petered out, she decided on full disclosure.

"Tori told me she was in love with me in college and still has feelings for me."

Kate rose on one elbow and stared at her. "What does that mean to you?"

Jo considered her answer carefully. "I love her. Always have," she acknowledged, sensing Kate tense beside her. "But I don't lust after her like I used to, nor do I fantasize about being with her romantically."

The memory of those few seconds last night, when she had done exactly that, flashed through her mind, but she pushed it away.

"Why not?" Kate challenged, her gaze unflinching.

Jo turned fully toward Kate, meeting her intensity with certainty. "Because I'm in love with you," she said, the words tumbling out for the first time. Jo realized how profoundly true they were.

A smile spread across Kate's face.

"Good answer," she murmured, snuggling back into Jo's shoulder, relaxing against her.

"She's dating a woman."

Kate's head popped up again. "And she's declaring her love for you?" she asked as her hand began a deliberate journey up Jo's inner thigh.

"I think she needed to get it off her chest and move on," Jo said. "As I have."

As Kate's hand continued its teasing exploration, Jo's thoughts drifted far from Tori to current pleasures.

❦

On Monday, David and Colin were pleased to hear that Jo had signed up 45 plaintiffs, including all three wrongful death cases. The explosion and fire had added fuel to their lawsuit, but they still lacked objective evidence that World Petrol had violated national and regional air quality standards.

"We can demand they turn over any environmental monitoring data during pre-trial discovery, but we'll never know if they're giving us all they have," David said.

Jo bit her lip and fidgeted, holding back details of the data Tori said Jude could provide. Until it arrived in the hands of the government regulators, it held little value for their lawsuit. The information burned inside her, making her fingers tap nervously against her thigh.

"Tori gave her talk at MD Anderson's Grand Rounds. There may have been a petrochemical industry plant in the audience, playing down her findings. As they often do with all studies that threaten their way of doing business," she said.

She wished Colin would leave so she could talk with David in private.

"Did you discover anything to substantiate your theory that World Petrol played a role in Dr. Nelson's arrest and the theft of her data?" David asked.

Colin rolled his eyes.

Irritated, she turned to David, shutting Colin out of her field of vision. "Brian Kirkland, her defense attorney, hired a private investigator to try to identify the anonymous tipster and determine who was behind the theft. The probable thief works for a private security firm and is likely also tapping her phone. Brian notified the police. However, we don't yet know who hired the security firm or the identity of who tipped off the FBI that Tori resembled the bank robber."

David shook his head, his expression thoughtful. "Who else would be interested in spying on her and stealing Dr. Nelson's cancer study data except those it threatened?"

"Exactly," Jo said.

"What do the police say? Have they arrested the thief?" David asked.

"Not that they've said."

"Well, I hope this private investigator uncovers tangible, hard evidence of World Petrol's involvement. Dr. Nelson sure needs it, and so do we," David said.

Colin snorted. "So, you've got nothing."

A flush traveled from her chest to her face. *Whose side are you on?*

David ignored him, opened his notebook, and picked up his pen. "Let's review your list of plaintiffs and their medical issues. We'll have to decide whether to file a mass toxic tort or a class action. As you know, not all of them will have legal standing or have health problems we can prove are related to living near the refinery. I prefer the former. We'll try the wrongful death cases separately."

Noting Jo's expression, he said. "I know. Some of them might be very disappointed."

"I'll leave you to it," Colin said, snapping his notebook shut and rising from his chair.

After he had closed the door, Jo asked, "Whose side is he on, really?"

"Ours," David assured her with quiet confidence. "He acts as our resident prosecutor, helping us build strong cases."

A smile softened his features as he added, "His bedside manner sucks, I know. You've done great work here, Jo."

CHAPTER 45

AFTER JO LEFT, Tori spent the day at the allergy clinic, treating patients affected by the refinery fire. She rang Dr. Ellen Grenoble from the office, which was much more convenient than driving to a pay phone.

Ellen picked up right away. After preliminaries, she said, "I've carefully reviewed everything. You've done an excellent job with your data analysis, and the draft of your paper requires very few modifications. You really didn't need my input."

"Thank you, Ellen. You're my insurance that it will be published and taken seriously."

"You mean in case you're convicted? I can't believe that will happen. I'd hate to take the credit for all your hard work."

"I told you someone broke into my house and stole my computer and study data. It's likely the guy who's been following me, who we know works for a private security firm. The police have not made the connection yet, though. I'm under siege here, Ellen. The study data is much safer with you in Boston."

A heavy silence followed before Ellen responded, her voice softened with empathy.

"It's all so weird, Tori. I'm so sorry you're going through this. Of course, I'll publish your research independently if necessary."

"You're a good friend, Ellen."

Each word expressed her gratitude, fear, and the desperate hope that her work would survive—even if her reputation didn't.

✍

The following Monday, August 12th, Tori continued treating World Petrol workers, Oilton residents, and other patients who had discovered her new location. Despite her former clinic's refusal to refer callers to her new office and slowing the release of her patients' medical records, she was rapidly rebuilding her practice.

Early that afternoon, Jude showed up for an appointment. She reported that although the wheezing had resolved, a dry cough persisted.

When Tori pulled the stethoscope from around her neck and listened to her chest, Jude turned and caught Tori off guard, putting her hand behind Tori's head and pulling her in.

Tori's breath hitched, and she let the stethoscope drop as their lips met for a lingering kiss that made her knees weak.

Coming to her senses, Tori pulled away and straightened, her voice barely above a whisper.

"Really, Jude, not here. It's—unprofessional."

Jude looked pleased with herself.

Tori's pulse still raced, and she marveled at Jude's effect on her. "But I do wonder why I deprived myself of this for so long."

Jude's rakish smile reached her eyes. "Because this properly indoctrinated Catholic girl needed the right butch to come along and open Pandora's box," she teased.

"That you've done, all right." Tori composed herself and

finished Jude's medical exam. "Two more weeks of the steroid inhaler should do the trick. You sound much better," she said, keeping a professional tone.

"Thanks, Doc." Jude hopped off the exam table, grabbed her shirt off the hook, and pulled it over her head. "By the way, I have something for you."

Her eyes narrowed. "No, Jude. Too dangerous."

"Wait, let me tell you. I never removed my external VOC monitors. I have tons more monitoring data. I also discovered records of PAHs, VOCs, and other toxins measured several years before my hiring. I downloaded copies."

Tori's heart sank, and she shook her head. "No, no. I told you to quit. You'll ruin your career."

"I *am* quitting. World Petrol, that is. I gave my notice when I returned to work after the fire," Jude said.

Tori's stomach tightened. "You're leaving?"

"I applied to graduate school. To study cell biology. And Tufts University accepted me. Someone dropped out after being accepted, and I got their spot."

Tori stared at her, open-mouthed.

"I didn't even know you'd applied."

"Yeah," Jude said, giving her a sheepish look. "I didn't want to tell you in case I received only rejection letters."

Tori rubbed her forehead, still reeling from the shock. "You're moving to Boston?" With difficulty, she let it sink in.

"I am," Jude said. "In five days."

The news rocked Tori's world. *Jude is leaving.* She slumped into a chair and brought her hands to her face.

Jude sat in the chair beside her, gently took Tori's hands away from her face, and lifted her chin.

"Come with me to Boston."

Tori's eyes widened. "What? My trial, remember?"

Someone knocked on the door. They pulled apart and shot up straight.

"Yes?" Tori said.

"Your next patient is here and is in exam room three," a female voice called through the door.

"Thank you," Tori called back. She rose. "I have to go."

Jude stood and clutched Tori's arms. "Ask the court for permission. Say you need to collaborate in person with that doctor at the Harvard School of Public Health. We can hand-deliver my environmental monitoring data to the EPA in Washington, DC—do it together."

"I don't know . . ." She was at a loss for words, the shock still reverberating through her. *Jude is leaving.*

Voices rose outside the door, brisk, efficient, professional.

All Tori wanted right now was to spend as much time as possible in Jude's arms, regardless of the risk of discovery.

"Can I see you tonight? I'll come to your place after work," Tori said.

Jude smiled and brushed her lips against Tori's.

"I'll be waiting."

CHAPTER 46

IN THE FOLLOWING days, Tori moved among her patients with practiced efficiency. Her hands were steady even as she continued to dismantle her lab piece by piece, watching her equipment disappear into strangers' vans.

BY NIGHT, SHE found solace in Jude's arms, memorizing the contours of her face in the soft light, storing away sensations like treasures.

By arrangement, Ellen FedExed a letter explaining why Tori needed to come to Boston to collaborate in person. Tori called Brian, and after some back-and-forth, the court required Tori to produce her return airline ticket and offer additional sureties, but ultimately granted her four days of travel.

Unspoken fears marred the days leading up to their trip. *These might be our last.* Tori couldn't bring herself to say it aloud, but the thought haunted her waking moments. Instead, they spoke hypothetically, their conversations circling the possibility of her conviction without quite touching its sharp edges.

She smiled at Jude's reassurances while mentally cataloging the exact green of her eyes and the specific timbre of her laugh—details to sustain her through the separation she increasingly feared.

✍

Saturday, August 17th, the day of their departure, dawned sunny and humid. Jude had sold her camper van and purchased a 1968 Ford Mustang. The body had some rust, but the engine had been rebuilt. Green with a gold racing stripe, Jude loved it. She'd also sold or given away many of her possessions, but what remained took up most of the back seat. The red duffle, containing years of damning environmental monitoring, lay on the floor behind the passenger seat, covered with her soccer gear.

Lingering in each other's arms too long had caused a late start.

"Let's hit it," Jude said. "Get as far as we can before midnight."

"Pedal to the metal," Tori urged.

"Yes, ma'am!" Jude slipped into the driver's seat and grinned at Tori as the V8 engine roared to life.

"Goodbye, fuckers!" Jude yelled out the open window as they sped along the freeway past the World Petrol refinery.

A burst of wild excitement exploded in Tori's chest, laughter erupting as she imagined escaping with Jude by her side, this woman who had changed everything. The radio blasted "We Are the World" and "Born in the USA," and Tori sang along at the top of her lungs, not caring how she sounded, feeling more alive than she had in years.

Darkness overtook them when they left I-20 to head north onto I-59 near Slidell, Louisiana. They pulled off the freeway at a deserted rest stop for a quick pee and to change drivers.

Jude handed over the car keys, and Tori got out. She had walked only a few feet from the car when a white van pulled into the rest stop and backed into a spot across from them. Tori's chest constricted, her breath catching in her throat as it often did lately when she spied a white van.

Then the beefy bald guy jumped out of the van and came striding toward them—brandishing a revolver.

World Petrol's goon. They know.

Tori's heart hammered against her ribs, and her breath came fast as she lunged for the safety of the Mustang.

Strong fingers clamped around her arm, yanking her backward. She struggled against his ironclad grip, feeling naked panic. His muscular arm throttled her neck while the cold metal of the gun barrel pressed against her temple.

"Let me go, you bastard!" she yelled, driving her elbow into his stomach with all her strength.

He grunted and wrenched her neck tighter.

Jude leaped out of the car and ran toward them, her face contorted with fury.

"Stop!" he yelled. "Or you both get hurt. Her first."

He shoved the gun harder against Tori's head.

Only two feet away, Jude froze, her fists clenched.

"Give me the monitoring data you stole from World Petrol," he growled at Jude, further tightening his arm around Tori's neck so that she had to fight for every shallow breath. His voice was like gravel against her ear, and she caught the stench of cigarette breath.

"Okay, okay," Jude said, her voice calm. "The bag is on the floor, in the back."

Jude bent to push aside the soccer gear and retrieve the duffel, her movements slow and deliberate.

Tori struggled against him, but he only tightened his grip around her neck so that she thought she might lose consciousness.

"Hurry up. Toss it over to me."

But instead of doing as he asked, Jude transformed into a

blur of motion, swinging the bag with unexpected force against his elbow and head. The gun clattered across the pavement.

Tori wrenched herself free, turned, and thrust the car key into the front of his throat. He gagged and stepped back but grabbed her arm. She brought her knee up into his balls with all her might.

He let go and doubled over, bellowing in pain.

"Fucking bitch!"

Adrenaline propelled Tori into the car. Jude seized the car key from her shaking hand, and the engine roared to life. They backed out, nearly clipping the man as he staggered toward his weapon. The tires screamed against the pavement as they accelerated toward the on-ramp and the freeway.

Tori glanced into the side mirror. The white van was turning onto the ramp.

"He's chasing us."

Jude smiled grimly, rolled down the window, and gave Van Guy a one-finger salute. Tori couldn't help but laugh—a release of tension, fear, and exhilaration. Despite the danger behind them, she felt invincible with Jude at her side.

Jude floored the Mustang, weaving, dodging, and changing lanes. An 18-wheeler looming on their right forced her to ease off the gas.

Tori watched as the white van grew larger in her side mirror. "He's two cars behind us," she said. "I can't believe it. Does he intend to chase us all the way to Washington, DC?"

"I hope not," Jude said, "because we're low on gas."

"We need a town with a well-lit, busy gas station." Tori checked the mirror. "He's right behind us."

"Fuck!" Jude smacked the steering wheel. "No Karen Silkwood for us!"

Tori studied Jude's profile—jaw clenched, muscles working

beneath tanned skin—as she executed a daring maneuver around the truck, threading the Mustang between two cars in the right lane. The van followed doggedly, though now separated by three vehicles.

"Let's give this bastard a run for his money," Jude declared, stomping the accelerator and sending them darting between lanes until the van disappeared from their mirrors. Despite its age and rust, the Mustang responded to Jude's touch with surprising power.

Tori scanned the highway anxiously. Where were the police when you needed them? Their speed had to be attracting attention. For once, getting pulled over might be their salvation rather than an inconvenience.

Leaning across the console, Tori checked the gas gauge. Her stomach dropped. The needle hovered ominously in the red zone. They were running out of options as quickly as they were running out of fuel.

Her pulse quickened when the white van reappeared, high beams flashing aggressively in her mirror like the eyes of a predator.

Five miles and countless lane changes later, they'd crossed into Mississippi with their pursuer still doggedly on their tail. The Mustang would soon sputter to a halt, and he'd be on them like a spider.

As they approached a small town, Jude's voice cut through Tori's spiraling thoughts. "Hang on, Tori, I'm going to take this exit at speed."

The world tilted as Jude hurled the Mustang onto the exit ramp at twice the speed she should have. The front bumper struck a guardrail, emitting a shower of sparks, and partially tore away. Tori's stomach lurched as the car wobbled precariously before Jude wrestled it back under control.

The explosion came first—a concussive boom that reverberated in Tori's chest.

She turned to see that the white van had crashed through the damaged guardrail and tumbled down the steep embankment, flames leaping upward.

Jude pulled over, white-knuckled and panting. Tori collapsed against her seat, eyes closed, and her body still flooded with adrenaline. When her limbs finally responded to commands, she got out of the car on shaky legs and began walking toward the black smoke.

Jude's tone was incredulous. "What are you doing?"

"I have to help."

"No, Tori, you don't. Police and fire are on their way. I hear the sirens."

CHAPTER 47

BY THE TIME Jude had filled the gas tank and duct-taped the bumper, the fire had been extinguished. An ambulance arrived, but they could not see what was happening in the ravine. Despite their excessive speed, no one arrived to question them. Jude convinced Tori they should move on lest they become part of a lengthy accident investigation.

They pressed on to Jackson, Mississippi, and fell into bed at a motel at midnight, exhausted. Before they left the following morning, Tori called Brian and told him about Van Guy—his threats and the fiery crash.

After expressing concern about their safety, Brian said, "James Hogarth no longer works for the security firm. He was fired for violating company policy and using illegal tactics. He's gone rogue and is working independently for someone."

"I don't think he'll bother us anymore," Tori said.

"No, it doesn't sound like it. I'll try to find out how he fared and let you know."

≪

They arrived at Logan Circle in Washington, DC, at nearly midnight. Jo listened wide-eyed as they told her about Van Guy's threats and the car chase.

"You're very lucky. I'm so glad you're safe," Jo said, guiding them to the guest room, where they both fell into a deep sleep as soon as their heads hit the pillows.

The next morning, a hearty breakfast of eggs, bagels, fresh berries, and yogurt awaited them. Jo greeted them warmly. "You look much more rested than you did last night."

Tori smiled. "Yes, I was dead to the world." Her longing for Jo was a distant memory. This morning, she felt comfortable in their friendship.

They gathered their things to leave for the long drive ahead. As they stood at the door, Jo said, "Jude, I'm delighted to have finally met you. You are one courageous woman."

Jude looked embarrassed. "So is Tori."

"That she is. Good luck today," Jo said, hugging them both.

≪

Driving from Logan Circle to downtown DC, Tori and Jude headed for Pennsylvania Avenue and the Federal Triangle, which housed the EPA headquarters, and parked three blocks away. As they approached the monumental architecture of the EPA's entrance, Tori marveled at the ornate facade featuring columns, porticos, and arched windows. It was imposing and grand. *I hope they fulfill their duty to the people of Oilton.*

Jude casually carried the red duffel, its contents representing the culmination of months of dangerous work. They stopped twenty feet from the entrance, and Tori threw her arms around

Jude, hugging her tight. "I'll wait at those benches over there," she whispered, her voice catching slightly. "I love you."

She sat on the bench, her face upturned and warmed by the sun, infused with a sense of satisfaction. Not only could she eventually use this data in her study, but it could also lead to the EPA suing World Petrol for Clean Air Act violations, with civil and criminal penalties. It would also provide ammunition for Jo's lawsuit and potentially secure justice for her patients.

Forty-five minutes crawled by like molasses before Jude emerged from the building, her face bright and smiling. Tori leaped to her feet, rushing toward her with eager steps.

"How did it go?"

"Piece of cake." Jude's voice rang with confidence. "Onward to Boston. I'll tell you about it in the car. But before that, just for good measure, I'll tip off *The Washington Post* and *The New York Times*."

On Tuesday in Boston, Tori's meeting with Dr. Ellen Grenoble was brief but fruitful. Ellen was delighted to learn that they could request environmental monitoring from the EPA for a follow-up study to correlate World Petrol's emissions with local cancer rates. Even Dr. Jeff Townsend expressed interest in participating, although he had not yet heard from Harvard's Institutional Review Board.

That night, Jude said, "Do you want me to return for your trial? I don't start classes until late September."

She pictured Jude and Jo in the courtroom, the two women who meant the world to her. Did it matter anymore if people knew she and Jude were connected? Clearly, the hired goon had known. But as much as she'd love to have Jude there, she didn't want to put her in further danger.

"Thanks, Jude, but I think you should stay the hell out of Texas."

Their goodbye at Logan Airport tore at Tori's heart, though she maintained a brave facade. They had discussed the possibility of her returning to Boston after the trial, a future that seemed both tantalizingly close and impossibly distant.

As she boarded the plane for Houston, the question haunted her: *Will Jude wait for me if I'm convicted?* Jude hadn't addressed this directly, maintaining an unwavering belief that the jury would acquit Tori at trial.

CHAPTER 48

TORI ENTERED BRIAN'S office on Tuesday, August 27th, her body buzzing with anticipation and dread. As she settled into the chair across from him, accepting his offer of coffee with a grateful nod, she felt like a character in a suspense thriller.

"That guy, Hogarth, who shadowed and threatened you, didn't make it. He died in the hospital three days ago."

"Oh." Regret for the man's suffering tinged her relief that the threat had passed. "Is there any news on who hired the security firm?"

Brian shook his head. "That's the problem. I subpoenaed the records from the security firm, which they ignored, but when I asked the judge for a writ to force compliance, he denied it as irrelevant to your case."

She huffed. "Really? Did you explain that someone has been desperate to put me out of commission?"

Brian drummed his fingers on the table, looking uncomfortable. "Yes, of course. The judge just rolled his eyes. He said our theory is circumstantial, based on inference, and is not directly related to whether you are guilty of the charges for which you were indicted."

"Were the police able to tie this Hogarth guy to the break-in and theft of my study data?"

"The PI said the police were trying to find him to bring him in for fingerprinting and questioning when he left town."

She blew out a quick breath. "Why were they so slow? Was my case such a low priority?"

Brian shrugged. "I'm sorry, Tori, but let's focus on what we do have. First, I need to contact your ex-husband. Do you know where he is?"

"Not exactly, no. He's been in touch about the divorce, though."

Brian frowned. "Can you tell me how to find him? I hesitate to call him at work and tip them off."

"I can give you his home phone number and new address."

"I want him as your witness, but I may have to subpoena him. I might not call on him, but I want control of Rick's presence or absence in case the prosecution gets any ideas."

"Better to head off any potential damning testimony," Tori's agreed.

"Exactly. Moving on, the FBI photo expert will explain to the jury that the photo lineup was presented to the eyewitnesses in a way that introduced bias. He will also explain his analysis of the robber's face and body build, as well as why he believes the woman in the video is not you."

She sighed, and her shoulders slumped. "But basically, it's just his opinion versus three eyewitnesses."

Brian leaned forward slightly. "We also have two of your colleagues testifying as to your reputation in the community."

"It's really not much, is it?"

Brian gazed at her. He opened his mouth, then closed it again. Finally, he said, "It's the best we have."

He picked up his pen. "Let's review your direct testimony."

As Brian coached her through the questions and answers, Tori felt like an actor rehearsing for the most critical role of her life. Every word, gesture, and facial expression had to be carefully calibrated. Brian's suggestion that she wear an open-collared blouse struck her as both practical and absurd. As if her future really hinged on the neckline of her outfit.

"Now I'll assume the prosecutor's role for your cross-examination," Brian said, and they began again.

Tori found that she was beginning to enjoy the role-play once she'd gotten the hang of it. But then Brian shook his head and held up his hand while she was in full flow.

"Give only brief answers and refrain from elaborating. If he presses you to say more, stay silent. He'll try to catch you out for any inconsistencies," he said. "The fact that you're a woman is in your favor, and the prosecutor is a brute. He's likely to get up in your face."

"Being a woman is an advantage? Since when?" Tori said.

"We're in the South, Tori. Juries will think it rude if he bullies you."

"Hmm," Tori said, still skeptical.

The session ended, leaving Tori emotionally and mentally drained. She felt trapped in a high-stakes performance where the line between truth and theatrics had become dangerously blurred. In this courtroom drama, she was an actor with Brian, the director. Her future depended on which side performed best.

∽

Labor Day approached, bringing with it the looming shadow of Tori's impending trial. The afternoon sun cast a mocking brightness over the city as Jo arrived in Houston.

In an attempt at normalcy, they ventured out for Mexican cuisine, but Tori's stomach roiled with anxiety. She was unable to finish her meal. As they sat in the vibrant restaurant, surrounded by the chatter of carefree diners, Tori felt increasingly isolated in her distress.

Her chest tightened when she thought of her career, reputation, and future in the hands of twelve strangers. She fought the urge to get up and pace the restaurant and swallowed the last of her beer, hoping for a calming buzz.

"I received the Final Decree of Divorce last week. I didn't have to hire an attorney. In the end, Rick was quite reasonable about dividing up our property, and I couldn't make a fuss. I will have to sell the house, though."

Jo's brow furrowed. "Oh dear."

"I'm not sorry. If I'm acquitted, I'll leave Texas. Go back to Boston." She dropped her fork and sighed. "It's strange, Jo. Brian was trying to contact Rick last week. He wants to subpoena him, but he can't raise him."

"Is he avoiding Brian?" asked Jo.

Tori pursed her lips thoughtfully. "Probably. I told Brian that Rick seemed to be around and gave him his new home number. Just before that, Rick left me a message asking me to call him. But I worry that he wants to rehash and reminisce about our marriage, to assure each other that we're still friends. I can't handle that right now. I'm not sleeping and am just about out of my mind with anxiety about this trial."

"Of course you are," Jo said. "He must know your mind is elsewhere."

At Jo's reassuring tone, Tori suddenly felt the tears well up. In a voice tight with emotion, she suggested they pay up and leave. Once they were in the car, she let the dam break. Resting her head on the steering wheel, she cried.

"I just can't go to prison," she sobbed. "It will ruin my

career—everything I've worked for. Jude will find someone else. I . . . I . . . just can't."

Jo moved across the seat and took her in her arms. Tori buried her head on her shoulder, and Jo patted her like a small child.

"Don't catastrophize, Tori. Brian and I have your back. This nightmare could all be over in a matter of days."

CHAPTER 49

TORI'S EYES FLEW open, her heart thundering in her chest as reality crashed over her like a tidal wave. Today, September 3rd, was the day of her trial. The weight of impending judgment pressed down on her as she stumbled to the bathroom, splashing cold water on her face in a futile effort to wash away her anxiety.

Her hands fumbled as she prepared her morning coffee. She limited herself to a single cup, acutely aware that appearing jittery or agitated in the courtroom could sway the jury's perception. With meticulous care, she donned the outfit Brian had advised—a blue blouse with an open collar, a simple black skirt, and low-heeled pumps. Every detail mattered when making a good first impression.

The silence upstairs told Tori that Jo was still asleep in the guest room. She poured a mug of rich French roast and knocked gently on Jo's door.

"Come in." Jo's voice was thick from sleep. "Oh, God. You're dressed." She sat up so abruptly that she banged her elbow on the headboard. "Did I oversleep?"

"No, it's still early." Tori set the coffee on the bedside table. When Jo motioned for her to sit, she perched on the bed.

Jo scrunched pillows against the headboard and leaned back, taking her first sip of coffee. "I understand you're worried." She placed a hand on Tori's arm. "Today will be tough listening to the prosecutor's case. But unless they pull something unexpected out of their hat, it's a weak one. We have our FBI photo expert, your testimony, and the character witnesses. Brian will do his best to select unbiased jurors. Don't let the prosecution get under your skin."

Tori straightened. "I'll try. But I'll want to punch that sanctimonious prosecutor whenever he opens his mouth." She had cried her tears earlier. Now, she held fear at bay with anger. She'd lurched back and forth between the two on an emotional roller coaster for days.

Jo smiled. "Savor your anger. It'll keep you strong. But don't let it show until we win."

The courtroom smelled faintly of varnish and old paper as Jo and Tori entered just before 8:30 a.m., when jury selection was to begin. Jo sat at the front of the public seating area, crowded with people intrigued by the novelty of a woman physician on trial for bank robbery. Tori and Brian took their places in front of the bar at the defense table. Tori sat stiffly, like a soldier about to go into battle. Her attire and demeanor radiated professionalism.

Brian looked his usual composed self, his expensive suit and dark-framed reading glasses giving him an air of quiet authority.

Across the aisle sat the prosecution team. The lead prosecutor, a balding man with a belly that strained against his suit buttons, had the wet cough of a smoker. His bespectacled assistant wore a dark suit and an ill-fitting tie, which he kept tugging at as if it might strangle him. Both men wore grim expressions.

"All rise," boomed the bailiff, his voice echoing through the room.

Everyone stood as an elderly judge shuffled into view, his robes swishing faintly with each step. He settled into his chair and peered over his reading glasses at the panel of prospective jurors. His voice was thick with a Texas drawl as he began.

"Good morning. I am Judge Herbert Elias, the trial judge in this case. You have been called to this courtroom as a panel of prospective jurors for the case of United States v. Victoria Nelson. This is a criminal case in which Victoria Nelson is charged with committing the crime of armed bank robbery in violation of federal criminal law."

The judge then explained and supervised *voir dire*, and for the rest of the morning, he allowed the prosecutors and defense to ask prospective jurors questions. Brian did his best to challenge for cause those who held stereotypical views of women and resented those who violated those roles by becoming physicians or robbing banks. Nevertheless, Jo noted with disappointment that the jury box was filled with eight men and only four women. Jurors were less likely to convict a defendant of the same sex.

Jo's rumination was interrupted by the judge's announcement.

"We will now break for lunch and reconvene at 1:30 p.m."

Upon their return from lunch, the judge began his instruction, "Ladies and gentlemen of the jury, now that you have been selected and sworn, we will begin with opening statements. Opening statements are not evidence. They are simply each side's opportunity to outline what they believe the evidence will show during this trial."

He nodded to the prosecutor. "The government may proceed with your opening statement."

The lead prosecutor rose. As he made his way to the front, Tori noticed how the jacket of his dark suit stretched tightly over his back and hips, and snakeskin cowboy boots peeked out from under his trousers.

He scanned the faces of the jury and cleared his throat.

"Ladies and gentlemen, the evidence presented in this case will show that on June 14, 1985, the defendant, Ms. Victoria Nelson, entered the Fallon National Bank of Texas with a clear intent to commit robbery. At approximately 11:15 a.m., she approached the teller and demanded all available cash, stating she had a gun. The teller, fearing for her life, complied with her demands. Ms. Nelson left the building with $6,555 in cash.

"You will hear testimony from bank employees who will describe the terrifying moments of that day and identify the defendant as the bank robber.""

The prosecutor scanned the jury again. Several glanced at Tori. All were listening attentively, their faces neutral.

"The Government will also present evidence that the defendant's behavior before the bank robbery had been unusually erratic and out of character, and that she was under tremendous financial pressure, thus providing motive for the theft."

Again, his gaze swept over the jury. "At the end of this trial, we will ask you to return a guilty verdict, as the evidence will leave no doubt that Ms. Nelson is responsible for this crime."

Tori watched his self-satisfied smirk as he returned to the prosecution table. Her chest tightened. *Erratic behavior? Financial stress?* Her mind churned with the possibilities. She resisted the urge to fidget. She was conscious of her pulse pounding in her neck and wondered if it was visible to others.

When the judge indicated, Brian rose to address the jury. He removed his glasses and smiled, looking each juror in the eye.

"Ladies and gentlemen of the jury, today you will be asked to consider the case of Dr. Victoria Nelson, a respected physician who has dedicated her life to healing others. The prosecution would have you believe that this physician, engaged in the busy practice of medicine, with no criminal history, a solid bank account, and no motive whatsoever, suddenly decided to rob a bank."

Brian chuckled as if in disbelief. His laughter was so natural and infectious that Tory saw a female juror suppress a twitch in the corner of her mouth.

"And where is the evidence?" Brian continued. "The FBI found none of the stolen money, no dye placed with it, no gun, and no clothes worn by the robber. All the prosecution has is notoriously unreliable eyewitness testimony. Here, we have a case of mistaken identity—an unfortunate error in a chaotic situation."

He paused before continuing. "The real culprit remains at large, and Dr. Nelson stands accused solely because she somewhat resembles that person. I ask you to look closely at the facts and remember that, in this country, we do not convict people based on innuendo or coincidences. We require solid evidence. And in this case, there is none."

Brian returned to the defense table and gave Tori a reassuring smile. Her pulse slowed.

CHAPTER 50

The following morning, the judge called on the government to present their first witness.

There was a short pause, and then the lead prosecutor hauled himself to his feet with visible effort, clearing his throat with a phlegmy rasp.

"The government calls Special Agent Brennan to the stand."

The FBI agent swaggered to the chair. Probably in his late twenties, his short, cropped copper hair and boyish good looks made him appear no older than a teenager. The prosecutor waited for him to settle, then asked him to identify himself and his position with the FBI before continuing.

"Special Agent Sean Brennan, on the morning of Monday, June 17, you arrested Ms. Victoria Nelson." It was a statement, not a question. "What led you and your fellow agent to arrest her?"

Relaxed and confident, the agent leaned back and crossed his legs.

"There was a bank surveillance videotape of the robbery from which we obtained still photos. She was identified as the robber in a photo lineup by three bank employees who witnessed the robbery."

"Let's take a step back a moment because this is an important point. You mentioned video surveillance footage. This videotape has been certified as having been obtained from Fallon National Bank. And it is from this video that you obtained the still photos?"

"Yes, sir."

The prosecutor nodded gravely.

"I'd like to ask the court's permission to show the video footage."

"You may proceed," the judge replied.

The surveillance tape flickered to life. Jo's breath caught as a woman approached the teller. Again, the woman's striking resemblance to Tori unnerved her—the same facial shape, jawline, and blonde hair protruding from a ball cap. She was about the same height, and the only discordant feature was the large belly protruding under the oversized blue shirt.

Jo let out her breath. They must be able to see that the woman is not slim-figured Tori.

When the tape ran out, the prosecutor wasted no time. His voice was sharp and deliberate, prompting the agent to sit up straight.

"What exactly happened when you showed the bank employees this tape and the still photos?"

"All three witnesses confirmed it was the robber."

"Then what did you do next?"

"We circulated the still photos taken from the video around the business district near the bank, asking if anyone recognized the person. No one responded at the time, but the following Monday morning, we received an anonymous tip claiming the woman in the photo resembled Dr. Nelson, a physician at

Novak-McKay Multispecialty Clinic. We put a photo from her driver's license into a photo line-up with other women resembling the woman in the video, and all three eyewitnesses picked Dr. Nelson out of the line-up."

The prosecutor had been coughing. He grabbed his water glass, gulped, and turned back to the FBI agent.

"How did Ms. Nelson seem when you came to her clinic to arrest her?"

"She looked shocked. She asked why she was a suspect. When we read her the charges and her rights, she protested that there must be some mistake."

"And what did you tell her?"

"We told her we'd discuss it further when she was at the FBI field office."

The prosecutor turned away. He gave off an air of having become bored by the agent's last two answers.

Jo, on the other hand, was listening intently.

"What did you learn from her interview?"

"She denied having anything to do with the robbery. She said she was working in her home office the morning of the robbery until she went to lunch."

"And did she provide a verifiable alibi—someone who can confirm that she was, in fact, working at home at the time of the robbery?"

The agent leaned forward. "No, sir."

A simple reply, but it was clear the prosecutor was aware of the dramatic effect it had as he paused to let it sink in. Jo glanced at the jury. Several were taking notes.

"Thank you, Agent Brennan. I have no further questions."

"Your witness, Mr. Kirkland," the judge croaked.

Jo watched Brian step toward the agent. His demeanor was quietly courteous, entirely focused.

"Good morning, Agent Brennan. I have a few questions for you today."

"Okay." The young man wasn't looking quite as comfortable as he had when talking to the prosecutor. They would have been in frequent contact, but this smartly dressed, brisk defense counsel was new to him.

"How many agents participated in working on this case?"

"Just me and my partner."

"Where is he today?"

"He moved off the case. Promoted and transferred to another department."

"Were you the officer who presented the photo lineup to the bank employees?"

"I was, yes."

"And did the photos in the line-up include the entire clothed body of each woman or just the faces?"

"Just the faces."

"I see." Brian rubbed his chin. Jo found it hard to tell if he was letting a few seconds pass to disconcert the agent or was genuinely thinking.

"Were the photos presented to each witness in separate rooms?"

"Of course."

"You said that three eyewitnesses picked my client out from that photo lineup?"

"Yes."

"And were the photos of the faces presented simultaneously or sequentially?"

Brennan began to look wary.

"Sequentially."

"Did you know which photo belonged to the suspect, Dr. Nelson, when you were presenting them?"

The agent looked uncomfortable and shifted in the chair. "Yes."

Jo could barely hear him. Brian spoke sharply.

"Speak up, please, so the court can hear you."

"Yes," Brennan said. The muscles in his jaw worked. All his cockiness had drained away.

He knows he may have screwed up.

Brian flipped a page on his legal pad without looking up. Jo guessed he was denying the witness any sense of reassurance.

"I'd like to review the physical evidence in this case. During your investigation, did you recover any fingerprints belonging to Dr. Nelson at the bank?"

"No." The agent seemed to feel the question was unfair. He added defensively, "But the bank robber wore gloves."

"Did you find the robber's clothes, as documented in the surveillance video?"

"No."

"Did you find the money stolen from the bank? Was any of the cash found when you searched Dr. Nelson's home, office, and car?"

The agent seemed reluctant to answer. "No."

"The teller placed a dye pack into the bundles of money given to the robber and activated it when the robber left the bank. Was there any evidence of dye in Dr. Nelson's house when the FBI searched it after her arrest?"

"No."

"Or in her car? Office? Or anywhere else?"

"No."

Jo felt a flicker of excitement and sat up straighter, admiring Counsel's change of pace. Each negative answer acted like a lifeline, pulling her closer to hope.

"Did you find a gun in Dr. Nelson's possession?"

"No."

"So, you found no physical evidence whatsoever linking Dr. Nelson to the bank robbery?"

The agent's shoulders slumped. "No."

Brian's tone sharpened. "Did you find evidence that Dr. Nelson had any motive to rob a bank? Any financial difficulties or a drug problem, for example?"

Brennan hesitated. His eyes slid sideways to the prosecutor.

"No, the FBI found no evidence of a drug problem or financial difficulty."

Brian turned away and let the agent's negative responses hang in the air as he picked up some papers from the defense table. He caught Jo's eye almost conspiratorially before he turned back to the witness.

"Thank you, Agent Brennan. No further questions."

Brennan sprang from his chair as if he could not exit fast enough.

The judge addressed the prosecutor, "Any redirect, Mr. Dillon?"

"No, Your Honor."

"Let's take a break. We will reconvene at 1:00 p.m."

During lunch, Tori experienced a moment of optimism after Brian's staccato, rapid-fire cross-examination of the agent. He'd demonstrated to the jury that the FBI had found no physical evidence whatsoever, nor had their investigation uncovered a drug problem or financial difficulty. Moreover, Agent Brennan had only shown Tori's face in the photo lineup and had known which photo was hers when he presented the lineup one by one to the bank employees, potentially biasing their response.

But back in court that afternoon, her optimism was shattered when the prosecutor rose to announce, "The government would like to call Mr. Richard Dynoski to the stand."

Tori gasped.

Brian leaped to his feet.

"Objection! We were not given any notice of this witness's testimony."

The judge gave the prosecutor a hard, disapproving look.

"Bailiff, please remove the jury."

While they filed out, Brian sought to reassure Tori. "If the judge allows him to testify, we could have grounds for a mistrial," he whispered.

Tori regretted not calling Rick back and urging him to return Brian's calls.

"Attorneys approach," the judge ordered. When they both stood before him, he said, "Why was this witness not disclosed to us pre-trial, Mr. Dillon?"

The prosecutor raised his chin. "Your Honor, this is the defendant's ex-husband, and it has only been recently that their divorce became final. We haven't been able to find him to serve the subpoena until this morning. There was no time to disclose this in discovery."

The judge frowned and narrowed his eyes.

"This is far from satisfactory. I would like to hear your proffer of this witness's testimony."

The prosecutor straightened his tie. "Yes, Your Honor. We want to call this witness to testify as to the state of mind and behavior of the defendant and her finances just before the robbery."

The judge appeared to deliberate, then came to a decision. "I will allow it. But I expect the defense needs time to prepare for cross-examination. Is that right, Mr. Kirkland?"

"Yes, Your Honor."

The judge sighed heavily.

"It's all very inconvenient for the court and the jury, and the prosecution's attempt to take advantage of the situation is noted. As we find ourselves in this position, the trial will resume on Friday." He banged his gavel. "Get to work, Mr. Kirkland."

CHAPTER 51

JO OBSERVED TORI as she perched on the edge of her seat in Brian's office. Her face looked drawn. Jo knew Rick's betrayal cut deep. How could that slimy little prick agree to testify for the prosecution against Tori? The timing couldn't have been worse. She wouldn't put it past Rick to have made sure their divorce became final just before the trial so that he could testify, rendering spousal privilege useless.

Brian returned with coffee mugs and offered one to Tori, which she declined with a slight shake of her head, saying she was already too wound up. He settled down with his notebook open, the pen ready.

"Obviously, we weren't prepared for this," Brian said, his voice measured. "Your ex-husband appeared to be quite hostile when I saw him in the office with you in June. At that time, he mentioned your long phone calls, your evening outings, and your late-night return. Is there anything else you'd like to share with me?"

His gaze locked on Tori, expectant and unwavering.

Tori sighed. "Our marriage was a sham. I needed a distraction to think, to do something out of my comfort zone. I started going out to The Lodge, a bar, and learned to line dance. I made friends who didn't know I was married or a physician. I felt light and happy when I was there. I rarely returned home before Rick was in bed." She glanced at Jo. "We weren't sleeping together anymore."

Jo gave her a gentle nod of encouragement. "Tell him about Jude,"

Brian looked interested. "The woman who worked at World Petrol who turned over monitoring data to the EPA?"

Tori nodded. "Our relationship was about more than friendship and the monitoring data." She drew a deep breath. "We became lovers."

If Brian was shocked by this revelation, his professional demeanor betrayed nothing. He rubbed his chin thoughtfully.

"I see," he said. "Was your husband aware you were seeing a woman, ah . . . romantically?"

Tori sighed. "I don't think so."

Brian drummed his fingers on the table. The intensity in the room was getting to Jo, and she rubbed her palms down the front of her thighs.

"If he does know, maybe he's being called to cast Tori's character in an unfavorable light in front of this conservative Southern jury."

"Maybe." Brian agreed. "But it is not relevant to the bank robbery, and the judge should not allow it. As regards the rest, I'll have to show how angry he was about the divorce and imply he's giving his testimony for revenge to cast doubt on its veracity."

"But he told me he isn't angry. Not anymore," Tori said.

"Hmm." Brian scratched his head.

"What about the fact that he works for World Petrol?" Jo asked.

The connection hung over them like a dark cloud. "Of

course, them again," Brian said, leaning his chin on his fist. "I'll try to make use of that. But I'm afraid this judge is not likely to allow me to introduce anything that sounds like a conspiracy theory and is not directly related to the bank robbery. And we've uncovered no solid evidence that World Petrol or their proxy orchestrated your arrest."

Jo bit her lip. *Even though it's at the heart of this case?* But Brian was an experienced defense attorney and in charge.

⌘

Back in court on Friday morning, the prosecutor called Rick to the stand.

From the public seats, Jo's eyes bored into him as he approached the witness stand. He was avoiding eye contact with anyone but the prosecution team. He wore a blue suit jacket and an open-collar white shirt without a tie. His face looked haggard, as if he hadn't slept for days.

The prosecutor didn't try to button his suit jacket as he approached the witness. While Rick answered routine pre-liminary questions in a flat monotone, she thought he looked nervous, pulling at his shirt cuff and jiggling one knee up and down in that irritating way he had.

She tuned into the prosecutor's questions.

"How long were you married to Ms. Nelson?"

"Ten years," Rick said.

"And how would you describe your wife during that time?"

"Normal, hardworking. Obsessed with her work." Rick said.

"Were you and your ex-wife having financial difficulties over the past year?"

Rick shifted in the witness chair. "My start-up was failing, and I'd run out of venture capital. I nearly declared bankruptcy before securing a temporary contract and eventually landing a job with a salary."

"What about Ms. Nelson? Was she having financial difficulties?"

"She had a good income from the clinic, but she also had expenses for setting up a laboratory and her cancer research that wasn't covered by grants." Rick folded his arms across his chest. "I don't know if she had money problems, but I doubt it. We kept our finances separate after I started my business."

The prosecutor raised his eyebrows at his response and changed the subject.

"I would like to inquire about your wife's behavior through-out your marriage. Did she come home from work to make dinner and do everything a wife usually does for her husband?"

Jo winced. *"Everything a wife does for her husband?" Is this 1985 or 1955? How is that relevant? Why is Brian not objecting?*

"Yeah, most of the time," Rick said, glancing for a second in Tori's direction.

"Did you have a happy marriage?"

Rick's brow furrowed. "I thought so."

"Did her behavior change in any way in the months leading up to her arrest?"

Rick took his time answering. "Yes."

"How did it change?" The prosecutor asked. Jo noticed how he had moderated the sneer in his voice, making him sound like a sympathetic therapist.

What a hypocrite.

"She started spending more time on the phone with her girl-friends," Rick said.

"Yes, and . . . ?"

"She started going out after work and staying out late—not coming home for dinner."

"I see." The prosecutor paused.

He's playing to the men on the jury, Jo thought.

"What do you think she was doing when she went missing, not coming home to fix you dinner?"

Jo's shoulders tensed. *Uh-oh.*

Brian jumped up. "Objection, your Honor. Calls for speculation."

"Objection sustained."

Rick looks pissed off.

"Mr. Dynoski, before your separation, were you and your wife sleeping together or in separate rooms?"

Brian jumped up again. "Objection. Irrelevant and an invasion of privacy."

The judge shook his head and addressed the prosecutor.

"I'll allow it, but you must demonstrate its relevance to her behavior before the robbery." He turned to Rick. "You may answer."

"We were sleeping in separate rooms," Rick said in a small voice. He looked so uncomfortable that Jo wondered whether the prosecution had pressured him into testifying against his will. After all, he hadn't come as a witness voluntarily.

"Were you worried your wife might be having an affair?"

Jo tensed again. *Don't let him get away with this.*

"Objection," Brian said. "Leading the witness. Not relevant."

"Objection sustained, as to leading the witness. As to relevance, you have yet to demonstrate it, Mr. Dillon," the judge said. "Where is this line of questioning going?"

"Your Honor. I am about to demonstrate it." He scanned the jury's faces, as did Jo. They appeared rapt.

"Mr. Dynoski, were you aware that your wife was having an affair with a woman? That she's a lesbian?"

Most of the jury rapidly switched their gaze to Tori.

Jo's breath caught. *Dirty trick. The thug must have communicated with the prosecutor.*

Rick's mouth had dropped open. "What? No!"

Brian jumped up. "Objection! Relevance! Speculation! I request that this whole line of questioning and answers be stricken from the record."

"Objection sustained," the judge said. "

The judge turned and addressed the court reporter. "Please strike from the record the last line of questioning and answers beginning with Mr. Dillon's question about whether Mr. Dynoski and the suspect were sleeping together." He also instructed the jury to disregard it.

But the viper had struck, and the damage was swift and lethal. The prosecutor made no effort to hide his smirk.

"No further questions."

"Your witness, Mr. Kirkland," the judge said.

Brian rose and took his time approaching the stand. He took off his glasses and gave Rick a hard stare.

"Mr. Dynoski, you said you thought your marriage had been happy."

Rick, looking shattered, stared at his hands. He lifted his head with a look of defeat. "I did . . . I mean, I thought it was. In retrospect, I realize we've grown apart over the last few years. We didn't fight much until recently. She worked long hours, but . . . she's a doctor."

"Right. With a busy practice, yes?"

"Yes," he said wearily.

"Does it seem reasonable that, as your wife approaches her mid-thirties, she might want to experience some of what she missed during her long and arduous medical training? Go out with her friends, socialize, not have to adhere to a rigid schedule when off work?"

"Yeah. That's what it sounded like when I asked her about it." Rick said.

Rick looks so much older with those drooping bags under his eyes.

"So, did you ever follow her and try to find out what she was doing in the evenings when she came home late?"

Uh, oh, dangerous, Brian.

"No. Never. I was too busy trying to avoid bankruptcy and looking for a job." Rick's tone had grown sharp.

Brian requested a sidebar with the judge, but Jo could not hear the conversation. He then turned to the witness.

"Do you have any evidence that your wife was having an affair with anyone?"

"No, I don't . . . We were married for ten years. I don't think she was having an affair . . . with anyone."

"Were you outraged and hurt when your wife asked for a divorce?" Brian asked gently.

The question seemed to ease some of the tension in Rick. He blew out his breath.

"I was. Yes. We had been together a long time. I went a bit off the rails. Tori was obsessed with her cancer study, and when she wasn't in her office working on that, she was out somewhere. I just . . . didn't understand what was happening and . . ."

"Thank you, Mr. Dynoski." Brian interrupted. "One more question. You said at the beginning of your testimony that you currently work in the IT Department at World Petrol."

"Yes." Rick's knee started jittering again.

"When did you start your new job?"

"Initially, I worked on a contract that started in May this year. Then it became a permanent position last month." Rick eyed Brian warily.

Brian's glance swept over the jury.

Jo noticed most appeared to be listening intently.

"Wasn't your ex-wife doing research that showed excess cancer rates in the vicinity of the World Petrol refinery?"

Jo squirmed. *Too early to show your hand, Brian.*

The prosecutor leaped to his feet. "Objection. Relevance."

The judge addressed Brian. "Mr. Kirkland, I don't see how the defendant's research study is relevant to her alleged crime."

"Your Honor, I intend to show its relevance later on with testimony from the defendant."

The judge hesitated, weighing his decision. "Objection overruled." He turned to Rick. "You may answer the question."

"Yes," Rick said, shifting his weight.

"Didn't you try to dissuade your wife from pursuing that study?" Brian asked.

The prosecutor levitated from his chair. "Objection. This is clearly not relevant to the crime."

Again, the judge hesitated. He sighed, closed his eyes, and curled his fingers around his chin. Looking up, he said, "Objection sustained."

Oh, shit.

Brian silently regarded Rick, who lowered his eyes.

"Thank you, Mr. Dynoski. No further questions."

Rick bolted from the witness stand.

Jo was puzzled. It had been an awkward twenty minutes, watching Rick on the stand. But there was something more. As the court adjourned for the day and began to empty, it came to her.

She'd been wrong. Rick really didn't want to testify against Tori.

CHAPTER 52

OVER THE LUNCH break, they met with Brian, and his assistant ordered sandwiches. Tori looked pale, her mouth pressed into a thin line. The prosecutor's lesbian question appeared to have rattled her.

"Don't worry," Jo said. "The judge instructed the jury to ignore it, and it's stricken from the record."

"Yes, but the jury heard it. I saw several react negatively. It's still in their minds."

True. The damage had been done.

Plus, Brian had floated a bit of the conspiracy theory on cross, and the judge's decision to exclude it did not bode well for bringing it up again.

Jo and Tori ate their sandwiches silently, each in their own world of worry, while Brian reviewed his prepared cross-examination of the eyewitnesses.

The prosecution called the first eyewitness to the stand, a middle-aged woman dressed in a dowdy brown suit.

"Please state your name for the court," he said.

"Sarah F. Jenkins."

"And where do you work?"

"Fallon National Bank of Texas."

She looked ill at ease, listing slightly to one side.

"Can you tell us what happened the day of the robbery that concerns us today?"

She took a deep breath. "It was around 11:15 a.m. No customers were present when a woman walked in with her hands in her pockets. Everything seemed normal until she approached my window and asked me to hand over all the cash I had. She said she had a gun."

"How did you react?"

"I was scared. But I tried to stay calm and follow protocol. I handed over my cash—I had more than usual—and slipped in a dye pack."

"Did she say anything to you while you gathered the money?"

"She told me to hurry. She seemed jumpy and nervous."

"What did the woman look like?"

"She was blonde, with shoulder-length hair, under a ball cap. She wore large sunglasses so I couldn't see the color of her eyes. No lipstick. She wore an oversized blue work shirt and tight gloves.

"I'm going to show you the surveillance video of the robbery." The prosecutor turned to the clerk. "Please turn on the projector."

Once again, the grainy videotape of the bank robbery appeared on the screen, followed by two still photos taken from the video. "Is this the person who asked you to hand over the money?

"Yes."

"Is this person sitting in the courtroom today?"

Sarah cast a quick, furtive glance at Tori.

"Yes."

"Can you point her out, please?"

Sarah Jenkins raised her finger and pointed at Tori at the defense table. She quickly lowered her hand.

Their case had taken its third significant blow. Jo glanced at Tori, who sat rigid, her face neutral.

"Let the record reflect that the witness pointed to Ms. Victoria Nelson, the defendant. Thank you, Ms. Jenkins. No further questions."

The prosecutor turned away, looking smug.

"Your witness, Mr. Kirkland," the judge said.

"Good afternoon, Ms. Jenkins. I have a few questions for you." Brian smiled engagingly.

She produced a tentative smile. "Okay."

"You said the bank robber told you she had a gun. Did you see the gun?"

"No."

"Did the woman who asked you to give her money look overweight to you?"

Sarah's eyes slid away. "I couldn't really tell. She had on this big, baggy work shirt."

Brian waited with an air of expectancy, but the witness said no more.

"You said you put a dye pack in with the money you gave to the robber. Did the FBI find the dye-colored money in the defendant's possession?"

The prosecutor leaped from his chair.

"Objection! Beyond the scope of this witness's knowledge."

"Objection sustained," the judge said.

Why did he ask that? He must have known the prosecution would object.

"Ms. Jenkins, after the robbery, the FBI showed you a photo lineup of the faces of women who resembled the woman in the bank surveillance video and asked you to choose which one was the robber. Did the officer's hand linger on one photo more than another?"

Sarah's brow furrowed. "Um . . . no . . . I don't think so."

"Did you see the expression on his face when he handed you each photo?"

The witness looked confused. "Um . . . probably. I don't really remember."

"Ms. Jenkins. Did the officer's body language change at any point when showing you each woman in the line-up?"

Sarah looked increasingly flustered. "I . . . I can't remember."

"Did the officer tap one photo or another when he presented them?"

"I . . . don't know."

"I see. So you don't remember if the officer indicated to you through body language or facial expression, which photo was that of the suspect, Dr. Nelson?"

Sarah's wide-eyed reaction, signaling comprehension, spoke volumes. She leaned forward. But before the witness could answer, the prosecutor jumped up, nearly tripping over his briefcase.

"Objection, your Honor. This calls for speculation about the motives of others."

"Objection sustained," the judge said.

What the hell? Jo counted the ways a guilty verdict could be appealed.

Brian scanned his notes and looked up. "Thank you, Ms. Jenkins. No further questions."

Brian sat, and Jo watched him whisper in Tori's ear. The witness had appeared tentative in identifying Tori as the bank robber, but she'd stuck to her story. Jo knew this was common among eyewitnesses, who had months to consolidate and reinforce their opinions. True or not, they came to believe the stories they told themselves.

The other two bank employees were called to the stand and confirmed that Tori was the woman in the surveillance video and photos. Brian's FBI photo identification expert would have his hands full, discrediting the eyewitness testimony with his image comparisons.

When the judge finally adjourned court for the day, tottering off to his chambers, Jo's mind raced ahead to next week's battle. So far, there had been significant setbacks, but the trial was far from over.

∽

Jo busied herself in the kitchen, preparing a simple but comforting meal—crisp Caesar salad and golden chicken tenders—while her mind replayed the courtroom scenes. She poured two glasses of chardonnay, the pale liquid catching the light as she carried them to the living room where Tori waited.

"It's not looking good, is it?" Tori said.

"Rick didn't do as much damage as I thought he might. And he looked wrecked," Jo said.

"Yeah, but the eyewitnesses confidently confirmed it was me in the surveillance video," Tori said.

Worry had etched itself back onto Tori's face—the telltale lines around her eyes deepening, her complexion ashen under the living room lights.

Jo leaned forward, her protective instinct taking over.

"We knew they would," she reassured Tori with a steadiness she didn't entirely feel. "Just wait until we present our side. In the meantime, you look like you've been run over by a truck. Why don't you go to bed early tonight? Get a good night's sleep."

CHAPTER 53

THE FOLLOWING DAY, Jo was still worried about her friend, who seemed listless. She looked as though she hardly slept. She tried to rekindle Tori's hopes, though she had her own doubts.

"It's going fairly well, don't you think?" Jo's voice carried a note of cautious optimism. "Despite those three eyewitnesses, Brian masterfully set the stage for our FBI expert to undermine their reliability. And Agent Brennan's monotonous recitation of the absence of physical evidence connecting you to the robbery? That must be planting seeds of doubt in the jury's minds."

Tori frowned, her fingers tracing patterns on the breakfast table.

"I'm still anxious about how the jury reacted when the prosecutor brought up my being a lesbian. I couldn't stay away from Jude during her final days in town. That Hogarth guy must have been feeding information about us to the prosecutor."

"Yeah, I know," Jo acknowledged, taking a thoughtful sip of her coffee. "But Brian will try again to bring up the conspiracy angle during your testimony. He's already flagged Rick's position at World Petrol and your cancer study."

She didn't mention her concern that the judge would likely find it irrelevant.

Tori's shoulders slumped. "But we have no proof that World Petrol orchestrated my arrest."

"All we need is to plant doubt in some jurors' minds that they might be involved," Jo reminded her, trying to rekindle hope.

"Unless they believe being a lesbian is the moral equivalent of being a bank robber," Tori murmured, looking away.

Jo studied Tori's downcast face before asking softly, "Are you?"

Tori looked up, confusion and alarm in her eyes. "Am I what? A bank robber?"

"A lesbian?" Jo held her gaze.

A smile bloomed across Tori's face. "Does loving two women and making love with one of them make me a lesbian?"

Jo grinned back. "Getting there," she replied, her voice warm. "But you don't have to label yourself if you don't want to."

But for the rest of the weekend, Tori seemed despondent, going to bed early, sleeping late, and eating very little. Jo worried that the fight had gone out of her.

When the judge declared the court in session Monday morning and the jury filed in, Jo's attention was diverted by movement at the back of the courtroom. Her eyes widened when she spotted Rick slipping onto a bench. She wondered why he'd made the effort to come. He'd been eager enough to bolt after giving his testimony the previous day. Her attention returned to the front when Brian rose to call the FBI photo identification expert to the stand.

The prosecutor leaped to his feet. "Objection, your Honor. The reliability of eyewitness identification is within the common knowledge and experience of the jury, and expert testimony on this subject would not assist the trier of fact."

Jo's hand went to her mouth to stifle a gasp. *What?*

"Oh, come on," she muttered behind her hand.

The judge asked the bailiff to remove the jury while he called the two attorneys to the bench. Jo hunched forward, straining to hear the discussion.

The prosecutor said, "The photo expert's testimony will do nothing but confuse the jury. Eyewitness testimony is recognized as adequate in Texas. The expert's methods are not widely accepted and don't meet the Frye Standard."

Brian countered with, "Eyewitnesses are influenced by how the photo line-up is presented. The lineup included only faces, and the defendant's body build is clearly different from that of the robber. The photo line-up effectively eliminated a key identifying characteristic that the witnesses could have observed."

His gestures became increasingly animated, and his face showed strain. "Also, the body language of the presenter can provide unconscious cueing. The photo expert will explain how this can occur and compare the measurements of the robber's face and body build to those of the defendant. His testimony is key to our defense."

Jo's fingers tightened around the edge of her bench. It was true that much of Tori's defense relied on convincing the jury that the arrest was a case of mistaken identity. All they had left were the two general character witnesses waiting outside the courtroom—and Tori's own testimony.

Jo couldn't see Tori's face, but her back was rigid, and the set of her shoulders suggested she'd clenched her hands tightly together on the table.

The judge signaled the discussion was over and read his decision to the court reporter for the record.

"I have considered the offer of proof by the defense of what testimony the FBI photo identification expert will provide, and how it would be relevant. However, I am excluding his testimony. While potentially relevant, the expert's testimony might confuse or mislead the jury. The three eyewitnesses are competent to judge for themselves if a person's photo and physical appearance match that of the bank robber without the aid of an expert. Furthermore, the accuracy and reliability of the methods used by photo identification experts are not well established. The eyewitnesses' testimonies are sufficient, and the defense has had the opportunity to explore any flaws in their acceptance during cross-examination."

Oh, my God. Jo was stunned by this setback. It was little consolation to think that if Tori were convicted, this judge was setting up the case for a potential reversal on appeal by excluding evidence bearing directly on the central issue in determining her guilt. She shifted forward to try to catch Tori's eye, and as she did so, she noticed something was terribly wrong.

Tori was leaning forward, breathing heavily, and clutching at her chest.

Jo stood up and ran forward, and without thinking, attempted to break through the bar that divided the public from the court, before the bailiff physically restrained her.

"This is no bluff," Jo shouted, extracting herself from the bailiff. "I'm calling 911!"

Brian helped Tori to the floor with gentle hands.

"Tori, hold my hand, and try to take deep, slow breaths," he said.

"I can't . . . lie flat . . . can't breathe," Tori whispered, grasping his arm, and trying to sit up.

Jo leaned over the bar, straining toward Tori. "I've called 911. The paramedics are less than five minutes away."

The judge, who at first appeared stupefied, rallied himself to say, "It appears that there is a medical emergency involving the defendant. This court will stand in recess until we receive further information regarding the defendant's condition. We will reconvene once it's appropriate to do so."

He banged his gavel but remained on the bench, while the jury filed out.

Brian wrapped a supportive arm around Tori, helping her sit upright. Tori pressed both hands to her chest, rocking back and forth as sweat glistened on her face.

"The pain . . . never had it . . . before," she gasped.

"Take deep, slow breaths, honey, we've got you," Jo soothed, leaning as far over the bar as she dared, her own heart racing. "Do you hear the siren? The paramedics are almost here."

Jo noticed with relief that Tori seemed to be breathing more easily. When the paramedics rushed in, Jo reluctantly stepped back from the bar while they assessed her.

"Her blood pressure is high at 160/100, and her pulse is 130, but she's in normal sinus rhythm," the female paramedic told them when she stood. "I gave her nitroglycerin, but we'll take her to the hospital for further evaluation."

Jo watched helplessly as they loaded Tori onto a stretcher, the receding adrenaline leaving her weak and shaky. When her request to ride in the ambulance was denied, she promised Tori, "I'll meet you in the ER, Tori. It's going to be okay."

Tori managed a weak nod in response.

As Jo collected her bag, she noticed Rick standing beside her, his arms hanging limply and his brow furrowed.

"Shall I come?" he asked.

"No. Make sure Brian knows how to contact you. We'll call you when we know what's going on," Jo replied, her mind racing ahead to the hospital and what might await them.

CHAPTER 54

JO HUDDLED IN the corner of the emergency department's waiting room as far as possible from a young man whose wet, hacking cough punctuated the tense atmosphere like gunshots. His glazed eyes and slumped posture suggested he was utterly wasted. Two frustrated toddlers wailed despite their mothers' increasingly desperate attempts at distraction. Directly across from Jo sat an elderly man with wild, tangled silver hair cascading into a long beard, both matted with grime. He rocked back and forth, clutching his arm while releasing low, guttural moans. Just as unsettling were the two women sitting silently across the room. Their vacant stares into nothingness revealed a resignation more haunting than all the noise combined.

The waiting room walls began to close around her. Jo was seconds away from bolting through the exit doors when salvation arrived in green scrubs.

"Jo Turner?" the nurse called out.

She leaped to her feet. "Yes?"

"The doctor has seen your friend, and we're waiting for the blood test results. Would you like to come on back?"

Following the nurse through the labyrinthine corridors, Jo

found herself in a large room sectioned off by hanging curtains. The illusion of privacy was shattered by an elderly patient next door shouting at their nurse, every word crystal clear through the flimsy divider.

But none of that mattered when Jo saw Tori sitting upright in bed. Color had returned to her previously ashen face, and two prongs of oxygen flowed into her nose. Tori greeted her with a smile.

"Hi, Jo. I'm okay. I started feeling better in the ambulance. My EKG is normal. I had either a panic attack or an esophageal spasm—or maybe both—brought on by stress. Esophageal spasm can mimic a heart attack. I'm sorry for scaring you. I've never had such pain before in my life, and I panicked."

A wave of relief washed over Jo as she grinned back.

"Yeah! Way to bring the court proceedings to a screeching halt and scare the hell out of me."

She bent over Tori to plant a kiss on her forehead. "I'm so glad you're okay."

But when she saw the imploring look in Tori's eyes, her momentary lightness vanished.

"I can't go into that courtroom again, Jo," Tori confessed, her voice dropping to a near whisper. "The judge is against me. He wouldn't let our photo expert testify. The eyewitnesses are unified in their identification of me. All we have left are my character witnesses willing to testify about my general reputation in the community, which is now in the toilet. It's not enough. I'm screwed."

Jo knew Tori was right. Without the FBI photo identification expert, Brian could only question the police methods used in the photo lineup. The judge had excluded their most crucial witness from proving their mistaken identity claim.

Even the character witnesses presented a risk if the prosecutor then called rebuttal witnesses.

"You'll take the stand," Jo insisted, trying to inject confidence she didn't feel. "Tell your story. Let the jury see who you really are."

"I can't. The prosecutor could bring up my erratic behavior before the robbery and even my relationship with Jude to bias the jury. I have no alibi. Three bank employees said it was me. What chance do I have?"

Jo squeezed Tori's hand, feeling the cool fingers beneath her warm palm. "You must testify, Tori," she urged, leaning closer. "The jury needs to hear how you've been followed and threatened and your study data stolen. This will suggest that your arrest may be part of a larger scheme to silence you. You can't just give up. It won't look good to the jury."

"You know as well as I do that the judge won't let Brian bring that up," Tori countered, her voice flat with defeat.

Their debate was interrupted as a doctor swept the curtain aside and approached with a clipboard. "Good news, Dr. Nelson. Your troponin is normal. You didn't have a cardiac event. Your diagnosis was correct. You probably had a panic attack and esophageal spasm."

Jo flashed a thumbs-up. Tori was already yanking the oxygen cannula from her nose, clearly eager to escape.

"I see you are ready to leave us," said the doctor, drily. "I suggest using peppermint oil or lozenges, or I can prescribe a proton pump inhibitor. You should also work on managing stress. It's a major trigger for both panic attacks and esophageal spasm."

"I'll stick with peppermint lozenges," Tori replied, and added pointedly, for Jo's benefit, "and I'll avoid the stress of testifying in court."

Jo sighed. The battle ahead had just gotten considerably harder.

❧

Once Jo had settled Tori on the living room couch with a glass of iced tea, she called Brian from the kitchen wall phone to let him know Tori was okay.

"Thank goodness. I was about to request a continuance."

Jo hesitated, her gaze drifting through the door to Tori, who sat hunched on the couch, looking smaller than Jo had ever seen her. She lowered her voice and turned to the wall.

"Tori says she doesn't want to testify."

"What? Why not?" Brian's voice rose. "As you know, jurors often expect innocent people to defend themselves in court. The judge will instruct them not to hold her silence against her, but some will still infer guilt if she doesn't take the stand. Additionally, I plan to bring up all the other issues related to stalking, threats, and the break-in to create doubt."

"She's worried about the cross-examination," Jo spoke low, willing Brian to follow her lead so as not to alarm Tori. "That prosecutor could introduce damaging, usually inadmissible evidence, and this judge might let him."

"What damaging evidence?" Brian's tone was sharp.

"Such as her hanging out in a bar with lesbians or even her complicity in stealing data from World Petrol. That might raise questions for some jurors about her moral character or the stability of her mental state before the robbery."

"Times have changed," Brian countered, but Jo heard the uncertainty behind his words.

Jo's eyes narrowed, remembering the jury's not-so-subtle response to the word "lesbian".

"Not everywhere. I observed how some jurors reacted when the prosecution brought it up."

"The judge instructed the jury to disregard it. He won't let the prosecutor bring it up again. That's not reason enough for her not to testify," Brian insisted, the defense attorney in him clearly battling with the reality Jo presented. "And the prosecutor never brought up her complicity in stealing environmental monitoring data. There's a good chance he doesn't know about it."

A deep sigh escaped Jo's lips as she glanced back at Tori, who was staring vacantly into her untouched tea. "She's adamant. I know it doesn't look good. I've explained that to her. Plus, she doesn't think the judge will allow her to testify about someone trying to silence her to prevent her from publishing."

"She's probably right," Brian admitted, defeat finally creeping into his voice. "The prosecutor will object, and this judge will probably sustain it. But I'd also planned to put to rest the prosecutor's implication that Tori suffered financial hardship."

Jo's mind raced through alternatives, desperately seeking a solution but finding none.

"Come into the office this evening if Tori is up to it," Brian said. "Maybe I can convince her to testify," though his tone suggested he doubted it. After a pause, he added, "Too bad I can't call you as a witness."

"Yes, I know," Jo replied, bitterness coloring her words. "Too much conflict of interest for the prosecutor to exploit."

CHAPTER 55

MONDAY EVENING IN Brian's office, the atmosphere was thick with desperation as Jo and Brian tried to persuade Tori to testify. But Jo could see that the fight had drained from her, replaced by a hollow resignation that frightened her.

"Without the FBI photo expert, what chance do I have? The jury is already prejudiced against me despite the judge's instructions. Even my ex-husband testified, saying I was acting strange before the robbery."

Jo felt a surge of protective indignation. "But you have a chance if we bring up the possibility that Big Oil framed you to keep you from publishing your study. The jury must already be incredulous that a physician making good money would put everything at risk to rob a bank for a paltry $6,000, especially a woman," Jo said, searching Tori's face for any sign of the determined and courageous woman she knew.

"This judge won't let us bring that up. And we have no hard evidence," Tori countered, her shoulders slumping further.

Brian's usually impeccable appearance showed signs of strain—stubbled chin, drawn face, fingers drumming nervously on the table. He wasn't giving up yet, though.

"We need to get in just enough to plant the seeds of doubt that you're guilty," he insisted.

"I just can't testify. Please don't ask me again. I appreciate all you've done, both of you—more than I can ever express." Tori said, her eyes welling with tears. She reached for a Kleenex and blew her nose. "Dr. Grenoble will publish my study and hopefully integrate the monitoring data with Dr. Townsend. I'm done. I'm taking my name off the paper."

Jo sighed, unable to hide her disappointment and confusion. "Oh, Tori, this is all wrong. I can't believe you're doing this."

"But I am," Tori said, holding Jo's gaze.

Jo barely listened as Brian outlined a modified plan for questioning the character witnesses. Her mind raced as she tried to understand what was happening beneath the surface.

That night, Jo was shrouded in a dark cloud of worry. She watched Tori sink into herself again, seemingly resigned to her fate. Jo's analytical mind wouldn't rest—there had to be something she was missing, some crucial piece to explain Tori's baffling reluctance to fight for herself. She racked her brain repeatedly, turning over every conversation and every detail of the case, searching for the answer that remained frustratingly out of reach.

On Tuesday, Tori attended the court but was silent and uncommunicative. She seemed to occupy as little space as possible in her chair at the defense table. Brian called the character witnesses, who portrayed Tori as a respected physician, a loyal friend, and an upstanding community member. Surprisingly, the prosecutor called no rebuttal witnesses. But Tori stood firm in her decision not to testify. Jo's heart sank as Brian rested Tori's case.

On Wednesday, the prosecutor's closing arguments unfolded just as Jo expected, emphasizing the compelling nature and consistency of the eyewitness testimony. He suggested the upheaval in Tori's life—financial pressures, marital discord, and impending divorce—likely led to a mental breakdown and the rash, impulsive decision to rob a bank. When he returned to his seat, Jo caught the satisfied smile on his face and the triumphant glance he shared with his assistant.

Brian approached the jury box with his shoulders slumped, apparently weighed down by injustice. Jo's shoulders tensed.

Once again, his eyes rested on each juror, but this time, his face was solemn. There was no infectious smile to catch and quietly return. His voice rose with barely contained outrage as he addressed them.

"Ladies and gentlemen of the jury, I want you to look at Dr. Nelson. Really look at her, please. This physician has dedicated her entire life to healing others and preventing illness. She diagnoses illnesses, treats workplace injuries, and assists patients in navigating their most challenging health issues. She has been a tireless advocate for her patients."

He moved closer to the jury, his voice dropping to an intimate tone.

"Now imagine this: a physician who has spent years building trust, known in every hospital and clinic in this community, with a thriving practice and financial security—would this person suddenly snap and throw away a lifetime of disciplined service and healing to become a common thief?"

His voice rose again with passionate conviction.

"The bank employees picked her photo from a lineup—yes. But only the faces were shown, and you could see for yourselves that the woman in the video had a different body type than Dr. Nelson. And we all know how fragile human memory can be. And what if the person showing the photos—one at a time, remember—already has their suspect in mind? How easy it would be for the agent to influence a witness's recollection by voice or body language. How many innocent people have been wrongly identified by witnesses who claim to be certain?"

Brian's fist clenched at his side as he paced back and forth.

"The Federal Bureau of Investigation, with all its resources and expertise, found nothing to incriminate Dr. Nelson. Not a single shred of physical evidence. No money. No dye-stained clothes. No weapon. There is no evidence to connect Dr. Nelson to this crime, except for an imperfect resemblance to the blonde, female perpetrator."

He turned to face the jury fully, his eyes fiery.

"Every day, Dr. Nelson walks into her clinic and faces patients struggling with ill-health, often caused by the dangerous places they work in. They trust her absolutely with their lives, their health, and their futures. She conducts research into the causes of illness to prevent these diseases. And now—based on nothing more than a questionable identification—you're being asked to destroy everything she's built and all she's strived to give back to the community."

He gripped the railing and leaned forward.

"The real criminal is out there, laughing at us, perhaps planning her next target, while we sit here contemplating the destruction of an innocent woman's life. Is that justice? Is that what we stand for? I implore you—don't let an innocent healer become a victim of mistaken identity. Don't let this community lose one of its most dedicated physicians to a tragic error in judgment."

He shook his head solemnly and returned to his seat. *A fine performance*, Jo thought. Hopefully, his eloquence could save her friend from a fate she appeared strangely resigned to accept.

≈

At home, Jo did her best to distract Tori while the jury deliberated, but found her friend distant and emotionless.

When Brian's call came late Thursday afternoon, Jo's stomach dropped. The jury had reached a decision—already.

Jo hugged her friend before they entered the courtroom. Tori's cheek was cold against her own.

Once again, Jo took her seat in the public area, and Tori sat ramrod straight at the defense table. The creak of the back door made Jo turn. She stiffened as she spotted Rick slipping onto a bench. Once again, she wondered what he was doing here. He'd shown plenty of discomfort when he'd been on the witness stand, but all that discomfort would have been for himself, she assumed. Why he'd bothered to turn up this week was a mystery to her. Was he so vindictive that he wanted to gloat over Tori's misfortune?

Her attention snapped away from Rick when the jury filed in and took their seats. Jo's trained eye didn't miss how not a single juror looked in Tori's direction—an ominous sign.

"Has the jury reached a verdict?" the judge asked.

"We have, your Honor," the foreperson responded, and Jo found herself holding her breath, her entire body tense.

"What say you?"

"We, the jury, find the defendant, Dr. Victoria Nelson, guilty of armed robbery as charged in the indictment."

Jo took in a quick breath. She gazed at Tori's back with wide, disbelieving eyes. Tori didn't look around. She didn't even move. Her whole being radiated eerie calm, her head held high in a stony silence that frightened Jo more than any other reaction.

Movement caught the corner of Jo's eye. Rick was halfway out of his seat, a look of horror frozen on his face.

The judge's voice seemed to come from a great distance as he addressed Tori.

"The court finds a factual basis for the guilty verdict. You will be remanded into custody immediately. Sentencing will follow."

He turned to the jury. "I thank the jury for your service."

With a finality that echoed through Jo's bones, he grasped his gavel and intoned, "This court is adjourned."

Jo pushed her way forward to the bar. As Brian and Tori exited, he said. "I'll appeal the verdict immediately and demand that you be freed on bail."

Tori said nothing.

Jo hugged her. "Stay strong. It's not over."

"It's over," Tori replied against Jo's shoulder, her voice so devoid of emotion it sent chills down Jo's spine. "Everything."

A burly court officer brushed Jo's elbow and pulled her away. The officer handcuffed Tori and led her from the courtroom.

CHAPTER 56

WHEN JO RETURNED to Tori's house, Orange Cat greeted her with an enthusiastic display—meowing insistently and weaving figure-eights between her ankles, his warm fur brushing against her skin. She reached down and patted him.

"Oh, Orange Cat, I am going to have to take you home with me. How do you think Sam will like that?"

With a deep sigh, Jo dialed David at the office. As she relayed the outcome of Tori's trial, she could hear the disbelief in his voice mirroring her own internal turmoil. His only consolation seemed to be that Drs. Ellen Grenoble and Jeff Townsend would salvage the cancer study that would otherwise be tainted in the wake of Tori's conviction.

Jo promised to be back in the office the next day or so, with the understanding she would return to Houston for Tori's sentencing.

❧

The period before sentencing seemed to take forever. Probation reports and sentencing recommendations needed to be given to the judge. Brian promised to let her know the minute he heard the judge was ready to deliver the sentence.

In the end, it took barely six weeks. Back in the courtroom on October 22nd, Jo sat rigid as the judge pronounced Tori's sentence: three years in federal prison. The words slammed into Jo like physical blows. She fought to maintain her composure, hot tears threatening to spill while Tori—brilliant, dedicated Tori—was led away in handcuffs like a common criminal.

∽

Brian moved with impressive efficiency, assembling a compelling case for bail pending appeal. His memorandum highlighted everything Jo knew to be true: Tori's spotless record, her deep community connections, and her consistent compliance with earlier court requirements. In less than a week, a miracle occurred. Tori was released on bail pending her appeal.

On Monday, October 28th, Jo waited anxiously outside the Federal Detention Center. When Tori emerged, Jo barely recognized her. Tori's usually immaculate appearance had deteriorated—her hair hung limp and oily, and her frame appeared to have shrunk inside her clothes, as though prison had begun consuming her from within.

In the car, Jo ventured, "How was it?"

Immediately, she regretted her question.

"I don't want to talk about it," Tori replied, her voice flat.

"Of course."

Jo's eyes flicked between her friend and the road, nearly causing an accident when the car ahead suddenly braked. The silence stretched between them until Tori broke it.

"I had a lot of time to think about my cancer study."

Surely she had more pressing concerns than her research? But before Jo could respond, Tori continued with devastating finality.

"As you know, I've taken my name off our planned submission to a professional journal. Dr. Ellen Grenoble and Dr. Townsend finish the study and publish it without me. They will be your experts."

Jo's heart went out to her.

"Oh Tori, you've worked so hard . . ."

Tori cut her off. "You'll never be able to hold the oil companies accountable if my name is on the paper."

"You deserve recognition for your hard work and all you've sacrificed."

The injustice of it took her breath away, but Tori wasn't finished. Her voice strengthened.

"As soon as you return to Washington, file a Freedom of Information Act request and obtain the monitoring data Jude provided to the EPA. Keep going forward with your lawsuit. That's what you can do for me now. And for my patients and all the others who've been harmed."

Jo pulled the car over, no longer trusting herself to drive safely. Tori's gaze captured hers—intense, focused, and determined.

"Promise me you'll carry on," Tori demanded.

"I will," Jo managed, wiping away a tear.

"And another thing," Tori continued, her tone brooking no argument. "You and the firm need to stop associating with me. From now on, Ellen will be your scientific contact."

"What? No way." The request stung.

"It's not a good look as you progress with your case."

"I'll be the judge of that," Jo retorted, pulling back into traffic. Yet even as she protested, she knew Colin would likely deliver the same pragmatic demand.

That night, they shared a quiet dinner. Jo had brought Orange Cat back with her, and his reunion with Tori was polite and understated. After dinner, Tori excused herself to retreat to the bedroom and call Jude. Jo remained at the table, weighed down by her thoughts and the request of her friend whose life had been tragically upended—just for doing what was right.

The next morning, Jo and Tori sat at the breakfast table, the bright sunlight streaming through the window starkly contrasting with their somber mood. Tori's eyes glistened with tears as she reached out to grasp Jo's hand.

"I don't know how to thank you for being there for me through all this," she said. "We've achieved so much for my patients and the people of Oilton." Her lips trembled. "But there's something . . ."

Tori's words hung in the air as the wall phone shattered the moment. Jo swiftly answered, shielding Tori from any unwanted intrusion. Brian's voice crackled with urgency at the other end.

"You need to come down here right away. Tori needs to hear this," he said, his excitement palpable.

"What is it?"

"It's better if you hear it from the source," he said, a smile in his tone.

"Okay, we'll be there soon."

She turned to Tori, who was clearing the dishes.

"Drop everything. We're going to Brian's office. He sounds more excited than I've ever heard him."

"Why?"

"He won't say until we're there. He says you need to hear it from the source."

Still in her bathrobe, Jo flew up the stairs to change. When she descended, fully dressed, Tori was waiting by the front door, car keys in hand.

In reception, Brian bounded down the hall to greet them. "You're not going to believe this," he said, leading them briskly to his office.

"Believe what?" Tori asked, her voice laced with skepticism.

"Rick is here."

She and Tori exchanged surprised glances.

Rick jumped up to greet them. "Tori, I'm so sorry. I didn't think you'd be convicted. I . . . " He reached out as if to touch Tori, then ran his hand through his hair.

Brian intervened, his voice firm. "Tell Tori what you just told me. From the beginning."

CHAPTER 57

TORI'S EYES NARROWED as she studied the man who had once been her husband. Rick slumped into a chair and bent forward, his hands clasped between his knees as if bracing himself for the impact of his words.

"Shortly after I started working for World Petrol, a lawyer from Risk Management approached me in the company's cafeteria and rambled on about how your study would lead to lawsuits and additional regulations that would harm the company's bottom line."

His confession hit home. She exchanged a look with Jo. Just what they'd suspected.

Rick continued, "He asked me if I could influence you to drop it. I said I'd try but knew you wouldn't, and you'd be pissed off if I told you I was working for them."

He looked up, finally meeting Tori's eyes.

"And I was," Tori said.

Rick's face sagged. "Yeah, I know." He straightened. "But after you told me about the break-in, I got suspicious."

"Tell Tori what you heard at work," Brian prodded.

"After we last talked and just before your trial, I was called to the medical department to resolve an issue accessing their internal database. I overheard snippets of a conversation between two of the medical administrators. But one said, "That woman doing the study of cancer around the refinery . . ." and I realized they were talking about you, so I tuned in. The other one said, "When they passed around the photo of the bank robber, Roger Barron called in a tip that the bank robber looked like her." They closed the door, and I didn't hear the rest. But it set off alarm bells for me."

Tori's stomach tightened, and she exchanged another knowing look with Jo.

Rick shifted in his seat. "I suspected then that World Petrol was involved in your arrest. I tried to call you, but you didn't return my call."

Turning to Brian, he said, "I knew you were trying to get hold of me to stand as a witness. But I didn't want the company to suspect I might be on Tori's side until I could find out what they'd been up to."

Rick faced Tori again. "I discovered that Roger Barron was the head attorney in the Risk Management Department. I could legitimately access limited internal documents, but not his. So, during your trial, I looked for ways to hack into Barron's internal memos and began reviewing them for references to you and your study."

Leaning forward, Brian said, "And what did you find?"

"It took a week or so after your trial ended, but eventually I found one addressed to a senior manager, marked as confidential, describing how Barron had alerted the FBI to Dr. Nelson's resemblance to the bank robber and how this might derail her cancer study. Then later I found another addressed to the same senior manager, saying, 'Our guy, Hogarth, has dealt a definitive blow to Dr. Nelson's cancer study, and it will not likely go public before her trial.'"

"So they *did* hire Hogarth," Tori said, exchanging another look with Jo.

"And paid him directly, even after the security firm fired him," Brian said.

"Yes, it took over three weeks hacking into another department's records, but I found payments to an outside security firm as well as direct payments to James Hogarth."

"Fantastic!" Jo said, grinning.

"There's more," Rick said. "A few weeks before the trial, another confidential memo from Barron to the senior manager stated that the judge presiding over Dr. Nelson's trial was in trouble. Barron worried he might be forced to retire due to his mounting procedural errors."

"Good news for your appeal," Jo said.

Tori's brow furrowed, and she said sharply, "Why did you testify against me?"

Rick sighed, and his eyes slid away. "When the prosecution called me at work to testify at your trial, I declined, saying we were still married, even though we weren't anymore. However, Barron came to my office after the prosecutor had called me. He said that the company's higher-ups would greatly appreciate my cooperation with the prosecutor and that I would be duly rewarded. He also said there'd be trouble if I said anything to support your case."

Rick looked at her with beseeching eyes. "I didn't want Barron to suspect I was trying to hack into his files. I tried not returning phone calls—both Brian's and the prosecutor's—but then they must have found out our divorce had become final, and the prosecutor subpoenaed me at work."

Rick paused and regarded Tori thoughtfully. "Is it true? Are you a lesbian?"

His question caught her off guard. After only a moment, Tori nodded, strangely liberated by this simple acknowledgment.

"Yes. It's who I am. I'm sorry, Rick. There's a lot you didn't know about me."

Rick sighed. "I realize that now." He appeared to need a moment to collect himself before he continued.

"Anyway, I tried not to say anything too damaging or to lie. And I needed more time to hack into Barron's computer, access the financial records, and download files without arousing suspicion. I had hoped to get at least some stuff over to Brian before you were called to testify. But then, you rested your case early, and I ran out of time." He shook his head. "I couldn't believe you were convicted with only eyewitness testimony."

"Do you have the memos and financial records now?" Tori and Jo asked simultaneously.

"I do," Rick said. "I've given them to Brian. I'm so sorry it took this long. Just as I was about to download them, Barron changed his passwords and added a layer of security. I had to start over again, finding a way to hack into his files."

"Thank you, Rick," Tori said, genuine gratitude softening her voice. "You continue to surprise me."

He nodded. "For months, I was angry, for sure. I didn't want to get a divorce. But World Petrol's trying to destroy your career by framing you for bank robbery and stealing your study data— that's beyond the pale. You must know I couldn't go along with it."

Tori sighed. "I wasn't sure at first. But in the end, I didn't think you would." She gave him a concerned look. "What will you do now?"

"I quit. World Petrol would fire me anyway after they

discover what I've done and try to ruin my reputation to make sure I never work for a big multinational corporation again. But that's just fine with me. I've seen how they operate, and it's not for me, although they certainly need someone with my skills to strengthen their digital security. A friend in California has an idea for software that will revolutionize the personal computer industry. I'll check it out. Even if nothing comes of it, other entrepreneurial opportunities will come along."

She smiled at him, recognizing that despite everything, there was still a core of decency in the man she had once married.

Brian looked as if he could no longer contain himself. "I don't doubt that our appeal will be successful, given this new evidence. The exclusionary rule, which bars evidence obtained via unconstitutional state action, doesn't apply to evidence unlawfully acquired by private individuals. This and the judge's procedural errors, particularly his exclusion of the FBI photo expert, will probably result in a mistrial—at the very least."

Jo reached over and grasped Tori's hand tightly. The pressure of Jo's fingers intertwined with her own anchored her to this moment of hope after months of despair.

This could all be over soon.

For the first time since her nightmare began, Tori allowed herself to believe in the possibility of freedom.

CHAPTER 58

ONCE DR. JEFF TOWNSEND reviewed Jude's environmental monitoring data that Dr. Ellen Grenoble obtained from the EPA, he reversed course. He eagerly joined forces with Ellen, bringing fresh energy to Tori's study that had often felt like a lonely crusade. For the next two months, the three of them crafted two compelling papers, ready for simultaneous submission to a prestigious medical journal.

Yet they hovered in a state of suspended animation, waiting for the outcome of Tori's appeal. Both colleagues adamantly insisted that Tori's name be listed as the lead author on the publications, a professional courtesy that touched her deeply.

In January 1986, Jo called Tori to inform her that World Petrol was facing multi-million-dollar fines from the EPA. They cited over 10,000 Clean Air Act violations at its Oilton refinery and chemical plant complex, resulting in the release of millions of pounds of carcinogens and other toxic chemicals into the surrounding air.

Jo's firm had also filed a mass tort lawsuit in collaboration with the EPA. Jo assured Tori that when the joint cancer study was published, it would be the cornerstone of evidence proving

harm to the community from World Petrol's emissions, providing further incentive for them to stop polluting.

So as not to abandon her patients, Tori planned for their
care should she go to prison. Occupational and environmental
medicine programs had sprouted up at schools of public health
nationwide, and she'd successfully recruited a physician with
compatible values to take over her practice.

It was everything Tori had hoped would happen—for her
patients, the people of Oilton, and her decades-old desire to be
a force for positive change in the world.

On March 10th, 1986, Brian called Tori to tell her that the
three-judge panel deciding her appeal was expected to render its
decision by midweek. She was not required to be present in the
courtroom. Jo flew to Houston to be with her when the decision
came in, but Tori had insisted Jude stay in Boston to study for
her upcoming exams.

Tori sat in a recliner on her deck, the sun warm on her face
and bare arms. Her backyard was bursting with colorful blooms:
azaleas, marigolds, zinnias, and the wildflowers she'd planted.
Butterflies, bees, and hummingbirds flitted among the blos-
soms, and birds chirped from nearby feeders and birdbaths. The
earthy scent of moist soil mingled with the sweet perfume of
blooming flowers wafted to her on a soft breeze. Orange Cat lay
at her side on a leash, his tail twitching back and forth as he eyed
nearby birds, though he was not allowed to stalk them except in
his dreams.

Tori sighed. She'd miss her springtime garden. She'd sold her
house, and the buyer would take possession in two weeks. She
sipped iced tea and let her thoughts wander. She'd accomplished

what she'd set out to do here. Things had worked out remarkably well. But one issue remained unresolved.

Jo joined her on the deck, holding a glass of iced tea. "Brian called to say he should hear from the panel about your appeal within the hour."

Tori caught the note of excitement in her voice, and her chest tightened with familiar anxiety. She practiced the breathing techniques Jo had taught her while Jo leaned back in the recliner, her hands behind her head. It calmed her to see her friend lying there at ease beside her.

"Six months ago," Jo said, "could you have imagined we'd be where we are now?"

"No, I couldn't." Tori shifted onto her hip to face her. "You know, I'm so grateful for your support. Not only the arrest and its aftermath, but personally, too. My coming out as a lesbian was difficult for me. I was very unstable before you came, churning with emotions like a volcano building to an eruption."

"Well, you seem to have recovered nicely," Jo said, smiling.

Tori's heart hammered in her throat, but she strove to keep her voice calm.

"Jo, there's something I need to say."

She saw Jo tense.

She's worried I'm still in love with her.

Tori smiled briefly. "Don't worry. This isn't a declaration of passion. I've moved on and hope to build a life with Jude, eventually."

Jo's face relaxed.

"What is it, then?" Jo took off her sunglasses and faced her.

Tori gripped her glass, took a deep breath, and opened her mouth to speak. "I . . ."

Orange Cat chose that moment to leap onto Tori's chest,

knocking her drink from her hand so the cool liquid spilled over her chest.

Jo jumped up and rushed into the house to get a towel.

Tori picked up a damp Orange Cat and set him down. "Way to go, Orange Thingy," she said. "I guess you don't want me to tell her."

She untied his leash, and they followed Jo indoors. Just then, the kitchen wall phone rang, and she startled. Tori lunged for the receiver with a trembling hand, and she and Jo pressed their heads together, the receiver between them.

"The judges have decided," Brian said.

Tori struggled to calm herself sufficiently to listen to what he was saying. His words seemed to be little more than procedural details and fresh evidence. Then came the moment of truth.

"The judges declared a mistrial and overturned your guilty verdict."

This was good news indeed. But would she have to go through the ordeal of another trial?

Before she could ask, Brian said, "But here is the best news of all. The prosecutor called me after the decision came in. Even he was appalled by the new evidence of World Petrol's meddling. The government has decided to drop the charges in the indictment. You're free, Tori."

Tori's knees buckled, and she grasped a chair for support. Jo's arms enveloped her, holding her close as a sob of relief escaped.

When they finished the call with Brian, they stood, wide-eyed, looking at each other, then burst into tearful laughter.

"It's really over," Tori exclaimed, her voice trembling with emotion. Everything was possible again.

◈

When they'd calmed down sufficiently from their initial euphoria and Tori had changed her wet shirt, Jo brought out an expensive bottle of champagne. Hoping for good news, she'd bought it while shopping to stock Tori's fridge. The friends settled on the couch in the living room, and Orange Cat leaped up and nestled between them. Jo absently stroked his back.

"What will you do now, Tori?"

Tori sipped her chilled champagne, and her gaze drifted into the middle distance.

"I can allow Ellen and Jeff to keep my name as lead author on our papers."

"Where it should be," Jo said.

"And I can finally leave Houston and go to Boston to be with Jude. Since I'm no longer a felon," her tone was a little dry, "perhaps I can rejoin the faculty at Harvard."

Jo smiled. "That's wonderful, Tori. I'm so happy for you."

But Jo sensed something was off. Her concern mounted when she noticed Tori's brow furrow and her eyes glisten.

"Tori, why aren't you as happy as I am?"

Tori gripped her champagne flute tightly, her lips trembling.

"I'm afraid . . ." she whispered, her voice barely audible.

Jo's concern turned into confusion. "Why? What's going on?" she pressed, her voice gentle.

Tori dropped her eyes, biting her lip, looking like she might cry.

"Just spit it out, Tori," Jo encouraged, her voice soft but firm.

A tear spilled down Tori's cheek.

"It *was* me in that video, Jo." Her voice cracked. "I robbed the bank."

CHAPTER 59

JO'S EYES WIDENED, her breath caught, and she swallowed hard. She swung around to face Tori. Disturbed, Orange Cat leaped off the couch.

"What? Fuck, no! Why?"

Tori took a large swig of champagne, leaned back, and stared into the middle distance, avoiding Jo's stunned gaze.

"I was in a state of turmoil over my marriage, my growing desire to be romantically involved with a woman, my cancer study, and my demanding practice—especially the laboratory, which would have cost a fortune to set up. I was trying to handle it all by myself, losing weight, and not sleeping. I started to self-medicate with diazepam. It's a benzo. Foolishly, I continued to increase the dose. Eventually, I consulted a psychiatrist, but I was embarrassed to tell her about the diazepam, so she never knew. She put me on amitriptyline, an antidepressant, and I took it for several weeks, along with the diazepam, even though it made me feel weird and hyper."

Tori sighed deeply and met Jo's eyes. "It's rare, but some people suffer behavioral abnormalities and disinhibition with these drugs in combination and act totally out of character.

Unfortunately, that's what happened to me. To the point that I thought it was okay to rob a bank."

So, she did have a drug problem. I should have dug further and not dismissed it.

Tori sighed again and continued. "I'd been so incredibly foolish and was aghast when I realized what I'd done. I couldn't tell anyone. My psychiatrist would be obligated to report it. I never went back to see her and immediately began tapering off both drugs."

Tori dropped her head into her hands. "I'm so ashamed."

Jo's tone was sharp. "But why didn't you *tell* me? We could have used it in your defense."

Tori lifted her head. "And when people found out I was a self-medicating drug abuser and a bank robber? I'd be convicted for sure. My credibility would be in the toilet."

Jo frowned. "That it would. But did that even enter your mind before you decided to rob the bank?"

Jo rubbed her forehead and reached for her glass of champagne. She felt sick, and her hand shook. She put the glass back without drinking.

Tori huffed a mirthless laugh. "No, not at the time. I felt powerful and in control. I had this crazy idea that I would rob a bank that did a lot of business with the petrochemical industry to fund my laboratory start-up—just payback for the industry's misdeeds. Then I wouldn't have to scrounge for grants."

"That *is* crazy. What about the physical evidence?" Jo asked, her head spinning.

"I never had a gun. I left the bank and dashed to the clinic garage, where I'd parked a few minutes earlier."

"Why did you say you were working at home that day?"

"I *was* at home early on. Working out how to rob a bank and get away with it."

"Oh, Jesus." Jo pictured her friend pacing in her office, plotting her crime. "Go on."

"After I robbed the bank, I hid behind a large truck in the garage, stripped off my dye-stained clothes, the pillow in my waistband, the gloves, and dark glasses, and placed them in a large paper bag. Then I threw on my long white coat."

"The cops would check all the dumpsters in the area. What did you do with the bag?"

Orange Cat jumped onto Tori's lap and faced Jo, his amber eyes fixed on her face.

"I noticed dye had stained some but not all the money, so I put on another pair of surgical gloves and separated the dye-stained money to go with the clothes and the first set of gloves. I put the paper bag inside a biomedical waste bag in the trunk of my car. I put on new gloves and moved the unstained money into a separate plastic bag."

All Tori's energy seemed to have drained away. She bent her head over Orange Cat, stroking him. But Jo needed to hear the rest.

"No one saw you? Then what?"

Tori looked up, her face drawn. "No one saw me. I drove to the hospital to dispose of the large bag in the biomedical waste container for incineration. Then, I headed home, showered and dressed in my normal clothes, and drove downtown again to meet Jude for lunch."

"All that before 12:30?" Jo was beginning to feel lightheaded. "Were you going to tell Jude what you'd done?"

"I don't know."

"What did you do with the rest of the money?"

"I arrived at the restaurant late. As you know, Jude didn't show, and I ate alone, thinking about what to do. After lunch, I drove to the Montrose Counseling Center—it provides mental health services to gay and lesbian youth—and discreetly left the plastic bag with the clean money just inside their door."

"You gave the money away?" This was getting even weirder. Jo rubbed her hands down her thighs. She didn't get it.

Tori sighed. "Clearly, I didn't get enough for my laboratory start-up, so I decided the money should go to another good cause." Tori sighed. "I know it sounds crazy. But at the time, my addled brain thought I could rob a bank and get away with it."

Jo frowned again and spoke sharply. "Which, in the end, you did." She looked away for a moment to collect her swirling thoughts, feeling very much off balance.

She faced Tori again. "Does Jude know?"

"Yes, I eventually told her." Tori flicked her hair out of her eyes and held Jo's gaze, tears welling again. "I'm ashamed of what I did—the self-medication, the bank robbery—and especially lying to you. But I couldn't bear the thought of losing your friendship and respect by telling you the truth. It was eating me up inside to the point I couldn't testify in my defense. I deserved the conviction. And I'd already turned over my study to Ellen, so I knew it'd get published—even if I was found guilty."

Jo had no words. Tori must have seen how hurt she was. She reached over and touched Jo's arm, her eyes lit with an inner fire.

"But I'm proud of getting my cancer study into the world, uncovering the harm the fossil fuel companies cause people and the environment. And for helping you make them accountable, so that they'll change. We've accomplished something truly significant together, haven't we? Just as I knew we would when we were in college."

Jo's emotions swirled—a complicated mixture of anger, hurt, and awe that made her chest tighten and stomach roil. She looked down at the cat, unable to hold Tori's gaze.

How could I have been so wrong? No matter how close you

think you are, can you ever really know someone? Tori was a far more complex person than the woman she thought she knew. But she'd always been a little blind where Tori was concerned.

Jo sighed and slowly raised her eyes to meet Tori's. As unhappy as she was with Tori's revelation, she had to agree. She nodded. "Yes, we have."

THE END

AUTHOR'S NOTE

The characters, corporations, towns, and events in this book are fictional, and any resemblance to real people, businesses, or locations is coincidental.

However, it is well established that cancer rates are significantly higher in areas around the Houston Ship Channel in Texas in comparison to other parts of the state and the nation. This region, home to several of the largest petrochemical and industrial complexes in the United States, has elevated cancer rates due to prolonged exposure to hazardous pollutants. This is also true of the 85-mile stretch between Baton Rouge and New Orleans, home to over 200 petrochemical plants and refineries, making it one of the most industrialized regions in the country.

The Houston Ship Channel and "Cancer Alley" in Louisiana have been described as "sacrifice zones" due to their disproportionate environmental burden on nearby communities. While industrial facilities significantly contribute to the regional and national economies, they also pose significant health risks to local populations.

ACKNOWLEDGMENTS

Readers are always at the top of my gratitude list. When I wrote my debut memoir, *Making the Rounds: Defying Norms in Love and Medicine*, I was an unknown author with no readers, consumed by anxiety about sharing something so personal with the world. However, many readers and reviewers commented that the book was "enthralling and brutally honest," "engaging and immersive," and "I did not want it to end." This gave me the confidence to study the writing craft further and try my hand at novels, combining real-life experiences with fiction. *Framed* is my third novel.

A book project is a long slog filled not only with energizing creativity but also with drudgery, revision after revision, and self-doubt. I am so grateful to the following people who, like supportive bystanders at a marathon, provided feedback and cheered me on. Thank you to my beta readers Linda M. Ford, Melanie Dawson-Whisker, Linda Moore, Ellen Barker, Kate Zeiler, David Logan, Elke Scrimshaw, Georgina Patko, Gretchen Staebler, Sandra Whiting, Dianne Kenny, Pat Henson, and the Lake Forest Park Writing Group: Linda Lockwood, Anu Garg, Helen Wattley-Ames, Mercedes Roberson, Sara Kim, and Connie Ballou. Special thanks also to my thriller coach, Kerry Savage, and attorneys Jody Weiner and Lori Duff. All gave feedback to help me create a better book.

Editors are crucial for clarifying and identifying mistakes that become invisible to authors after repeated readings. Thank you to my editors, Ruth Bullivant and Linda M. Ford.

As an indie author without a big publisher's publicity and marketing backup, I rely on readers like you to leave ratings, reviews, and comments on social media and book retail sites.

The connections and stories I share with readers remind me of why I write—to inspire, to offer hope, and to entertain. Here's to the power of words and the communities that support us.

ABOUT THE AUTHOR

Patricia Grayhall is a retired medical doctor and author of *Making the Rounds: Defying Norms in Love and Medicine*, published by She Writes Press, which garnered a starred review in *Kirkus Reviews* and was listed as one of their Best Indie Books of 2022. The memoir won the 2024 National Indie Excellence Award for LGBTQIA Nonfiction and Memoir, the 2023 Best Indie Book Award in LGBTQ Memoir, and the 2023 Readers' Favorite Book Awards Gold Medal in LGBTQ Non-Fiction.

She and her partner, Linda M. Ford, are the authors of the second-chance lesbian romance novel, *Golden Years and Silver Linings*.

Her first solo novel, *A Place for Us*, inspired by her experience of immigrating to Canada with her British partner, was published by She Writes Press in June 2025.

Patricia has published articles in *Queer Forty*, *The Gay & Lesbian Review*, *The Millions*, *Lesbian Game Changers*, *Women Writers*, *Women's Books*, and *Seattle Magazine*, among others. You can find numerous podcasts and radio interviews, articles, and blogs on her website at www.patriciagrayhall.com, where she enjoys connecting with readers.

Patricia splits her time between Seattle, Washington and Vancouver Island, British Columbia, where she enjoys hiking, wildlife, other people's dogs, and her second career as an author.

ARE YOU LOOKING FOR YOUR NEXT GREAT READ?

Try Patricia Grayhall's other books:

A Place for Us: A Novel

Golden Years and Silver Linings: A Lesbian Romance

Making the Rounds: Defying Norms in Love and Medicine